STEPHANIE BOND
LESLIE KELLY
LORI WILDE

SAND, SUN...

Seduction!

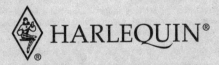

HARLEQUIN®

TORONTO • NEW YORK • LONDON
AMSTERDAM • PARIS • SYDNEY • HAMBURG
STOCKHOLM • ATHENS • TOKYO • MILAN • MADRID
PRAGUE • WARSAW • BUDAPEST • AUCKLAND

Recycling programs
for this product may
not exist in your area.

ISBN-13: 978-0-373-83734-2

SAND, SUN...SEDUCTION!

Copyright © 2009 by Harlequin Books S.A.

The publisher acknowledges the copyright holders
of the individual works as follows:

ENTICED
Copyright © 2009 by Stephanie Hauck.

PROPOSITIONED
Copyright © 2009 by Leslie A. Kelly.

FEVERED
Copyright © 2009 by Lori Blalock Vanzura.

Printed in U.S.A.

CONTENTS

ENTICED

Stephanie Bond

This story is dedicated to those of you still looking for romance; here's hoping you find it on a beach!

CHAPTER ONE

"ARE YOU PACKED?"

Kimber Karlton glanced up from the file she was reading and smiled at her paralegal, Anna, who stood in the door of her office. "Are you kidding? This is my first vacation in two years. I've been packed for a week."

"I'm so jealous—a week on a remote island in the Indian Ocean with a handsome man." The woman sighed. "It's so romantic, I could die."

"You can't die, Anna—what would I do without you?"

"Well, you'd be out of the loop on the office gossip, that's for sure." The woman's eyes danced. "Would you like to hear the latest?"

Kimber held up her hand. "No, thanks. I'm not interested in rumors."

"Not even if they're about you?"

Kimber pursed her lips, then set down her file. "Okay, what?"

Anna stepped forward and covered one side of her mouth. "Well, you didn't hear it from me, but word has it that Gil is going to propose to you on the island!"

Surprise barbed through Kimber and she unwittingly

released a pent-up breath she'd been holding for most of the three years that she'd dated fellow Atlanta attorney Gil Trapp. Despite working for the same firm and being on the same floor, they were both so busy they rarely saw each other these days. They had toyed with the idea of moving in together for the sake of convenience, but Kimber had resisted. Since puberty, her independent, divorced mother had drilled a message into her head: a woman should keep her own name, her own apartment and, if necessary, her own company, until a man made an offer that was too enticing to resist. And for months now, Kimber had secretly hoped that Gil would propose already so she could stop agonizing over whether he was "the one" and they could start their lives together on sound legal footing.

With a solid prenuptial agreement, of course.

Her heart raced, but still, she wasn't the kind of person who put faith in rumors. Kimber bit her lip, trying to hide her excitement from Anna. "Who told you that?"

"A little Bertie."

Roberta, Gil's paralegal. So it was true! Relief washed over her, and she laughed into her fingers. Then, mindful of her audience, she sobered abruptly. "You and Bertie can't tell anyone else. After all, Gil might change his mind."

"He's not going to change his mind," Anna scoffed. "Look at you—you're young, beautiful, talented and successful. If you ask me, Gil's crazy not to have snapped you up before now."

Kimber smiled, but a little bubble of apprehension rose in her chest. It was a common question among her friends and family—why hadn't Gil proposed yet?

Weren't things going okay? Weren't they happy? What was he waiting for?

"I guess he was waiting for the perfect setting," Anna offered as if she'd read her boss's mind.

"I think you're right," Kimber agreed with a nod.

This time tomorrow they'd be lying in hammocks under palm trees, watching azure water wash over pink sand, sipping frozen drinks, far, far away from civilization. The long flight to the other side of the world would be worth it. The Maldives were a group of several hundred islands off the Indian coast. Each island was so tiny and remote that only a small percentage of them were inhabited, and fewer still welcomed tourists with exclusive accommodations. It was a once-in-a-lifetime destination—the ultimate backdrop for a marriage proposal.

"When are you leaving the office?" Anna asked.

"Gil had a meeting in Alpharetta. He's picking me up in one hour, so fingers crossed that nothing pops up or falls apart in the next sixty minutes. Thank goodness the Pennington divorce is put to bed."

Over the past year, she'd spent more time with Della Pennington than she'd spent with her own mother. Della had been heartbroken over her husband's request for a divorce. Kimber personally thought the woman was a little soft in the head—it wasn't healthy to be so invested in a man. True, her husband, Gerald, had been evasive about his reason for wanting a divorce, but in Kimber's experience, that usually indicated a girlfriend waiting in the wings. But Della had kept insisting that her husband didn't really want the divorce.

"Heaven help us all," Anna said. "I didn't think that

divorce would ever be over. I couriered the final papers this morning."

"Good." Even after months of arbitration and many billable hours, Della Pennington was in deep denial. At times Kimber had felt more like a therapist than a legal counselor, coaxing the woman to accept the inevitable. She hoped that the reality of receiving the final papers hadn't been too traumatic, but Della was going to have to face reality sooner or later. Kimber pushed her thoughts away from the dissolution of the Pennington marriage and back to her goal of getting out of the office on time.

"I purposely didn't schedule any appointments this afternoon," Kimber explained. "I'm just going to finish paperwork."

Anna grinned. "I will personally block the door if anyone tries to get in your office."

"Thanks, Anna." Kimber waited until the paralegal left before pumping her fist in the air and giving a little squeal. Gil was going to propose! When she came back from Maldives, she'd have a ring on her finger and a wedding to plan. So many details. They'd have a big ceremony, of course, and she'd wear a Marchesa gown. And in practical terms, it made more sense to sell her condo and move into his house. But plenty of questions swirled in her head. Would she take Gil's name? Would one of them have to leave the firm? And would they change their minds about remaining childless?

Reminding herself she still had paperwork to wrap up, Kimber forced her focus back to the file she'd been reading. But after scanning the same paragraph three times, she gave up and picked up the phone, trying to look serious as she dialed, in case anyone glanced into her glass-walled office.

"Tinsel Travel, this is Elaina."

"Hi, sis."

"What's wrong?"

Kimber frowned. "What makes you think something's wrong?"

"Sisters know these things. Don't tell me you're sick. You can't miss this trip, Kimber. The Maldives are the most exclusive vacation spot my agency offers."

"I'm not sick, and I'm not going to miss the trip. Relax, the cat's out of the bag."

"What cat and what bag?"

"Ha, ha. The fact that Gil plans to propose while we're on the island."

Silence boomed on the other end. "He does?"

"As if you didn't know."

"Uh, Gil didn't say a thing to me."

"Sure. Whatever you say." Kimber knew her older sister was hanging on to the lie to keep Kimber guessing. As a travel agent, Elaina had planned hundreds of surprise getaways and knew how to play dumb.

"Did Gil tell you he was going to propose?" Elaina asked, her voice suspicious.

Fishing for information—a dead giveaway, she knew. "No, his paralegal told my paralegal."

"Oh. Well…if he does propose, what are you going to say?"

Kimber frowned, then laughed. "I'm going to say yes! What do you think I'm going to say?"

"I don't know—that's why I asked. Do you really want to marry Gil?"

Hurt flashed through Kimber's chest. Elaina and Gil had never exactly clicked, and if she didn't know better, she'd think Elaina was trying to plant doubts in her head. Then she smiled in realization—it was all part of the gag to keep from spilling the beans. Her sister had probably helped pick out the engagement ring. "If I didn't want to marry Gil, why would I have dated him all this time?"

"Don't ask me," Elaina said.

Kimber laughed at her sister's attempt at diversion. "A heads-up would've been nice, but luckily, I packed all my best lingerie. Still, maybe I should dash home and get another cocktail dress out of my closet."

"Kimber, Maldives is so remote, the trip alone will be taxing. By the time you get there, all you'll want to do is relax. You won't need a cocktail dress. In fact, you'll barely need *shoes*."

"Uh-oh," Kimber said, thinking of all the chic outfits she'd packed. "I'll be a tad overdressed."

"Don't worry, you can pick up some casual things when you arrive. This is your chance to loosen up a little, sis. Take advantage of it."

Elaina was always telling her to let go and lighten up. Kimber had to bite her tongue to keep from reminding her sister that she'd contributed to Kimber's uptight personality by being the older wild-child sibling. When Kimber had seen how much angst Elaina had caused their mother, she'd fallen into the role of the obedient child. Maybe she was wound a little tight, but it worked for her. Meanwhile, Elaina lived with her longtime boyfriend Mike, who epitomized the word "dreamer." Kimber resented how hard her sister worked in comparison to her partner, but she held her tongue to keep sisterly peace.

"Just for you, I'll try to loosen up," she said lightly.

"You packed lots of sunscreen, didn't you? Someone with your complexion wasn't meant to be so close to the equator."

A wry smile curved Kimber's mouth. "I'm stocked up." She was accustomed to protecting her pale skin. She only hoped the humidity on the islands didn't turn her wavy hair into a mass of brown frizz. "If there's nothing else you have to tell me," Kimber said in a singsongy voice, "I'll let you go."

"No, there's nothing else. Have a great time, sis."

Elaina's voice sounded concerned, and Kimber realized her sister was worried about the engagement no longer being a surprise. To put her at ease, she murmured, "Everything is going to be wonderful, thanks to you."

"I hope so," Elaina said, sounding unconvinced. "Call me if anything goes wrong."

Kimber laughed. "In that case, don't expect to hear from me because this is going to be the vacation of a lifetime—nothing is going to go wrong on this trip."

At the knock on her door, Kimber lifted her gaze to see Anna standing there with a stricken look on her face. Next to her stood the immaculately coiffed Della Pennington, holding a large white envelope in her elegant, diamond-studded hands.

"Gotta go," Kimber murmured, then disconnected, unease stirring in her chest. She conjured up a smile. "Mrs. Pennington, so nice to see you. Is there a problem?"

Della Pennington burst into tears. "I need your help."

"I tried to explain that you have to leave soon," Anna offered.

But her client's tears alarmed Kimber—normally the woman was like a little oak tree. "It's all right. Come in, Mrs. Pennington." She stood, grabbed a couple of tissues from a box and motioned for Anna to close the door on her way out.

She guided Della to a chair. "I see you received the final papers. I'm sorry, I should've called and warned you."

Della dabbed at her shimmering eyes. "No, dear, it's fine. I knew this day would come." Suddenly she smiled. "These are happy tears because a divorce will no longer be necessary."

Panic blipped in Kimber's chest. "Has something happened to Mr. Pennington?"

"Yes, as a matter of fact. I hired a private investigator to follow him."

Kimber swallowed hard, worried that Della had uncovered a girlfriend and had snapped, doing something terrible. "And?"

"And I found out about the brain tumor."

Kimber blinked. "Brain tumor?"

"I knew something was wrong with my Gerald, and it turns out I was right. He was hiding it from me."

"Is Mr. Pennington going to be okay?"

Della sighed. "The tumor is benign, but it's growing and affecting his mind, which is why he started all this divorce nonsense in the first place."

Kimber's chest filled with wonder. "All those times you defended your husband, I thought you were in denial. After all he put you through, you still believed in him."

Della's bright blue eyes shone with wisdom. "When

you truly love someone, my dear, common sense goes out the window. If you follow your heart, you might get hurt, but you'll never go wrong." She winked, then sobered. "Now I have another problem. Gerald refuses to have an operation that surgeons say will save his life."

"Do you think the tumor could be preventing him from making an informed choice?"

"Yes. Which is why I need to have Gerald's medical guardianship assigned to me as soon as possible." She clasped Kimber's hands. "I realize you're about to leave town on vacation, but you understand our situation better than anyone, and time is of the essence. Will you help me, dear?"

The flash of regret over changing her travel plans lasted only a heartbeat. Mr. Pennington's life was on the line. Kimber squeezed Della's hands. "Of course. I'll get the forms ready. After that, it's only a matter of getting them signed by your husband's doctors and finding a sympathetic judge. Let me make some phone calls and start putting things in motion, okay? With luck, we might be able to wrap this up in a couple of hours. You can wait in the lounge and Anna will get you whatever you need to be comfortable."

The woman's shoulders fell in relief and her eyes teared up again. "Thank you so much. I'm sorry to disrupt your plans."

"Don't worry about it," Kimber soothed. "I'll still have time to catch my flight."

As the woman left her office, Kimber picked up the phone and dialed Gil's cell phone. After several rings, he answered.

"Hi, sweetheart. I'm on my way."

She made a mournful sound. "Slight change of plans. Something came up with a client that I need to handle."

"Oh, no," he said, disappointment resonating over the line. She could almost hear the wheels turning in his head, thinking about all the details he had to take care of once he reached the Maldives. If she knew Gil, he was planning a big production before getting down on his knee to propose. He didn't like surprises, interruptions or delays.

"Don't worry," she added quickly. "I should still make it to the airport in time to catch our flight to Singapore."

"Are you sure?"

"Yes. You go on ahead. I'll see you there."

"Promise?"

"Absolutely."

CHAPTER TWO

"NO, NO, NO!" KIMBER YELLED as the traffic in front of her slowed to a halt. "Don't stop—I'm going to miss my flight!"

On cue, her cell phone rang. It was Gil, frantic.

"Kimber, where are you? We're going to be boarding the plane soon."

"I'm stuck in traffic on the connector. I'll be there as soon as I can."

"I can't believe you let this happen. We've been planning this trip for months!"

She closed her eyes briefly. "I know, Gil, and I'm sorry. But Della Pennington—"

"Oh, God, her again? Kimber, you let that woman take up too much of your time."

"This was different, Gil. She found out her husband is sick. She needed my help to get medical guardianship so he could have surgery—"

"So how far from the airport are you?"

Kimber frowned at being cut off, then told herself that Gil wasn't as callous as he was behaving—he was just upset. He was trying to get her to a romantic destination so he could propose, and fate was conspiring against them. "If traffic starts moving soon, I'll be there in about fifteen minutes."

"Okay, call me when you get here."

"I love you," she murmured, but Gil had already ended the call. She sighed. He had a right to be upset with her. The trip was costing them a small fortune, after all, and although she wasn't supposed to know about it, their vacation represented a huge step in their relationship and in their lives. And Gil was so fastidious he was probably nervous about every detail.

Which was why, when fifteen minutes later she'd moved only a mile down the interstate, instead of calling Gil, she called her sister.

"Tinsel Travel, this is Elaina."

"I spoke too soon," Kimber said without preamble. "Something came up at work. Is it possible to get me on a later flight to Singapore?"

"You're kidding, right?"

"I wish."

The clicking of a computer keyboard sounded in the background. "Let's see, you and Gil are booked from Atlanta to Houston to Moscow, with a layover in Moscow before flying on to Singapore, then to Maldives."

"Mmm-hmm," Kimber murmured, chewing on her nail and throwing up a prayer.

A couple of minutes later Elaina said, "Okay, the good news is there's one seat available on a flight leaving from Atlanta three hours from now."

"Great!"

"The bad news is that it's in coach and you'd be connecting in Chicago, then Hong Kong before going on to Dubai."

"Dubai?"

"From there you'll take a puddle jumper to Maldives."

"I can't even travel to the islands with Gil?"

"No, but the good news is that Dubai is actually closer to Maldives than Singapore, and you'll have shorter layovers, so you might even get to the islands before him."

"Oh, that's…not awful," she said, her mind racing. At least his patience wouldn't be tried further by having to wait for her there.

"I'm afraid it's the best I can do," Elaina said.

"Okay," Kimber said in desperation. "Book me and text me the details."

"I'll have to make separate arrangements for a local flight from Dubai to the Maldives, and that could take a while, so call me when you land in Dubai."

"Thanks, sis." She disconnected the call and steeled herself before phoning Gil. He answered immediately.

"Where are you? I'm already seated on the plane!"

"I'm so sorry, hon—I'm still sitting in traffic."

"This is a disaster," he said, and she pictured him jamming his hand into his hair.

"It'll be fine. I just talked to Elaina and she got me on alternate flights." But when she explained that he'd be connecting in one continent, and she in another, a strangled noise came over the line.

"Kimber, I can't believe you managed to mess this up. This is *no* way to start a vacation. I'm so irritated!"

"I know," she soothed, knowing his blood pressure had spiked. "And I'm sorry we're not traveling together. When I get to the airport, I'll text you my new itinerary. And I'll be waiting for you in the Maldives with a cold drink."

"Okay," he groused. "But I'm not happy about this."

"Me, neither," she said, not wanting him to be in a bad mood when he proposed. "But everything's going to work out fine. You'll see. I love you."

He sighed. "I love you, too."

She ended the call, antsy and sick to her stomach for foiling Gil's plans. It was sweet of him to go to so much trouble. She was glad she'd gotten things worked out for Della Pennington before she left, but she had a feeling she'd be paying for that sacrifice for a while to come.

She had plenty of time to think about how she was going to make things up to Gil while sitting in traffic for another hour. Their sex life wasn't home-movie material, but that was only because when they were together, they were usually too tired to be creative. She intended to reverse that trend with her extra suitcase of lingerie.

Mercifully, traffic began to move and she arrived at Atlanta Hartsfield-Jackson Airport in time to check her two large Louis Vuitton bags and grab a snack before boarding the plane. Unfortunately the "last seat available" was also the least desirable seat on the aircraft— the center seat in the last row, next to the lavatory. Wedged between two men. One guy overflowed into her seat and the other guy snored like a walrus. The two-and-a-half-hour flight to Chicago wasn't too bad, but she was dismayed to discover they were also her seatmates on the subsequent fifteen-hour flight to Hong Kong. The first-class seats she and Gil had booked taunted her. Right now Gil was probably stretched out horizontally after being tucked in with a warm blankie and a nightcap.

Kimber stuffed tissue in her ears and dozed as best she could around the snoring and the bathroom door banging open and closed, but it was the most interminable flight she'd ever been on. The hands on her watch seemed to crawl, even as she adjusted them when they crossed time zones. Thankfully, she got to change planes in Hong Kong and was seated beside a window, but her stomach sank when a woman with two small children took the seats next to her. The toddlers were fussy from the start, and their wails only grew louder as the flight progressed. Trapped against the wall, Kimber couldn't avoid flying baby food and toys. She had apple juice poured down one of her legs, and her head pounded from one of the children banging on the seat tray with a truck. To top it all off, the fickle air-conditioning left her sweating in her sticky seat.

She was so miserable she wanted to cry. True, compared to a brain tumor, disrupted travel plans were a relatively small matter, but this was her engagement—her future was on the line. And since leaving Atlanta, she had leapfrogged an entire day and was operating on next to no sleep. She longed to take a shower and crawl into bed. Only the enticing image of an island paradise kept her going. Hours later, despite the fact that her eyelids felt like sandpaper, she was able to rouse herself enough to observe the spectacular sight of the city of Dubai lit up beneath them, sparkling in predawn light.

Kimber gasped, enchanted by the exotic skyline of soaring buildings, a mixture of onion domes and ultra-contemporary silhouettes. A pinkish-yellow glow emanated from the city. The effect was magical. Regret pinged through her that she wouldn't get to experience the city that she suddenly found captivating. That would have to wait for another trip, another time.

As soon as the flight landed and began to taxi, she turned on her cell phone and punched in Elaina's number. After a few rings, her sister's sleepy voice came over the line.

"Hello?"

"Sis, it's me. Sorry to wake you, but I just landed in Dubai."

"How were the flights?"

She shot a glance toward the woman with the toddlers, who had finally cried themselves to sleep. "Over, thank goodness. Did you get a flight arranged for me from Dubai to the Maldives?" Kimber rubbed her bleary eyes. She reminded herself that a hammock over a blue lagoon awaited her.

"Yes, I found you a flight."

Kimber squinted at her sister's odd tone. "But?"

"But it's a private charter, so it's a bit more expensive."

"At this point, I don't care. Where do I meet the plane?"

"I'll let the pilot know you're there, and I'll phone you back."

"Okay." Kimber ended the call and swallowed a caffeine capsule to make her more alert.

She was one of the last people to deplane and it took nearly an hour to retrieve her two large suitcases from baggage claim. She was pulling the bigger and heavier bag from the conveyor belt when Elaina called back.

"The pilot will meet you in one hour outside customs."

"How will I know him?"

"He'll be wearing a green hat that reads 'M Charters.' His name is Finn Meyers."

"He's American?"

"Right. My agency has worked with him before, and he's reliable. Kimber, just one more thing."

"Yeah?"

"People in that part of the world are more laid-back than Westerners. You might need to…go with the flow."

Kimber frowned. "I can flow."

"Uh-huh," her sister said, sounding doubtful. "Call me when you get to your island paradise to let me know you arrived. Meanwhile, try to have fun."

"Right," she said in a mocking voice. "Thanks, sis." Kimber ended the call, then punched in Gil's number. She left a message with details about the chartered flight and that she'd meet him in the Maldives, at the bungalow they'd reserved. "I love you," she murmured. "This is going to be a great trip. Really."

The line at customs snaked as far as she could see. Heavy with fatigue, she leaned on her luggage, waiting for the caffeine to kick in. The airport was unexpectedly beautiful—even opulent. It was like a combination atrium and shopping mall. She got glimpses in the distance of contemporary architecture, shiny retail stores and towering palm trees planted indoors. The impressive, immaculate airport was obviously meant to be the gateway to a progressive city.

While she admired her surroundings, Kimber shifted from foot to foot in discomfort. The high-heeled pumps hadn't been the best choice for travel, although in her defense, she'd dressed for the roominess of a first-class cabin. Her pale skirt suit looked a little the worse for wear, too. She'd considered removing her panty hose in the plane lavatory, but frankly, she hadn't had the energy. Kimber repaired her chignon as best as she could without a mirror, and hoped she had time to visit a ladies' room, freshen up and change clothes before meeting the pilot.

But it was not to be.

Getting through customs took longer than she'd anticipated, so long, in fact, that nearly two hours had elapsed by the time she reached the other side. She stopped and dropped her luggage, whirling around to catch a glimpse of a green hat. Across the way, a man sat sprawled in a seat wearing cargo pants and a loud, flowered shirt, his arms crossed and his legs stretched out in front of him, a green cap pulled down over his face.

Kimber stepped closer and squinted at the hat, relieved to see that it read "M Charters." She cleared her throat several times, hoping to wake him, but he didn't stir. She lightly tapped his arm and although a zing went through her fingers at the feel of the firm muscle beneath the bronzed skin, he didn't move. Irritated, she reached forward and lifted the bill of his cap.

His arm shot out and long, strong fingers circled her wrist. His brown-eyed gaze leveled on her. "What do you want?"

She gasped. "I'm sorry. I believe you're my pilot."

A sardonic smile lifted his mouth as he looked her up and down. "I'll be anything you want me to be, lady."

She frowned and yanked her hand back, straightening. "Mr. Meyers?"

"Finn," he corrected.

"I believe you were hired to take me to the Maldive Islands?"

"Are you—" he pushed the cap back on his head of shaggy, dark blond hair and reached into the pocket of his loud shirt to pull out a scrap of paper "—Kimber Karlton?"

"Yes."

He grinned. "Bet you got that name in prep school."

She frowned. "Can we be going, please? I'm in a hurry to meet my boyfriend."

He made a rueful noise. "Boyfriend, huh? Too bad."

She tingled with awareness as his gaze raked over her. Chalking it up to the caffeine finally kicking in, she bristled. "Mr. Meyers, I'm exhausted and I'm really not in the mood for your lame attempts at flirtation."

He sighed. "You're right—that wasn't my best line, but it's pretty damn early in the morning and I haven't been to bed yet." Then he chuckled. "Well, not to sleep, anyway."

Her eyes flew wide. "You're going to fly a plane on no sleep?"

He gestured to the seat he occupied. "I caught a catnap while I was waiting. Don't get your panties in a twist."

She blinked, then set her jaw. "May we get going?"

"We may," he said, then pushed his long body to his feet and took off walking toward the exit.

"I have bags," she called after him, gesturing to her luggage.

"I'm not a porter," he said over his shoulder. "And you should never pack more than you can carry."

Kimber gaped at his receding back. The man was

rude beyond belief. Despite her sister's endorsement, she was tempted to fire Finn Meyers and find other arrangements. Then she reminded herself that the goal was to reach the Maldives and get her marriage proposal. Suffering an ill-mannered pilot was a small sacrifice.

Resigned, she picked up her heavy suitcases and trudged after him.

CHAPTER THREE

FINN MEYERS resisted the urge to look over his shoulder to see if Fancy Pants was following him. When Elaina Karlton had begged him to take the job, she hadn't mentioned that her sister was so…hot.

Or she might be if she unclenched a little.

When he exited the airport to the outside, he put on aviator sunglasses against the glare of the early-morning sun. Hangovers were a bitch, but he wouldn't have had that last shot of tequila if he'd known he'd be flying a charter this morning.

Then he chuckled to himself. On second thought, he probably would've had that last shot regardless.

Whistling tunelessly under his breath, he made his way across crowded crosswalks toward the car park, enjoying, as always, the colorful diversity of the people, the vehicles, and the languages around him. After years of living in and around Dubai, he still felt as if he was on vacation in an exotic land.

"Mr. Meyers!" he heard from behind him. "Wait!"

Finn winced. It was the occasional brush with spoiled, uptight Americans that reminded him why he'd left his home country. Finn turned to see the prim

Kimber Karlton trying to keep up with him in those ridiculous high heels, struggling with her enormous suitcases. Conceding that losing her would be inconvenient, he folded his arms and waited until she caught up to him.

She was a slender whip of a woman, her skin as pale as nonfat milk. Much of her long brown hair had come loose from its knot. Because she was overdressed, the heat was already taking its toll. Her skin was shiny with perspiration, and each cheek sported a scarlet splotch. She pushed the wayward hair back from her face and settled her stormy, blue-eyed gaze on him. "I could use some help here."

"You're doing fine," he said, clapping her on the shoulder. "Besides, my SUV isn't much farther."

"And then what?"

"Then we'll drive to the airport where my plane is parked. By the way, I hope you don't get airsick easily." He turned and headed in the direction of his vehicle, squashing a pang for the woman. He was hired to do a job, and that was that. Stormy blue eyes be damned.

KIMBER WANTED to scream. Or cry. She was exhausted and starved, and her suitcases weighed a ton. Meanwhile, Finn Meyers strolled along in front of her as if he hadn't a care in the world. And from the look of his broad-shouldered physique, he could easily have managed one of her cases, if not both.

She reminded herself to focus on her goal, reaching the Maldives, where she would reunite with Gil and they would have the vacation she'd dreamed about.

Finn Meyers must at least be a safe person, otherwise her sister wouldn't have recommended him.

Unchivalrous, yes, but safe.

Kimber took a deep breath and reached for the handles of her luggage, juggling the bulky purse on her shoulder and grimacing against the sting of blisters on her feet. She glanced from side to side in an attempt to soak up all the sites she could, but in her effort to keep up with Mr. Meyers, she was left with little more than impressions of vibrant clothing and the lively exchange of Arabic and other languages she couldn't identify.

Meanwhile, people stared at her openly, and she wondered what kind of spectacle she must present— dressed in distinctive, impractical western clothing and disheveled beyond respectable boundaries, especially for a woman. Knowing that she was so out of her element and at the mercy of Finn Meyers made her speed up a little to keep him in sight. She gritted her teeth against the aching muscles in her arms, but she'd let her arms fall off before she'd ask for his help again.

At last he stopped at a faded, butterscotch-colored Toyota FJ Cruiser with a white top. She shuffled up with her load a few minutes later to find him leaning against the SUV studying his fingernails.

He looked up. "You're moving awfully slow for someone who's in such a big hurry."

She released the handles of her bags with a noisy exhale, then straightened. "Do I look like a pack mule?"

"Actually, in this part of the world, it would be a pack camel, and…" He looked her over head to toe, lingering on her breasts and her legs so long that they tingled beneath his appreciative gaze. "No, you don't look like a mule or a camel, although the humps—"

"*Could* we get going, please?" she cut in with a glare.

"Sure. Let me load those bags for you." He hoisted the suitcases as if they weighed nothing and tossed them in the back of the SUV without so much as a grunt. They landed with sickening thuds.

"Be careful!" she said. "All my stuff is in there."

"So like an American to pack your entire wardrobe," he said, then gestured to her suit. "I hope you brought something more sensible than that outfit."

She yanked at the wrinkled lapels of her jacket and lifted her chin. "I did. I assume there'll be someplace for me to change once we arrive at the other airport?"

"Er, sure," he said congenially.

She opened the passenger door of the SUV, looking forward to the comfort of a roomy, upholstered seat, then stopped and stared at the space that was empty except for a dozen or so empty beer cans.

Finn, who had swung into the driver's seat, glanced over. "Oh. I had to take out the seat for cargo. Here you go." He reached behind his seat and pulled out a blue, plastic milk crate, then plopped it down where the passenger seat should have been.

Kimber's mouth fell open. "You don't really expect me to sit on a milk crate, do you?"

He shrugged. "It's that or the floor. Or I can drag one of your big-ass suitcases up here for you to straddle."

She frowned. "I'll sit on the crate."

"I thought you might."

She used a handle to pull herself up into the SUV and settled gingerly on the crate before closing the door. He cranked up the engine and she scarcely had time to plant her feet among the beer cans before they lurched into motion.

Kimber gripped the door handle and the center console to steady herself. If she craned her neck, she could barely see over the dashboard. Meanwhile, the hard ridges of the crate were practically assaulting her. She winced and shifted, finding no relief.

"Wouldn't hurt so much if you had more padding down there," he offered.

Kimber shot him a glare. "You shouldn't concern yourself with my behind."

"I thought that was my job—delivering your behind to the Maldives to…meet your boyfriend, did you say?"

"That's correct." Gil would be landing in Singapore soon. He was disappointed, rightfully so, that they wouldn't be arriving together. But she'd make it up to him with the leopard-print bra and crotchless panties. The extra suitcase of lingerie would be her saving grace.

Finn stopped the SUV at a pay booth and removed his wallet. "By the way, the bill for parking in the short-term pay lot for all this time will be added to your tab."

"Fine," she mumbled.

While he flirted shamelessly with the young attendant, Kimber had a chance to study him more closely. He had what some might consider a nice profile of bold, clear features, but it was compromised by the day's worth of dark beard that gave credence to his story of staying up all night. He appeared to be in his mid-thirties, but he had the loose posture and demeanor of someone ten years younger. Everything about him—the cluttered vehicle, the loud shirt, the lack of manners—

was in opposition to everything she believed in about pushing oneself to excellence and integrity. It was beyond her how some people could set their personal standards so low.

When the attendant passed him a receipt, Kimber noticed the woman had written her name and phone number on it. He pulled away, seemingly satisfied with himself. Kimber rolled her eyes.

The SUV windows were down, ushering in hot, arid air. Her hair blew in disarray, but she was too tired to care. She stretched up to see out the windows and take in her surroundings. Dubai was a dense city, with towering skyscrapers and elevated highways. Construction cranes were everywhere, speaking to the rate of progress.

"First time in Dubai?" he asked.

"Yes."

"Great city, great people," he said, then reached behind his seat again. This time, he withdrew two yellow apples. "Want one?"

She practically pounced on it, then bit into it greedily.

"What do you do back in the States?" he asked, then bit into his own apple.

"Attorney," she said between bites.

He made a rueful noise in his throat. "Too bad." He turned his attention back to the road, blatantly unimpressed.

Kimber frowned and concentrated on devouring the apple and not falling off the crate. "How far to the other airport?"

He shrugged. "It depends on traffic. And it's actually more of an airstrip than an airport."

She didn't care as long as they could get airborne sooner rather than later. Kimber gnawed the apple down to the seeds.

"Hungry much?" he asked with a grin. He took her core and tossed it out the window.

"Thank you," she mumbled self-consciously, then removed a handkerchief from her purse to wipe her hands. She felt his gaze on her, sizing her up. It made her squirm because she knew he didn't approve of her, that he thought her, her luggage and her occupation were frivolous. She withdrew a compact and groaned inwardly at her pale, makeup-less reflection. She swiveled up her pink lipstick for a quick fix, but when she tried to apply it, the SUV swerved, leaving her with a bright streak on one cheek.

Kimber gasped and Finn burst out laughing.

"You did that on purpose," she accused, wiping at her cheek with the handkerchief.

"Put that stuff away," he said. "No one here cares what you look like."

She stiffened at his rebuff. "I care."

"Ah, loosen up, Fancy Pants."

She frowned. "Don't call me that. And don't tell me to loosen up."

"Get told that a lot, huh?"

"*No.*"

He laughed, which only irritated her more. She refused to look at him, concentrating, instead, on the scenery. Dubai could have been any large city in the States, except for the onion-dome architecture, soaring palm trees and the road signs written in Arabic. Another difference was that everything looked new and was tinged with a beautiful golden-pink sheen from the mesmerizing sky palette. And despite the streets being clogged with vehicles and the sidewalks being packed with people, the pace was decidedly slower. Fewer honking horns, more chatter. The reduced tempo could be attributed to the pervasive heat, she knew, but she also recalled Elaina's comments about life in this part of the world being more relaxed.

It was an existence alien to Kimber. In fact, anxiety crowded her chest at the thought of all the billable hours a company would forgo in a week's time, the business that wouldn't transpire, the items on a to-do list that wouldn't get done. The relative lethargy would drive her mad.

"Can't you go any faster?" she asked, glancing at the speedometer.

"Nope," he said cheerfully.

But soon they'd left the city behind and were moving through a less dense area. Tree copses and sparsely grassed fields became more common, interspersed with pockets of residential areas. When Kimber spotted a small plane rising in the distance, she breathed a sigh of relief. They must be getting close. Good thing, too, because her rear end was numb and, she feared, might be forever imprinted with the waffle design of the plastic crate.

"Here we are," he said congenially, then slowed and turned onto a paved road that stretched across a field.

The going was bumpy, though, and Kimber sucked in breaths against the keen pain of bouncing on the crate. After an interminable length of time, a large, long, metal building came into view—the hangar, she assumed. Finn slowed the vehicle and pulled into a parking lot populated with Lamborghinis and Rolls-Royce and Bentley limousines.

Obviously many private planes were housed there.

She groaned in relief when the SUV came to a stop, but it was a few seconds before she could lift herself off the insidious crate. To his credit, Finn did walk around and open her door. But to her dismay, Kimber practically fell into his arms trying to climb out.

"Whoa," he said, steadying her.

Their gazes locked and she was struck mute by the merry light in his brown eyes. It was so unfamiliar, this glib cheerfulness. The lines on either side of his mouth spoke of the ease with which he smiled and laughed. It was unsettling…and suspect. Kimber became aware of his warm hands on her waist and arm, and she jerked away. The man was probably used to seducing every woman in his path with a tickle and a grin.

She stepped back and smoothed her hands over her wind-whipped hair. Her suit was a mass of wrinkled fabric, her soft leather pumps were scarred and dusty, and her panty hose sported a two-inch wide run. "Where can I change clothes?"

Finn moved to the back of the SUV and removed her bags, setting them on the ground. Then he withdrew a black duffel and hooked it over his shoulder. "You can change right here."

She looked around the parking lot crowded with cars. "Here? Isn't there a bathroom inside the hangar?"

He made a rueful noise. "Not for female types, I'm afraid. The facilities are primarily for pilots and employees, all of whom pee standing up."

"So I'm supposed to change clothes right here in broad daylight?"

"I'll hold up a towel for you." He grinned. "And I won't even look—unless you want me to."

Outraged, Kimber lifted her chin. "No, thank you. I'll wait until we land."

"Suit yourself. Let's go."

He closed the SUV hatch and took off walking toward the hangar, leaving Kimber openmouthed. "Aren't you going to help me with my luggage?"

He turned around, but kept walking backward. "That whole not-packing-more-than-you-can-carry thing still stands."

Kimber gritted her teeth in frustration, then retrieved her suitcases and followed him, telling herself that her time with the odious Finn Meyers was almost over. A few more hours, then she never had to lay eyes on him or his flowered shirt again.

CHAPTER FOUR

FINN'S MIND AND BODY were clicking away as he walked toward the hangar. He was loathe to walk away from paying work, but Kimber Karlton was more of a handful than he'd anticipated.

Sure, she was the run-of-the-mill high-maintenance American female—he'd expected that. What he hadn't expected was his perverse need to rankle her, to push her buttons, to bring her down a notch. Maybe she reminded him a little too much of himself at one time.

Or maybe he was simply homesick for that independent feminine sexuality that seemed exclusive to American women. Kimber Karlton had the mind of an attorney and the body of a cocktail waitress. Every man's dream.

And nightmare, he reminded himself with a mental shake. Her sister Elaina was compensating him well, so he'd best keep his mind on business.

He shouted hello to Arif, the young man who had towed Finn's Cessna 152 from the hangar.

"Hello, Mr. Finn. She is ready to fly."

"Thank you, Arif."

Something behind Finn had caught the young man's

attention. Finn turned and watched as Kimber struggled toward them with her two suitcases. "I hope *she's* ready," he muttered.

"The lady is your passenger?" the young man asked. "I will help her."

"No." Finn stopped him. "You'll offend her if you offer to help. American women want to do everything themselves."

The boy nodded solemnly. "I have heard this about American women." He studied Kimber with blatant interest, then turned back. "But she is pretty, yes?"

Finn frowned. "Trust me, Arif. They only look like that to get you into their cage, then they will eat you alive."

Arif laughed. "That is not just American women, Finn. That is any woman."

"You have a point, my friend."

"With all that luggage, are you sure you don't want to take your larger plane?"

"Yes, I'm sure."

"But—"

"I'm sure, Arif." Finn extended a one-hundred-dirham note. "Load the smaller suitcase only."

Arif's eyes widened, then he took the money. "Yes, sir." The young man handed Finn a log to record his flight plan. "When will you return?"

"As soon as possible," Finn said. But when Kimber dropped her bags next to the plane and lifted her defiant blue gaze to his, he muttered, "And not soon enough."

KIMBER LOOKED over the toy plane that Finn stood next to and her stomach bolted. "*This* is your plane?"

"Yep."

"It's a tin can with a propeller."

His mouth quirked. "Don't worry, the rubber bands holding it together are strong."

She swallowed hard.

"Kidding, okay? It'll get us up and down."

"In a horrific fiery freefall?" Kimber lifted her arms and shook her head. "I can't ride in a plane this small." She waved vaguely toward the hangar. "Get another, preferably adult-size."

He scowled. "This is it, Fancy Pants. If you'd rather take your chances getting a seat on a commercial flight, just say the word and I'll take you back to the airport." He made a rueful noise. "'Course, my fee still stands."

Kimber bit down on the inside of her cheek. She was sleepy, hungry, grungy and at least one of the other seven dwarfs she couldn't think of at the moment, but she was determined not to cry in front of this man. She'd just keep reminding herself that within a few hours, she'd be in paradise with Gil and they would laugh over her misadventures with the slackard pilot. She angled her head. "Will I have to sit on a milk crate for the duration of the flight?"

Finn grinned. "No."

She took a deep breath, then puffed out her cheeks in an exhale. "Okay."

Finn looked her up and down. "Looks like you weigh what, about a buck twenty-five?"

"Yes…why?"

He tapped the log. "I need to record the cargo."

"Cargo?" She arched an eyebrow. "Let me guess—you're not married?"

"Nope."

"Shocker."

Finn gestured to the young man standing next to him who had been watching their exchange with avid interest. "Kimber, say hello to Arif."

"Hello, Arif," she said, sticking out her hand.

"Hello, miss." He blushed and shook her hand.

Finn turned to her. "After I finish the preflight check, we'll be ready to go. You can go ahead and get in."

Arif helped her into the plane. The cockpit was the size of a love seat. Her heart thudded in her chest and her hands felt clammy. The heat inside the metal plane was oppressive. From her purse she removed a moistened towelette and dabbed at her hairline. Unfortunately there wasn't a mirror over the visor, or even a visor. But she was too tired to care what she looked like. And as Finn had so elegantly put it—no one here cared.

Certainly not him.

She watched him through the windows as he circled the plane, checking the underside of the wings, withdrawing into a tube a clear liquid she assumed was fuel, then holding it up to analyze it. This was a side of Finn she hadn't yet seen—thoughtful and methodical, a man who knew his stuff. It made her feel safe. And it made her wonder how and why he'd ended up here in Dubai.

Not that it wasn't a glorious place as far as she'd seen. An exciting place, to be sure, and Finn Meyers was certainly the adventurous type. But despite his happy-go-lucky nature, there was something aloof about the man, something intriguing…

The pilot-side door opened and he jumped inside.

"We're ready to take off." He pointed to a compartment on her side. "Airsick bags are inside if you need one."

"Where are the parachutes?"

"Ha, good one. Don't worry—we won't be that high."

"You mean, if we fall out of the sky, we'll still be okay?"

"No, I mean if we fall out of the sky, we'll hit the ground before we could deploy a parachute."

Kimber sat back in her seat. Dear God, what had she gotten herself into?

Finn put on headphones and started the engine. The nose propeller whirred to life and became a blur. The noise was so loud, it settled the question of whether she might catch a nap on the way. Her teeth rattled from the vibration. The plane began a slow taxi out to a runway. Finn was talking to someone in the tower throughout. Suddenly the plane surged forward and they were airborne. There weren't any armrests to grip, so she dug her fingernails into the seat. She closed her eyes tight as the feeling of weightlessness took hold in her stomach. Focusing on breathing in and out took her mind off the fact that they were hurtling through the air in a windup plane.

"Open your eyes," Finn shouted with a laugh. "You're missing out on the fun part."

Slowly Kimber opened her eyes and oriented herself. She swallowed and waited a few seconds to see if her stomach was going to revolt. When it didn't, she peered out the window to see they were circling back over the small airport. From the runway, Arif waved with both arms. And next to him on the ground....

Kimber's eyes went wide. "We left one of my suitcases!"

Finn made a clicking noise with his cheek. "Yeah… about that—we didn't have room."

She gaped at him. "But those are my clothes! What am I supposed to wear?"

He jerked his thumb over his shoulder. "You still have one suitcase."

"But it's full of…" Lingerie and bathing suits and other frivolously optimistic things, like strawberry-flavored body liqueur.

"Full of what?"

"Nothing." Her mouth tightened in anger. "You had no right to leave my suitcase behind!"

"I'm the pilot—I had every right. This plane only holds 520 pounds."

She did the math in her head and frowned. "How much do you weigh?"

"One eighty."

"With my weight, that's barely above three hundred. My suitcase couldn't weigh more than forty pounds—that's way less than 520!"

"But that's not counting the wood."

She lifted an eyebrow. "What wood?"

He sucked in air. "Guess your sister forgot to tell you about that part."

She set her jaw. "What part?"

"I have to make a pit stop in Sri Lanka to pick up wood for my house."

She blinked. "Come again?"

"I'm building a house and I can get wood in Sri Lanka that I can't get anywhere else. I told your sister that was the deal—we stop in Sri Lanka on the way to Maldives."

"Can't you take me to Maldives first and stop in Sri Lanka on the way back to Dubai?"

"No can do. The wood will be gone by then. It's a special shipment—I have to get there today."

Kimber tamped down the panic bubbling in her stomach. "Okay, that shouldn't take more than a couple of hours. We could still be in Maldives by late afternoon, right?"

"Uh...no."

"Why not?"

"Because I have to go to a remote place to get the wood. But don't worry—I'll fly you to Maldives first thing in the morning."

Indignation shot through her. "That's unacceptable!"

He shrugged. "Sorry. That was the deal."

"But my boyfriend is expecting me in Maldives this evening!"

"So call him."

She closed her eyes and swallowed the vile words that sprang to the back of her throat. "Of course I'll call him, but the point is, I want to be there tonight, not tomorrow morning!"

"Ah, come on—what difference will a few hours make?"

"A big difference!" she cried.

"Have you ever been to Sri Lanka?"

"No," she mumbled.

"So look at it as an unplanned adventure." He grinned. "Besides, you and your boyfriend would both be too tired to enjoy tonight, anyway."

She gasped. "How dare you!"

He winked. "We need to get you something to drink as soon as we land. That'll help loosen you up."

Kimber leaned her head back on the seat, numb. She didn't know whether to laugh or cry, and she didn't have the energy to do either. Gil would be furious at yet another delay—how would she explain a pit stop with another man in Sri Lanka?

Finn suddenly let out a whoop. "What a beautiful day to fly! Hang on, Fancy Pants, we're going over."

"Don't—" But her reprimand was cut short when the plane went into a roll. The breath was pulled from her lungs, and she felt as if her eyeballs might pop out of their sockets. This was it—she was going to die before Gil could propose. No prenuptial agreement, no Marchesa wedding dress. Just her jet-lagged, mangled body amongst a handful of metal and a loud, flowered shirt in someone's backyard in Dubai.

And just when she'd begun to make peace with her untimely death, the plane righted. Her eyeballs sprang back into place, and her stomach leveled. And it dawned on her that Finn had rolled the plane on purpose.

She opened her mouth to scream at him, but inexplicably, a laugh bubbled out, instead. Kimber rationalized she must be getting loopy from the lack of sleep. She could *not* find this guy entertaining, not when he was standing between her reaching Gil and his proposal.

Finn grinned. "I knew you had a fun streak, Fancy Pants."

At the pure joy on his face, Kimber's heart buoyed crazily. She wondered if she'd ever been that happy in her life. His abandon stirred her, and she couldn't help but smile back.

"We'll have fun in Sri Lanka," he said. "You won't regret it, I promise."

He reached out and gave her knee a squeeze. Unbidden, desire struck her midsection. She inhaled sharply against the tightening of her breasts, the quickening in her thighs. Finn's outrageous behavior was dangerously enticing.

Then another thought struck Kimber—where would they spend the night? And how much could she really trust this sexy, overgrown man-child?

CHAPTER FIVE

"WELCOME TO SRI LANKA," Finn said, spreading his arms wide as if he owned the country. "Actually, this is Colombo, the largest and most urban city in the country."

Kimber peered out the window of the taxi, marveling at the mix of cultures and colors and aromas. She closed her eyes. "Something smells heavenly. Good enough to eat!"

"I'm hungry, too," Finn said, then tapped the driver on the shoulder. He paid the man and they alighted in the middle of a narrow street crowded with taxis, bicycles and pedestrians.

"Follow me," Finn said.

As if she would let him out of her sight. He threaded through the crush of bodies, and she trotted to keep up. He stopped in front of a food counter and scanned the offerings. Kimber looked at the faded pictures of prepared dishes, but she was lost.

"Trust me to order for you?" Finn asked.

She nodded and covered a yawn. Fatigue pulled at her shoulders.

His expression softened. "We'll get something to eat, walk around a bit, then go back to the apartment for a nap."

Her pulse jumped. "Apartment?"

"Belongs to a friend of mine. He lets me use it when I'm in the city. It's small, but it's clean and convenient."

"I'll get a hotel room," she said.

"Nonsense, there's plenty of room for both of us."

Kimber decided not to worry about the close quarters and accommodations until she had to. If she found the apartment untenable, she'd make other arrangements.

While Finn ordered their food, she stepped away and pulled her cell phone out of her purse. Thank God she had service, but her battery was running low. Estimating she had enough juice for one call, she decided her best bet was to phone Elaina in case Gil was still in transit. According to his itinerary, he should be arriving in the Maldives right about now, assuming *his* trip hadn't hit any snags.

She dialed Elaina's number, squashing the voice in her head whispering that she hadn't called Gil because she didn't want to face his wrath. Thinking of him waiting for her in the Maldives, fuming, made her queasier than flying.

"Tinsel Travel, this is Elaina."

"Hi, sis."

"Kimber! How's it going?"

"Not great. The pilot you hooked me up with has his own agenda. He brought me to Sri Lanka—and he said you knew about it."

"Oh. Well…he might have mentioned a stop before Maldives, but Sri Lanka's not really out of your way."

"But he won't take me to Maldives until tomorrow."

"Well, that's not so bad. Sri Lanka is wonderful."

"Except that Gil is waiting for me in Maldives!"

"He'll just have to wait one more day. It'll be fine."

"The pilot also managed to lose one of my suitcases."

"But you have one left."

"Full of lingerie!"

"So buy some new things. These things happen when you travel. Remember what I said about going with the flow?"

"Yes." Kimber massaged the bridge of her nose to keep the tears at bay. "My phone's almost dead. Will you call Gil and tell him that I'll see him tomorrow?"

"Sure, no problem."

"And, sis…you don't have to mention to Gil that I'm in Sri Lanka with a man."

"Why not? It might do the android some good to think he has a little competition."

Kimber gasped. "Finn is no competition!"

From a few feet away, Finn called, "Hey, Fancy Pants, come and get your lunch!"

"Is that him?" Elaina asked. "Did he just call you Fancy Pants?"

"I have to go," Kimber said. "My phone's dying. Bye." She stabbed a button to disconnect the call, then groaned. She turned and marched up to Finn, who was juggling two plates heaped with food.

"Don't call me that," she admonished, taking one of the plates and the bottle of water he handed her.

He grinned and headed toward a long counter where people were eating standing up. "It got your attention, didn't it?"

Fragrant spices wafted from the plate, tickling her nose. "What is this?"

"Typical Sri Lankan lunch," he said, setting down his

plate and making a place for her to stand next to him. He pointed. "There's rice in the middle. Around the outside is meat curry, fish curry and vegetable curry. And the sauce is a gravy made with coconut milk."

Kimber's mouth watered. "Where are the utensils?"

"We don't need them," Finn said. Using his fingers, he mixed one of the curries with rice until it formed a bite-size ball, then popped it into his mouth. His expression was one of pure rapture. "That is so good," he said thickly. "Try it."

She made a face. "I should at least wash my hands first."

He guffawed. "Come on, try it."

Kimber hesitated, then picked up a mound of rice with her fingers and dredged it in the fish curry until it made a passable blob. She brought it to her mouth, losing half of it in the process, but managed to get a taste. "Yum—I taste saffron and…cardamom?"

"Very good," he said, nodding. "You'll get the hang of it."

She made another rice ball with the vegetable curry and put it in her mouth.

"Uh—watch that one," Finn warned.

Too late, green chilies burst into flames on her tongue, incinerating her mouth. Kimber's eyes went wide, then she swallowed, coughing and wheezing.

Finn laughed, then stopped her from reaching for her bottle of water. "That'll only make it worse—eat more rice to diffuse the chilies."

She did, wiping at the tears rolling down her cheeks. Slowly the heat dissipated, then she drank deeply from the bottle. "You set me up," she accused.

"I just didn't realize you were going to inhale the food before I could warn you. Sri Lanka has some of the spiciest dishes in the world."

A willowy young woman dressed in a yellow sari walked by, staring at Finn. He stared back and watched her walk away.

"Speaking of spicy dishes," Kimber said dryly.

He grinned. "Can't blame a man for looking."

Kimber glanced around at the exotic women all around them, as colorful and fragrant as tropical flowers. Next to them in her rumpled suit, she felt like a weed. "The women here are lovely."

He shrugged. "Yeah." Then he looked up. "But there's something to be said about a pair of big blue eyes and freckles."

She swallowed the food in her mouth without chewing. He liked her eyes? She covered her nose. "I don't have freckles."

"Oh, yes, you do." A smile tugged at his mouth. "With your complexion, you should wear sunscreen this close to the equator."

She gave him a wry smile. "It's in my suitcase you left behind."

"They have sunscreen here. I need to get some toiletries, too. We'll shop after we eat."

She nodded, marveling at how her anger with him over the delay had dissipated. He and Elaina were right—she should just enjoy the experience. Like the amazing food. By the time she finished eating, she had learned how to combine small amounts of the different curries with the rice for the most delicious mouthfuls.

"That was wonderful," she said, licking her fingers.

"Glad you enjoyed it," he said, then patted his stomach. "We'll both be ready for a nap by the time we get to the apartment." He disposed of their plates and she followed him along the sidewalk. The crowds had increased and she found it harder to keep up with him. He stopped and waited for her. When Kimber caught up, he clasped her hand in his.

"Just for safety," he said, so nonchalantly she didn't question it.

Besides, it felt pleasant…and right, being here in this exotic place with a man who knew his way around and appreciated the local customs.

"I'm surprised at all the English I hear," she commented.

"Yes, a lot of English is spoken here, but the official languages are Sinhala and Tamil."

"Do you speak them?" she asked.

"Just enough to transact business."

"You mean pick up women?"

"That, too," he agreed, then led her across the street to a textile market. "Do you see anything here you like?"

Kimber was awestruck by the panels of gorgeous handwoven and hand-dyed cloth used for saris. "It's all beautiful—but I'm not sure I could pull it off."

"Of course, you can," he said, then pointed to a deep-blue cobalt cloth with a yellow border. "How about that one?"

She nodded. "It's lovely."

"We'll take it," he said to the woman tending the booth.

Kimber fingered a pair of loose, flax-colored linen pants with a drawstring.

"Do you want those, too?" he asked.

She nodded, then chose a soft, white linen blouse to match. "The quality is incredible," she said, rubbing the fabric between her fingers.

"It's what they're known for," he said, then removed his wallet.

"I'll pay you back," Kimber said. "In fact, put it on my bill."

He hesitated, then nodded. "I can do that."

They stopped at another booth for a pair of soft leather sandals, and she found a beautiful scarf to tie back her hair. At a retail store they picked up toiletry basics, and by the time they checked out, Kimber was fighting to keep her eyes open.

"How about that nap?" Finn asked, flagging a taxi.

She could only nod. During the taxi ride, though, she could no longer fight it. Her eyes closed for good, and she leaned until her head met something soft and warm and enticing. Kimber succumbed to sleep, smiling.

FINN LOOKED DOWN at the woman who had snuggled up next to him and sighed. This was getting complicated. Maybe the stopover in Sri Lanka hadn't been the best idea, but he was counting on Kimber Karlton's prickly exterior to maintain a healthy distance between them.

He hadn't planned on her being…fun. And…sexy.

The taxi pulled up at the apartment. Finn shook Kimber, but she didn't respond. He handed the driver the door key and asked him to get their packages. Then Finn scooped Kimber up in his arms and carried her inside, depositing her on the only bed and removing her silly, travel-worn shoes.

He tipped the driver, then locked the door, yielding to a yawn of his own. Sleep would do them both some good, he decided, crawling onto the bed with her.

She turned and curled into him, and he rested his hand on the curve of her hip.

Yes, after a nap they would both be thinking more clearly.

CHAPTER SIX

KIMBER WAS LYING in a hammock under two perfect trees, swinging slightly, with an ocean breeze kissing her skin. She groaned with pleasure and licked her lips. She was so thirsty. Across the beach, Gil walked toward her, carrying a tray with a tall pink drink and a little blue box. Her ring! But when Gil reached her side, instead of reaching for the ring box, she reached for the glass. She was so thirsty…so thirsty…

She moaned past a dry throat and began to rouse from her relaxed state. She felt a warm body lying behind her and smiled. Gil. All the trouble getting to the island had been a bad dream…

She reached down and covered his hand with hers. Normally Gil wasn't a spooner. He liked to have his space in bed and lots of pillows. It felt nice having him tucked up behind her, his morning erection pressed against her.

He groaned, and Kimber's eyes popped open. It wasn't morning…and that didn't sound—or feel—like Gil. She blinked at the unfamiliar blue room and yellow curtains, trying to orient herself. Her mind raced. Her plane was diverted to Dubai, Elaina had arranged for a pilot to meet her…

Finn Meyers.

Her last memory was of being in a taxi, riding to an apartment to take a nap…

Oh, dear God.

Behind her, he shifted and pulled her closer to him. Kimber leaped from the bed and backed up against a wall.

On the bed, Finn started awake and lifted his head. "Huh? What's wrong? Are you okay?"

She narrowed her eyes. "How did I get here?"

He sat up and pulled his hand down his face. "You fell asleep in the cab. I carried you inside."

"You carried me?"

He frowned. "Yeah, and for the record, you felt heavier than 125 pounds."

"*Why* are you in bed with me?"

"Because it's the only bed in the apartment."

"I thought you said there was room for both of us!"

He gestured. "It's a big bed!"

She crossed her arms. "You were…lying too close."

He laughed and shook his head. "Oh, no—you're the one who cuddled up to *me*, Fancy Pants."

"*Stop* calling me that."

He sighed. "Relax. It was just a nap, nothing happened."

She ran her hands up and down her arms and looked around. "Where is this place? Does anyone know we're here?"

He swung his legs over the side of the bed and stretched his arms up high in a yawn. "We're in a nice residential neighborhood. If your body winds up in a ditch somewhere, the taxi driver will probably remember us since he had to help me get everything inside because you were comatose." He pointed to her right. "Through that door is a small kitchen, a TV and a phone if you feel inclined to call for help." He pointed to her left. "Or through that door is a bathroom and a shower that has decent water pressure." He lifted his hands. "Your choice."

She pursed her mouth, then fled to the bathroom.

"Save me some hot water," he yelled after her, "or I might be tempted to climb in with you."

Kimber closed the door and looked for a lock, but there was none. The bathroom was tiny, with a commode, pedestal sink and curtained shower. She turned and caught a glimpse of herself in the mirror and screamed.

A knock sounded at the door. "Are you okay in there?"

"Uh, yeah. I saw a bug. I'm fine." But her reflection was enough to scare anyone. Her face was pale except for huge freckles across her nose and cheeks, and mascara had smeared under her eyes, leaving her looking like a raccoon. Her hair was a big, brown bush. It wasn't her best look.

She glanced around and realized Finn had set her suitcase, purse and the packages she'd bought next to the shower. A pang of guilt stabbed at her for accusing him of trying to take advantage of her.

Then she frowned. If not for him, she'd be with Gil right now, in that hammock she'd dreamed about, with a diamond solitaire on her ring finger. Finn Meyers didn't deserve any credit—or slack. After all, she was footing the bill for this little side trip that was delaying *her* vacation.

The nap had done her a world of good, she decided as she stripped off her panty hose and suit and stuffed them all in the small trash can. She was already feeling more alert and capable of dealing with Finn Meyer and the beach-bum charm that apparently worked with most females.

But not this female.

She turned on the shower and stepped underneath the spray, uncaring that the water was still cool. Despite her shivering, Kimber groaned with pleasure to have the past two days' worth of travel washed away. A handful of shampoo and a bar of soap did wonders for her energy level. She scrubbed until her skin stung, then with Finn's threat to join her ringing in her head, she rinsed quickly and wrapped her hair in a towel. She opened the suitcase, frowning at all the frilly lingerie, rummaging past thongs and corsets and string bikinis for practical undies. Then she dressed in the new linen pants and shirt and pushed her feet into the soft sandals.

After smoothing sunscreen over her freckles, she dusted her face with powder and stroked mascara over her lashes. She drew back and studied the blue eyes Finn had commented on. They were her best attribute, she conceded, among her other passable features. Elaina was the beauty of the family, which probably had lent to her wild ways. Kimber had been happy to fade into the background and bury her nose in a book. Boys had never really noticed her. She didn't date at all in high school, and very little in college. There had been no time for a social life while going to law school. Gil Trapp had been her first serious relationship, and they had seemed well suited to each other from the beginning. They had settled into a routine so quickly and so easily she had never doubted their happiness.

She gave herself a mental shake. And she wasn't doubting it now. But she needed to call Gil and let him know she was okay. Knowing Gil, even if Elaina had reached him, he'd still be worried sick about her…and about his foiled plans.

Pushing the troubling thoughts from her mind, she removed the towel and combed conditioner through her long hair, leaving it to dry naturally. She emerged from the bathroom feeling like a new woman.

"I thought you'd drowned in—" Finn looked up from an upholstered chair in the sitting area and did a double take "—there." His Adam's apple bobbed. "Wow. You look…different."

"Thanks," she said dryly. "It's amazing what a little soap can do."

He was still staring. "Uh…there's beer and water in the fridge."

"Would it be all right if I placed a long-distance call on a credit card?"

"Sure." He pushed to his feet, holding the black messenger bag she'd seen earlier. "I'll just take a quick shower."

He stole another glance her way before leaving the room, and she smiled with feminine satisfaction. It felt good to be appreciated. Gil never—

She stopped the thought before it materialized. She would not compare her longtime boyfriend to a man she'd met—she squinted—was it only this morning? She felt as if she'd known Finn much longer.

The man had a way of making time crawl.

Kimber located the phone and fumbled her way through a conversation with an operator, who placed a call to Gil's cell phone.

On the second ring, he answered. "Hello?"

"Gil, it's me!"

"Kimber? Where the hell are you?"

She frowned at his tone. "I'm in Sri Lanka. Didn't Elaina call you?"

"Yes. The question is, why didn't *you* call me?"

Anger sparked in her stomach. "Because my battery was dying, and I thought I had a better chance of reaching her. And I'm fine, thanks for asking."

"Elaina told me you were fine. And don't get cross with me, Kimber. This is all your fault."

She pressed her lips together. "Being sidelined in Sri Lanka isn't my fault."

"If you'd been on the flight with me, none of this would've happened."

"We went over this, Gil. I couldn't leave Mrs. Pennington in a lurch."

"So you left me in a lurch, instead."

"I didn't plan it this way," she said quietly.

"I don't understand—Sri Lanka isn't that far. What's keeping you from traveling on to Maldives?"

She paced the small kitchen, trying to think of something to say that wouldn't further incite Gil's anger.

The door opened and Finn emerged wearing the cargo pants…and nothing else. His dark blond hair still held the comb marks, and the brown hair on his broad chest sparkled with droplets against tanned skin. Long, muscular arms and flat abs were simply a bonus. Kimber gawked.

"Kimber? Are you there?" Gil demanded.

She turned her back on Finn to gather her composure. "I'm sorry, what did you say, Gil?"

A frustrated noise came over the line. "I asked why you can't come directly to Maldives now, instead of waiting until tomorrow morning."

"Mechanical problems," she said, thinking it was easier to lie than to explain that Finn had offered to show her the countryside while he shopped for wood. "How is Maldives?"

"Just grand," Gil said morosely. "I'm glad I brought a book."

"Me, too," she said cheerfully. "I should hang up—this is probably costing a fortune. But I'll see you tomorrow, sweetie, okay?"

"Okay," he grumped. "Bye."

She opened her mouth to tell him she loved him, but he'd already hung up. She replaced the receiver slowly, then turned around. Finn, thank goodness, had donned a T-shirt.

"Everything okay?" he asked.

"My boyfriend's worried, is all."

He grinned. "Did you tell him you were in good hands?"

"Somehow I don't think that would've made him feel better."

"What's his name?"

"Gil."

He gave a little laugh. "Figures."

Kimber frowned. "What's that supposed to mean?"

A honk sounded outside.

"There's our driver," Finn said. "Ready?"

"Let me grab my purse." She jogged to the bedroom to get her purse and swung it over her shoulder. On the way back to the entrance, though, she forced herself to slow down. She shouldn't be so excited about spending the afternoon with someone other than Gil.

But she was.

CHAPTER SEVEN

"WHAT KIND OF HOUSE are you building?" Kimber asked Finn as they bumped over a rural road. She sat in the middle of the cab of a small, clattering pickup, jammed up against Finn to give the driver room to shift gears. The wizened little man driving the truck hadn't said a word since they'd climbed in.

"A small one," Finn said. "But I'm doing everything myself just the way I want it."

"What's the wood for?"

"A banister I'm building. I'm using as many different indigenous woods as I can. And here I can get teak, mahogany—even ebony."

"Sounds beautiful," she offered.

"I think it'll be nice when it's finished."

"Do you live alone?" she asked, then lifted her camera to take a picture of the passing scenery.

"No, there's Ally."

Kimber couldn't explain the stab of disappointment she felt—so the man was living with someone, what was it to her?

"Ally's my cat," he added.

She laughed. "You don't seem like a cat person."

"I'm not, but she just showed up one day and I can't get rid of her."

"So she adopted *you*."

"Something like that. I guess you live with your boyfriend?"

She shook her head. "We both have our own places in Atlanta. We work together, so living together just seems…too much." Something they'd have to sort out after they were married.

"Is The Varsity still in Atlanta?"

The Varsity, an Atlanta landmark, was reportedly the largest fast-food restaurant in the world. "Yes. You know The Varsity?"

"I've been through Atlanta a time or two."

"Where did you live in the States?"

"Everywhere," he said vaguely. "I guess I've always been a nomad, although I've been in Dubai longer than anywhere else—six years."

"How did you and my sister start working together?"

"I know her partner, Mike."

"Oh." Kimber pretended to adjust her camera. She should've known—it took a dreamer to know one.

"You don't like Mike?" Finn asked.

"Mike's a good guy," she said. "I could never understand why he didn't marry Elaina."

"They seem content, last I heard."

She shrugged. "I always thought she could do better."

"I guess Elaina didn't," he offered cheerfully.

Kimber lifted the camera and continued to capture scenes outside the truck window—the rugged, rolling countryside that could be alternately sparse and lush, and the colorful laundry lines that flanked many of the modest homes dotting hills that were studded with palm trees. Finn played tour guide, pointing out the major-industry crops of tea, coffee and rubber. She continued to be impressed by his knowledge and love of the area and acknowledged that she'd led a very insular existence.

An hour later they pulled up next to a home dwarfed by the large truck stacked high with wood sitting next to it. A stocky man and two preschool-aged children emerged from the home. Finn waved and climbed out to greet the man with a handshake. Kimber alighted gingerly, wanting to stretch her legs. Finn and the man began speaking in a language she didn't understand, and at his fluidity, she guessed that Finn had downplayed his command of the local language. The two men moved to the truck and Finn began to inspect the logs with his large hands.

Her mind went to his hand being parked on her hip during their nap. In sleep, his body had responded to hers…and hers to his. But she chalked it up to the fact that she and Gil hadn't been together in a while because of their busy schedules. And Finn would probably respond to any warm woman, she observed wryly. The man seemed to be built for physical pursuits and pleasure, and he probably approached lovemaking with the same zeal as flying—doing barrel rolls and whooping throughout.

Instead of disgusting her, though, the idea sent a zing of excitement through her. If she were inclined toward sexual experimentation, she imagined that Finn Meyers would be willing.

Finn was handling a long slab of wood with care, holding it up to peer down its length. He stroked the surface of the wood with such concentration and purpose the moisture disappeared from Kimber's mouth. Would he stroke his partner with such precision?

Finn looked up and caught her staring, then gave her a wink that flustered her. She averted her gaze and pulled out her camera to snap more photos. The view at this vantage point was inspiring—the landscape rocky, with splotches of bright color where clumps of purple and white flowers had managed to take root. The late-afternoon sun was high and hot, but a nice breeze at this altitude moderated the temperature. She inhaled deeply to fill her lungs with the clean, clear air, and exhaled slowly. She rarely took time to enjoy the outdoors when she was home in Atlanta, primarily because Gil was allergic to almost anything that grew, but she vowed to change that part of her life when she returned. Elaina belonged to a hiking club, and often asked Kimber to go on day trips. The next time, she'd take her sister up on the offer.

At the horizon was a strip of navy blue water, the Indian Ocean. Across the ocean to the west, Gil was waiting for her. She could practically feel his irritation reaching out to her over the miles.

A tug on her shirt tore her attention away from her thoughts. She looked down to see the two children, their eyes and teeth bright against brown skin. A girl and a boy, perhaps five years old, who looked so much alike she wondered if they were twins.

"Hello," Kimber said with a smile. "How are you?"

They didn't seem to understand her, but from behind her back, the little girl revealed a necklace woven from the purple and white mountain flowers. She offered it to Kimber.

"How beautiful!" she exclaimed, then touched her chest. "For me?"

The little girl nodded, and Kimber crouched to allow the girl to lift the necklace over her head.

"Thank you," Kimber said, fingering the simple, yet beautiful creation. She pointed to the camera and gestured between herself and the children. "May I take your picture?"

The children smiled and moved to stand together— they obviously knew what the camera was for.

She snapped the photo and thanked them before they scampered away from her. When she looked up, Kimber found Finn watching her with a smile on his face. On impulse she lifted the camera and snapped a photo of him. He held up his hand to ward off more pictures, then pulled out his wallet to pay for the boards and logs that had been set aside. He also pulled coins from his pocket and made a show of pulling them out of the ears of the little ones before placing them in their tiny hands. They laughed in delight. The stocky man helped Finn load the wood into the bed of the truck they'd arrived in. Kimber made her way back to the vehicle, grateful that she'd seen a little slice of daily life in a place she might not have otherwise been exposed to.

"Thank you for bringing me," she said to Finn when they'd settled back into the truck.

He seemed surprised. "You're not angry you're not in Maldives?"

"You worked me into a trip you'd already planned. I'm the interloper here."

"Still, this isn't what you'd planned. And your boyfriend must be upset."

"He is," she agreed. "Gil doesn't like surprises."

Finn laughed. "Surprises are why I get out of bed in the morning."

"The two of you couldn't be any more different," she said, trying not to notice how good it felt to be wedged up against him. He'd settled his arm across the back of the seat to give them more room, but it actually made for more intimate seating.

Finn's mouth set in a line and she realized that she might have unintentionally offended him by comparing him to Gil. "What's on the agenda for this evening?" she asked to change the subject.

"There's a festival in town—I thought it would give you a chance to wear your sari."

"I don't know how to wear it."

"I'll help you," he said with a grin, then wagged his eyebrows.

She elbowed him, glad he was back to his lewd self. This Finn she could handle. It was the Finn who was building his own home, who'd taken in a stray cat and who could make children laugh that had her off balance.

By the time the driver dropped them at the apartment, the sun was setting. Finn instructed the man to deliver the wood to the airstrip, then followed her inside. Kimber checked her cell phone and winced.

"What's wrong?"

"I forgot to charge the battery. Gil has probably been calling all afternoon." From her purse she pulled out the charger and a converter, then plugged it into a wall outlet. Worry gnawed at her over the grief she must be causing him. Gil didn't deserve to have his plans ruined.

"It should be charged by morning," Finn assured her.

"Let's get changed. If you don't mind a short walk, we can skip a taxi."

"That sounds good," she said, then bit her lip. "But the sari…"

"Put on the little top that came with it, and the petticoat, then I'll help you tie it."

Kimber waited for him to make a lascivious remark, but he didn't. She escaped to the bathroom to don the thin petticoat, which was simply a long, thin skirt the same color as the length of blue cloth and fastened with a drawstring waist. A midriff-baring top in a similar color came next. She picked up the beautiful sari, which was easily six yards long, and walked out.

To her surprise, Finn had donned a loose, white cotton shirt embroidered with geometric designs. With his shaggy dark blond hair and bronze skin, he looked wild and untamed…and incredibly sexy.

"The shirt suits you," she murmured.

"Thanks." Finn stared at her in the flimsy garments, then cleared his throat. "Now let's get you dressed." He reached for the blue sari and unfolded it. "The edge with the border just brushes the floor. The plain edge gets pleated and tucked into your petticoat, like this." He folded the edge of the cloth into pleats, then tucked it inside the drawstring of the petticoat. His warm fingers skimmed her navel and stomach, sending little tremors of pleasure through her midsection.

"Then wrap it around your waist once." He held her gaze while he slowly enveloped her with his arms to wrap the entire length of the fabric around her.

Kimber swallowed hard as he invaded her personal space, sliding his hands over her hip and lower back.

Her skin sang where he touched her, sending alarms to other parts of her body. He smelled of sandalwood and earthy male scents, and his eyes were slightly hooded, as if he knew exactly how he was affecting her.

"I get the feeling you've removed a few saris in your time," she said wryly.

Finn laughed, his breath fanning her cheek. He pulled the remainder of the fabric back to the front and under her right arm, then over her left shoulder to fall down her back. Then he produced a small safety pin, and Kimber held her breath while he secured the fabric to her blouse at her shoulder. Her breasts felt tight and heavy, and despite the fact that she was standing completely still, her heart seemed to be getting a workout.

"There," he said with a little pat, admiring his job. "Not bad at all."

Welling up with pleasure, Kimber brushed her hand over the luxurious fabric of the sari. "I feel…exotic."

"You look exotic," Finn said quietly. He reached for the flower necklace that she'd set on the table next to the bed and lifted it over her head. "Perfect."

She smiled up at him, and the mood suddenly changed from friendly to electric. Kimber's breath caught in her throat as Finn lowered his head. But just before his lips met hers, she stepped back. "I can't, Finn. When I get to Maldives, my boyfriend is going to propose."

Finn's eyebrows went up. "Oh. You know this?"

"Someone close to him told me. It's supposed to be a surprise."

"Well…congratulations."

"Thank you." She wet her lips. "Maybe we should get going."

Finn nodded, then grinned. "Let's go celebrate your impending engagement, Fancy Pants."

She punched him in the shoulder, but was relieved that he was back to his old self. The night air was warm and thick as they walked the few blocks to the festival. They heard the activities well in advance of seeing them. Bonfires lit the sky. Music and ceremonial dances with flamboyant costumes were a treat for the senses. For dinner, Finn introduced her to more local food—spicy fish kabobs, rice cooked in banana leaves, and pudding with fresh coconut.

Kimber tried to forget about the near-kiss, but it was on her mind all evening. Part of her was relieved she hadn't let Finn kiss her, and part of her longed to know what it would feel like. It was just the island atmosphere, she told herself, the spice-infused air and the fervor of celebration. It made her want to... loosen up.

"Try this," Finn said, handing her a cup of dark liquid that looked like soda and taking one for himself. "It's a local drink called *arrack*. It's mixed with Coca-Cola."

Kimber took a sip and nodded. "It's good."

"And strong," Finn warned. "Go easy."

But as the night progressed, the tempo of the festival increased, and the *arrack* went down smoothly. Her senses became keener and everything seemed bathed in a rosy glow. The sari made her feel sensual and glamorous. She swayed back and forth to the music, and when a local urged her to dance with the crowd, she jumped in, throwing her arms up and shouting along with them. She spotted Finn on the periphery and waved for him to join her. "Come on, Finn! Dance with me!"

Finn watched Kimber with a sense of growing dread. Fancy Pants was good and drunk, and she would feel like hell tomorrow. And while it was nice to see that the woman had a wild side, that she could forget herself and simply enjoy the moment, he knew himself well enough to know the desire growing in his belly was dangerous—to himself.

He had a job to do, and developing feelings for her was a distraction he didn't need. Thank goodness she'd had the good sense to stop that kiss earlier. He would have to be stronger from here on out. The fact that public displays of affection was culturally frowned upon in Sri Lanka worked in his favor because right now he wanted to touch her so badly his hands shook.

She came running up to him, her eyes bright and her smile wide. "Finn! Come on, dance with me!"

He allowed her to pull him out into the crowd, telling himself he needed to keep an eye on her because many admiring eyes had turned her way. Kimber was a glorious sight, laughing and gyrating her lithe body to the music, her long, dark hair swirling around her shoulders. She was so far from the prim, prickly woman he'd picked up at the airport he could scarcely believe she was the same person. When the dance ended, Kimber clapped wildly, then fell into him. "Finn, I've never had so much fun in my life!"

"I'm glad, Fancy Pants," he said, supporting her weight. "I think it's time to leave. The walk back to the apartment might help you sober up."

She agreed cheerfully, but chattered and skipped like a child all the way back. She made him laugh, and he wondered how much she'd remember tomorrow morning. When he unlocked the door and helped her inside, she turned in his arms and pulled his head down to hers for a fervent kiss. Her mouth was ripe and sweet, her tongue insistent. She felt like the answer to every question he'd ever asked.

Warning bells sounded in Finn's head to stop, but when Kimber moaned into his mouth, he was lost.

CHAPTER EIGHT

WHEN KIMBER OPENED her eyes she felt as if she'd been hit by a bus.

Or maybe getting hit by a bus would hurt less, she decided with a groan. She turned her head to see a pair of big, bare feet lying next to her in the bed and jerked herself upright.

A mistake. The movement sent pain detonating through her head. "Ow, ow, ow!"

The feet moved, then under the covers, legs, and hips moved. At the foot of the bed, Finn raised his head. His hair stuck up at all angles. "Good morning to you, too."

Kimber pulled back against the headboard. "Omigod, omigod, omigod. What did we do?"

He frowned, then rubbed his eyes. "We didn't do anything, although, for the record, *you* wanted to."

"What? That's ridiculous!"

"You mean, ridiculous that someone like you would want to sleep with someone like me?"

She frowned. "I didn't say that."

"But you were thinking it," he said, pushing himself out of the bed. He wore white boxers, and although she'd already gotten a good look at the top half of his body, the bottom half seemed to be holding up its end of the bargain, too. When her gaze fell on his erection straining the front of his shorts, she gasped and looked away.

"Didn't mean to offend your sensibilities," he muttered, limping toward the bathroom. "There's aspirin on the kitchen counter. Drink plenty of water. I wouldn't want you to be hung over when I deliver you to your boyfriend today."

The bathroom door closed and Kimber stuck out her tongue. But the effort only sent thunder rolling through her head. She winced and gingerly climbed from the bed, relieved to see that she was still wearing panties and the top that went under the sari, but rattled to find the sari itself neatly folded and lying on a chest. Along with the flower necklace the children had made for her, now slightly wilted. Since she didn't remember coming home last night, she doubted if she would've had the presence of mind to so neatly fold the garment, which meant that Finn had undressed her.

And she did have a dim memory of kissing him, which meant he could've taken liberties if he'd wanted to.

Apparently he hadn't wanted to.

Kimber bit her lip, torn. Sure, she was relieved that the man hadn't taken advantage of her diminished condition, but what did it say about her that a hound dog like Finn Meyers wasn't interested?

Realizing she wasn't making sense, she pulled a sheet off the bed, wrapped it around herself and trudged to the kitchen. She downed three aspirin, drank a bottle of water and felt marginally improved. But disturbing flashes from last night kept coming back to her— dancing like a nymph, hanging on to Finn, throwing herself at him. He must be laughing at her.

But at least he was ready to be rid of her. She checked the time—8:00 a.m. The flight to Maldives would take less than two hours, so with any luck, she'd be having lunch with Gil today in their private bungalow on their private beach. And they'd still have three days together in paradise. She checked her cell phone and was glad to see it had charged. She'd wait to call Gil just before they took off in case he was sleeping in or their plans changed.

Then she gave a little laugh—what were the chances of the latter?

When Finn emerged from the shower a few minutes later, she passed him without speaking. Buoyed by the thought that she would finally get to the Maldives today, she showered and dressed quickly, donning the linen pants and shirt from yesterday. She'd have to buy more clothes when she arrived. She pulled her hair back into a ponytail and tied it with the scarf. If she looked her best when Gil saw her, it might help to alleviate some of his irritation.

"I'm ready," she announced, carrying her suitcase into the living area.

Finn sat in a chair watching TV, his face set in a scowl. "We have a problem."

Her heart blipped. "What?"

He gestured to the screen where black storm clouds and pelting rain were being shown. She didn't understand the language the newscasters were speaking. "Where is that?"

"It's heading our way, unfortunately."

"What does that mean?"

"It means we can't fly to Maldives today."

Her jaw dropped. "What? Why not?"

"Because a metal plane and electrical storms don't make good bedfellows." He didn't add "just like us," but it hung in the air between them.

Kimber counted to ten, then took a deep breath and exhaled slowly. "Okay—there has to be another way for me to get there. A train, maybe, or a bus?"

"We're surrounded by water, Fancy Pants, and there's no bridge."

"Okay, what about a ferry?"

"Not at this distance. There are some chartered trips to the Maldive Islands, but they won't go out in bad weather."

"Can you drive a boat?"

"Technically, a person *steers* a boat, but yeah."

"Can we get our own boat, then?"

He looked dubious. "It would be a rough ride."

"Fine by me."

"And it might be a little pricey."

"You can put it on my tab. How soon could we get there?"

He scratched his jaw, now dark with beard stubble. "Depending on how long it takes to find a boat, and if we can skirt the weather…I could probably have you there by tomorrow morning."

Her shoulders fell in dismay. "*Tomorrow?* Another day's delay?"

He shrugged. "Sorry, that's the best I can do. Maybe Elaina can find you something with her connections."

Kimber brightened. "That's the best idea you've had

since I met you, Finn Meyers." She pulled out her phone and punched in Elaina's number, doing the math of the time difference in her head—Sri Lanka was a half day ahead, so it would be yesterday evening in Atlanta.

"Tinsel Travel, this is Elaina."

"Sis, it's me."

"Oh, hi! You must be in Maldives."

"Uh, no. Grounded in Sri Lanka by an electrical storm. Finn can rent a boat and take me there, but we wouldn't arrive until tomorrow morning. I was hoping you could find something better."

Elaina made a rueful noise. "Give me a minute and let me check a couple of things online."

Kimber turned her back to Finn and lowered her voice. "Please, sis, you have to find something. If I have to call Gil and tell him I'm going to be delayed another day, I don't know what he'll do."

Elaina scoffed. "Are you afraid if you piss off Mr. Perfect that he won't propose, after all?"

"No," Kimber said, but it came out sounding less certain than she felt. "But this is supposed to be our vacation."

"You haven't been enjoying yourself?"

"Well…yes," Kimber admitted. "But this isn't what I planned."

"Some of the best things in life are unplanned," Elaina said in her older-sister voice.

Kimber frowned. "Can you find me a way off this island or not?"

"Uh, no. Sorry."

"That was quick—are you sure you checked everything?"

"Your best bet is to go with Mr. Meyers."

She pinched the bridge of her nose. "How am I going to break it to Gil?"

"You'll think of something. I hope this is the worst thing you'll have to deal with in your relationship with Gil."

The comment sounded more like a warning than advice, but Kimber chalked it up to her headache. "Okay, thanks for trying."

"Cheer up—crossing the Indian Ocean in a boat with your own personal guide isn't such a bad thing. Try to have fun."

"Yeah, whatever," Kimber said. "I have to go." She ended the call and massaged her aching temples.

Behind her, she heard a drumming noise that needled her headache. She turned to find Finn drumming his fingers on the table and wearing a cocky expression.

"What's the verdict, Fancy Pants?"

"Stop." She held up her hand, took a deep breath, then exhaled slowly. "If you call me that one more time, I will throw you overboard."

He smiled. "Just call me Captain Finn."

She lifted her chin in the air. "I'll be waiting outside."

FINN'S SMILE FADED when the door closed behind Kimber. He sat back in the chair and expelled a loud breath, then lifted the remote and turned off the TV coverage of an electrical storm raging in South America. Thank goodness Kimber didn't speak Tamil, or she would've realized the storms in the news footage were far, far from Sri Lanka.

He rummaged in his pocket for the printout of the e-mail he'd been carrying, and read it for the umpteenth time.

Dear Finn,
My sister Kimber is on her way to Maldives for a marriage proposal from a man I'm convinced is wrong for her, and I want her to have time to think about it. Please do whatever you can to stall her arrival. Kimber has never had any fun, and that's my fault. She saw the grief I gave our mother, so she turned into the perfect child, wanting to please everyone. This is my gift to her, and I'd consider it a personal favor if you would help me. I know I'm asking a lot, but Mike says you're the right man for the job. I'll cover all your expenses. Just keep Kimber away from Maldives for as long as you can. Then no matter the outcome, I'll be content knowing she didn't rush into anything.

Best,
Elaina Karlton

Finn wiped his hand over his mouth, then refolded the note. He hoped to hell Elaina knew what she was doing. She'd certainly made one miscalculation by believing him to be the right man for the job, because he was pretty damn sure he wasn't supposed to develop feelings for Kimber.

Racked with self-condemnation, Finn pushed to his feet and stuffed the note in his pocket. He'd planned for them to arrive at a different port than Male—the main port in the Maldives—and blame the weather or navigation charts, thereby delaying her arrival by yet another day. But at this point, the best thing for Kimber was to get her to her boyfriend…and away from *him*.

CHAPTER NINE

KIMBER STARED UP from where she stood on the dock. "*This* is the best boat you could find?"

Finn nodded, grinning. "She's a classic." As he slapped the side of the big, ugly wooden vessel that was supposed to take them to the Maldive Islands, a chunk of white paint fell off and splashed into the water below.

"If this is the boat from *Gilligan's Island,*" she said, "I'm not getting on."

He extended his hand. "It's called coming aboard. Watch your step."

She handed Finn her suitcase, then put her hand in his and allowed him to pull her up onto the deck of the cracking, peeling wooden boat. "Are you sure she's seaworthy?"

"Guess we'll find out," he said with a grin. "Did you call Phil?"

She frowned. "*Gil.* And no, I haven't called yet."

"Not too many cell towers in the Indian Ocean," he offered.

Kimber sighed. "I guess I'm dreading it. I know he's going to be upset."

"Can't blame him there," Finn said. Then his expression turned almost serious. "It'll be okay. Tell him I'll have you there in time for breakfast tomorrow, I promise."

She smiled. "Okay, thanks." She punched in Gil's number and waited nervously while it rang.

"Hello? Kimber?"

"Yes, it's me, Gil."

"Are you on the island already? Shall I send a water taxi to the marina?"

"Uh…no. Actually, there's been another delay."

"What?"

"An electrical storm—all planes are grounded." At the sound of an engine overhead, she looked up to see a small plane fly over. Kimber frowned and looked at Finn, who was on the dock untying ropes that kept the boat moored.

"So what does that mean?" Gil practically shouted.

"I'm coming by boat," she said cheerfully. "I'll be there first thing tomorrow morning."

"Tomorrow? *Tomorrow?*"

Kimber exhaled. "Sweetie, it's the best I can do."

A strangled noise came over the line. "This is unacceptable!"

Kimber almost laughed because she remembered saying the same thing to Finn when he told her about the side trip to Sri Lanka. And she remembered what he'd said. "Sorry…that's the deal."

"That's all you have to say?" he asked.

"Yes. Goodbye, Gil. I'll see you when I see you." She disconnected the call and turned off her phone.

And felt better than she had in ages. Like Elaina had suggested, she intended to enjoy this adventure.

She looked up just as Finn jumped from the dock to the boat deck. "How'd it go?" he asked.

"Fine," she said with a nod. "Finn…I saw a plane fly over just now. I thought a storm was coming in."

"Uh, it must be going in the other direction."

She looked up and turned in a slow circle. "The sky looks clear as a bell."

"Storms in this part of the world blow in fast—I think it has to do with the equator." He clapped his hands together. "How about a tour of the boat?"

"Okay." She followed him down a short staircase into the bowels of the boat.

"Galley kitchen, fold-out couch and head," he said, pointing.

"Head?"

"Bathroom. With a shower. This baby was really ahead of its time, design-wise."

As happy as she was to hear about the shower, she was most concerned about the fold-out couch and the sleeping arrangements.

He followed her line of sight and must have read her mind. "I'll be in the cockpit most of the night. The bed's all yours."

"Good," she chirped.

"Ready to shove off?"

"I guess so," she said, following him back to the top deck. "Can I help?"

"Watch starboard and make sure I don't get too close to that boat when I back out."

"Starboard?"

"Right side," he said with a wink. "I'll take port."

"That's the left side?"

"You catch on quick." Finn ducked behind the cockpit and turned the ignition key. The engine sputtered, coughed, then caught, spewing black smoke from the exhaust.

Kimber squinted. "Are you sure this tub will get us to Maldives?"

"If we sink, I'll swim you there on my back."

She smiled, but squashed a little pang—Finn was obviously eager to be rid of her. And who could blame him? She'd done nothing but complain every step of the way. She scrambled to make sure the floats between the boats kept them from touching as he backed the boat out of the slip and into open water. They turned around as gracefully as a washtub, but once they were headed out to sea, Finn slowly increased their speed. Soon they were clipping through the dark blue water at a good pace, leaving a frothy wake.

She stood at the rail in front of the boat, sticking out her tongue to taste the salt spray and watching birds swoop around them. The sun was a big, apricot-colored orb, bathing everything with the most incredible light. She took several pictures, then smiled up at the sky. There were still no signs of storms, but she was mindful of Finn's warning that bad weather could roll in quickly. She closed her eyes and enjoyed the wind on her face for the longest time, freckles be damned. She felt alive.

She turned to take a picture of Finn at the cockpit, but when she found him in the frame, her heart caught unexpectedly. He'd turned his green hat backward so it wouldn't blow off and moved his sunglasses up to the hat so he could study a map. He held a radio in one hand, probably communicating their position or destination. She watched emotions play over his face as he concentrated and alternately glanced up to the horizon and down at his radio to check and relay information. He looked over at her and flashed a grin.

Kimber inhaled sharply. How was it possible that his face had become so important to her in such a short time?

"Want to see where we're going?" he called.

Tingling with awareness of burgeoning feelings for him, Kimber joined Finn in the cockpit. He maintained the throttle while referring to a map stored under a clear acrylic dashboard to keep it flat and dry. He was using a ruler, compass and dry erase marker to chart their course.

"We're here," he said, pointing to a dot on the coast of Sri Lanka. "And we're going here, to Male." He pointed to another circle next to a tiny island west of Sri Lanka.

"The Maldives airport is in Male, right?"

"Right. It's probably the best place to meet up with your boyfriend. From there it's just a hop and a skip in a water taxi that will take you to your private quarters."

In light of her recent revelation about Finn, she felt uncomfortable talking about the accommodations Gil had made for them. "Where did you learn all this?" she asked, gesturing vaguely to the boat and the big steering wheel.

Finn smiled fondly. "My dad. He was a Navy pilot— I grew up around boats and planes."

"Ah, so that's why you moved around so much."

He nodded.

"Are your parents still living?"

"Yeah, they're retired in Pensacola, Florida. I get back to see them when I can."

"Any other family?"

"I have a sister in Birmingham. She's married with two girls. How about yourself?"

"I never knew my father—he died when we were young. My mom and sister are in Atlanta."

"So you plan to stay in Atlanta after you're married?"

She shrugged. "I suppose so."

"What kind of law do you practice?"

"Property law, mostly probate. And divorce, of course."

"Do you enjoy it?"

She nodded, then told him about the Pennington case. "I might be apologizing the rest of my life to Gil for screwing up our vacation, but I'll never regret missing my plane to help my client."

She half expected him to make a joking remark. Instead, he said, "And she'll never forget it."

"I think when I change jobs," she mused, "I might look into family law."

"You're changing jobs?"

"I don't think it's a good idea to work with one's spouse, so probably. How about you? What took you to Dubai?"

He shrugged. "I wanted to be where everything is happening, and right now, that's Dubai."

"So you don't think you'll ever move back to the States?"

"I never rule out anything. I like being able to pick up and go whenever I feel the urge."

"Ever been married?"

"Nope."

Kimber laughed. "You said that as if you don't ever intend to be."

"Yep." Suddenly Finn pointed. "We have company."

Kimber turned her head and gasped. "Dolphins!" Two dolphins raced alongside the boat, jumping out of the water in tandem.

They saw other sights as the day wore on—a giant tortoise, several swordfish and countless schools of smaller fish throughout the forests of vibrant coral that thrived a few yards below the surface of the crystal-clear water. Kimber learned to keep her camera close at hand. They lunched on sandwiches and fruit that Finn had packed, and chatted amiably about music and movies and books. Kimber acknowledged to herself it was good they would be parting ways in the morning, because the more time she spent with Finn, the more things about him she discovered she liked.

To top off an amazing day, they chased a matchless sunset of pinks and blues and oranges. Kimber realized sadly that she didn't want the day to end. But the sooner she reached Gil, the sooner she could shake this growing infatuation with Finn.

"Are we on schedule?" she asked. They were surrounded by darkness, with only the moon and the lights of the boat to reflect on the inky water, and her eyes were growing heavy.

"Actually, we're ahead of schedule. If we drop anchor in another hour or so, we could both get some rest and head out at sunrise. That would still put us in Maldives about 8 a.m."

She nodded, stifling a yawn. "Sounds good."

He laughed. "Why don't you go to bed? The sheets and pillows are in the overhead compartment."

"What about you?"

"Leave a pillow and blanket out for me. I'll sleep up here."

She stood, feeling tense over things she shouldn't be feeling, but wanting him to know that she'd had the time of her life.

"Good night, Finn."

"Good night, Fancy Pants."

She went below and located the cabin lights and the linens. The couch folded out to make a comfortable double bed. She set aside a blanket and pillow for Finn. Then she changed into the most modest of the lingerie outfits she had—red tap pants and a camisole—and climbed into bed, expecting to be lulled to sleep immediately by the rhythmic movement of the boat.

Instead, she lay there, eyes wide open, mulling over the desire coursing through her body for the man above deck.

It was crazy, a passing attraction to a man with whom she'd shared close quarters for the past two days. Finn Meyers was unlike any man she'd ever known—it was only natural she would be intrigued by him and his raw sexuality. Especially since he'd flirted so outrageously with her.

Snatches of erotic memories played over and over in her head—waking up spooned together on the bed, Finn dressing her in the sari, their near-kiss, their real kiss and the sight of him crawling out of bed wearing only his boxers.

Her body responded to those memories, softening and warming. Her breasts ached and her thighs tingled. The boat engine sent a vibration through her sensitized body that only heightened her desire for release. She was toying with the idea of self-gratification when the boat engine slowed, then stopped. Without the noise of the engine, the silence was profound.

The boat's own wake set it rocking for a few seconds, then she heard the sound of something heavy being lowered into the water—an anchor, she realized. A few minutes later, Finn crept down the stairs, no doubt assuming she was asleep. She could make out his silhouette in the light that shone into the cabin. Her heart pounded so loud she was sure he would hear it.

He had gathered the blanket and pillow and turned to go when Kimber made a split-second decision.

"Finn."

He froze, then turned. "Yeah?"

"Don't go."

He took a step closer. "Are you sick? Or scared?"

She swallowed hard. "No. I just want you to stay. Make love to me."

His breath came out in a half groan. "But what about…?"

"I'm not engaged yet."

"Kimber…are you sure?"

"I'm sure."

He abandoned the linens and pulled his shirt over his head. The shoes came off next, and when Kimber heard the zip of his fly, she realized this was really going to happen…and she wanted it so much.

After the pants were discarded, Finn crawled in on top of her and met her mouth in a hard, hungry kiss. His erection was already stiff against her stomach, her body equally as ready as his. But he took his time kissing her mouth and neck before removing the camisole and feasting on her budded breasts. He sighed against her skin and laved her nipples before drawing them, one after the other, into his mouth. Fire rained over her body.

She cried out and arched into him, running her hands down his muscled back and beneath the waistband of his boxers. He kissed a trail down to her navel, then shimmied the tap pants down. She pushed at his boxers and used her foot to drag them off—she just wanted his naked body on hers.

"Do you have a condom?" she asked.

"Yes, thank God." He ripped open a packet and rolled it on, then slid his body over hers, settling between her knees. "I've wanted you ever since I laid eyes on you."

"And now that you've got me?" she murmured.

He thrust into her and she groaned at the exquisite fullness. They kissed and lapsed into a slow, deep rhythm that grew more intense with each meeting of their bodies. The slow hum vibrating in her belly grew to a throbbing bass that Finn coaxed to the surface.

"There's no one here but us—I want to hear your pleasure."

She sighed and mewled and clung to him as the orgasm swelled to near excruciating tension, then screamed his name when it broke over her body like pounding surf. "Finn…Finn…oh, yes…yesssss…"

Finn set his jaw in restraint, wanting Kimber to experience her climax to the fullest before he lost control. But hearing her cry his name triggered a primal response in him. Every muscle in his body contracted for a mighty thrust. He shuddered, pumping into her with a desperation he'd never experienced before. Before the last of the spasms had rocketed through his body, he already wanted to make love to her again.

CHAPTER TEN

KIMBER WOKE UP smiling. She rolled over and curled into the place where Finn had slept next to her, still warm from his recent departure. Wan light filtered through the cabin door, and she could hear him moving around above deck. She pushed to her feet and wrapped a sheet around herself. Sometime between the first time they'd made love and the third time, she'd decided not to go to Maldives. She wanted to stay with Finn, whatever that meant—a new home, a new job, a new wardrobe, a new language. She'd fallen head over heels in love with him. Gil was a good man, but the two of them had never had what she felt with Finn.

Giddy, she moved to the stairs to coax him back to bed. Under her foot a piece of paper crackled. It was folded and curved, as if it had been in Finn's wallet or pocket. She unfolded the paper and realized it was the printout of an e-mail message. She started to refold it when she noticed Elaina's name.

Kimber read the note and went numb, then sat staring at the words, willing them to change. But every time she reread it, the meaning was the same.

At the sound of footsteps on the stairs, Kimber

looked up to see Finn, already dressed. The sight of him made her shrink a little inside.

"I didn't mean to wake—" He saw the piece of paper she held and closed his eyes. "Kimber, let me explain."

"No need," she said thickly. "It's all right here in black and white. I was set up by you and my sister. She purposely rerouted my flights. This was all a ploy to keep me away from a man she doesn't think is right for me."

Finn jammed his hands onto his hips and looked down, but didn't say anything.

"There was never a side trip to Sri Lanka for wood?"

He sighed. "I needed the wood, but it didn't have to be that day."

"So on top of everything else, there was plenty of room in that plane for my suitcase."

He pursed his mouth. "Actually, I could've flown my bigger plane."

Her eyes went wide. "So you could've flown me and my luggage in your bigger plane directly to Maldives, but you didn't."

"I was just doing what your sister asked me to do."

"So there was no electrical storm yesterday?"

"Not here."

"And what was supposed to happen next? Was the boat going to—" she drew quotation marks in the air with her fingers "—break down?"

"No."

"And what was last night? Another delay tactic?"

He had the good grace to look ashamed. "No. I'd decided on my own to take you to Maldives this morning no matter what."

She felt like the biggest fool in the world. To think she was seconds away from telling Finn she was in love with him, and all this time, her sister had been paying him to spend time with her.

"Well, since you decided to take me to Maldives this morning no matter what, we'd better get going."

"Kimber—"

"Please don't say anything," she said. "Please don't make things worse than they already are."

Finn pressed his lips together, then nodded and turned to climb the stairs.

Kimber felt as if someone had taken a knife to her heart. She hugged herself, determined not to break down, determined not to let Finn know how the gag had wounded her. She took a shower in the cramped bathroom to wash him off her skin, then dressed in the linen pants and shirt, now a little worse for wear. She wouldn't be as fresh as a daisy when she saw Gil, but it would have to do.

She remained below deck, swinging back and forth between anger and self-recrimination. She couldn't bring herself to call Elaina because she was afraid she'd say something she would regret. And the kicker in the whole situation was that every time she moved, her muscles ached from having sex with Finn. All. Night. Long.

The engine slowed, sending Kimber's pulse higher. She hauled her suitcase up the set of stairs, ignored Finn and looked out over the bow. Ahead was a marina with a sign identifying Male. She pulled out her phone to dial Gil's number, but spotted him pacing the dock.

She'd know those plaid shorts anywhere.

She moved to the front of the boat and waved her

arms. He saw her and waved back. She felt Finn's gaze on her back, but she refused to turn around. She wouldn't give him the chance to apologize even if he was so inclined. She just wanted never to see him again.

FINN WAS ABOUT to come out of his skin. Kimber loathed him, rightfully so for what he'd helped perpetrate against her. But he didn't want her leaving thinking that the sex had been part of the scam. Her boyfriend, the stiff-looking guy in the plaid shorts, was waiting for her on the dock and they were closing in fast. He had to do something quick.

So he killed the engine to float in the last twenty yards.

He left the cockpit and went to the front of the boat where she stood at the rail. He reached down to uncoil a bow line to toss to her boyfriend when they got close enough. They were at fifteen yards.

"Kimber, I'm sorry about what I did. I should've called it off before we…before I…" He sighed. "What I'm trying to say is that last night was for real, at least it was for me."

She turned her head. She didn't say anything, but he had her attention. Ten yards.

"Go back with me," he said. "I know you don't have any reason to believe me, but I'm crazy about you, Fancy Pants. I don't know what all we'll do together, but whatever it is, it'll be great."

She slowly wet her lips. "That's it? That's supposed to entice me to go with you?"

Five yards. He swallowed nervously. "I'm afraid so."

"Throw me the line!" Gil yelled from the dock.

Kimber turned her head in dismissal. "I believe my sister will cover your expenses. Goodbye, Finn."

Shot through with disappointment, Finn threw the line, and Kimber's boyfriend caught it neatly. He was tall, a corporate type with a side part and two-hundred-dollar running shoes. He looked relieved and happy to see Kimber. After tying off the line, he pulled the rail close enough to allow her to disembark. She fell into his arms and he pulled her into a bear hug. Then he whisked her and her suitcase into a waiting water taxi, and they zoomed away in the direction of any one of hundreds of private islands where Gil had an engagement celebration waiting.

Finn felt sick. He'd finally met the right woman—beautiful, smart, funny, sexy—and he had screwed it up royally.

CHAPTER ELEVEN

"I CAN'T BELIEVE you're finally here," Gil said, squeezing her hand.

"Me neither," Kimber said over the noise of the water-taxi engine.

"I'm not angry with you anymore. I know you can't help doing things to make me crazy, but I'm willing to overlook them."

Kimber blinked at his casual, cutting remark. She studied the face of her longtime boyfriend…and realized in a moment of clarity that his wasn't the face that made her heart race.

"Gil, we need to talk."

"Wait," he shouted, reaching into his pocket. "Let me get this out before anything else happens." He held up a blue, Tiffany's ring box, then opened the hinged lid to reveal an enormous diamond solitaire, glinting in the sun. "Kimber, will you marry me?"

Her eyes watered. It truly was the most beautiful ring she'd ever seen. Even Elaina would be won over. Her heart filled for all the years she and Gil had shared, and for all the effort he'd gone to for a memorable proposal. He must love her very much.

"No, Gil, I can't marry you."

He was smiling and leaning forward to kiss her when he drew back. "What?"

"I'm sorry," she yelled, "but I don't love you enough to marry you."

He looked incredulous. "Since when?"

"It doesn't matter," she said, patting his hand. "I'm so sorry for messing up this entire trip. I know you'll find someone someday who will appreciate you more."

The taxi pulled up to a small dock. "This is your stop, sir."

Gil looked around, still apparently confused.

Kimber reached forward and closed the box. "Enjoy the rest of your vacation, Gil."

Looking dazed, he stood and stepped out onto the dock, still holding the ring box. "But where are you going?"

"I'll have Elaina find me a place somewhere," she shouted as the taxi pulled away. "Don't worry!"

"Back to the Male dock, miss?" the driver asked.

"Yes, please." She leaned her head back and stared at the sky. The lack of pollution here made everything so vibrantly hued. A few days ago she'd been ecstatic that Gil was finally going to propose. Now he had, and she'd turned him down. Timing was truly everything. If she hadn't agreed to help Della Pennington, she wouldn't have missed her plane and would at this moment be engaged to Gil, none the wiser that her life was wanting.

And something Della had said came back to her: *When you truly love someone, my dear, common sense goes out the window. If you follow your heart, you might get hurt, but you'll never go wrong.*

Kimber sat up. She loved Finn. It made no sense, but it was true. She had to follow her heart and see where it took her.

With her heart pounding, she tapped the driver's arm. "Hurry, I need to catch a boat before it leaves!" The man bumped up the speed a notch, and Kimber sat on the edge of her seat, craning her neck to see Finn's boat. But when the taxi pulled up to the dock, the spot where his boat had been was empty.

Her heart sank.

The driver pointed. "Isn't that the boat over there, ma'am?"

She whirled around to see gas tanks, and Finn filling up his boat. Of course he would need fuel for the return trip. She tipped the driver, hauled her suitcase out of the taxi and dragged it around the dock to the gas pumps.

Finn was on the boat untying the lines from the dock when she skidded up. "Sir, I need a ride back to Dubai."

He turned and stared at her. "Why Dubai?"

"Because that's where everything's happening."

He smiled and nodded. "So I've heard."

She dropped her suitcase and crossed her arms. "My bag please."

"I have this rule about luggage," he said.

Kimber raised her eyebrows. "Oh?"

He jumped out onto the dock and pulled her into his arms. "You should never pack more than I can carry."

She smiled up at him. "I like that rule."

He thumbed the curve of her cheek. "Why'd you come back, Fancy Pants?"

"Because I want to wake up and be surprised every day."

He nuzzled her neck. "Well, there are a *few* things you can expect on a regular basis."

"*Now* I'm enticed," she murmured.

* * * * *

PROPOSITIONED

Leslie Kelly

To Stephanie and Lori—it's been a delight working with you. Piña coladas are on me.

CHAPTER ONE

"YOU KNOW WHAT I *really* want? What I'm most in the mood for? Sex on the beach."

Liz Talbot managed to hide a bored sigh, ignoring the salacious smile on the face of the husky blond guy sitting in front of her. After eighteen months working at Trinity's Surfside Bar, which sat on the edge of a breathtaking, sugar-white-sand beach on the tropical island of St. Lucia, her only reaction to the unoriginal pickup line was resignation.

If she had a nickel for every time she'd heard that very same come-on from some sleazy tourist, she'd own this place. Instead, she just served up the best margarita on the island for Dark Age wages and fairly good tips.

"You know? Sex? On the beach?"

Nudge nudge, wink wink. As if she hadn't gotten it the first time. Why did she put up with this again?

Then she glanced toward the side of the building and saw nothing but turquoise water, lit up with thousands of tiny, sparkling jewels of sunlight that danced on the gentle waves. Above it, expansive blue sky, a few cotton-candy clouds and a sun the soft yellow of buttercup petals.

No walls separated the inside from the out. No barriers stood between a regular day and the most beautiful scenery on the face of the earth. The exquisite landscape was simply accepted as the status quo around here; sheer loveliness wrapped up in the normality of daily life.

She'd gotten so accustomed to it she almost didn't remember how a gray sky at dawn had depressed her. Had a warm day in March really once seemed a precious gift? And she could barely conjure up a picture of what melted snow—darkened with gravel and road salt—looked like piled up along the sides of a bumper-to-bumper highway.

That was why she did it. Sleazy guys with sad come-ons notwithstanding, living here was worth it. This job most definitely beat sitting in an office doing the nine-to-five tango and all that went with it back in Boston.

Been there. Done that. Never going back.

"I hear it's the best kind," her customer added when she didn't respond, his poor, sun-baked brain obviously not registering her complete lack of interest and her mild disdain. "You think you might be up for that? I bet you professional bartenders know how to make it sweet and smooth."

Gee, how sexy, witty and intriguing. Her poor feminine brain just wasn't made for such alluring banter. She really needed to rip off her clothes and fall to the nearest flat surface in sheer, unadulterated lust.

That, or thrust a pair of toothpicks in her ears to gouge out the echoes of the nine-hundred-million other times she'd heard the same line from guys who looked just like this one.

Thinning hair and a bright red spot on his crown. *Check.*

An equally red face. Not merely from his existence as a blowhard or the two drinks she'd served him, but proof of the reckless lack of regard for the tropical sun. *Check.*

Loud, flowered shirt, open halfway to reveal a hairy chest. Glazed eyes that said he'd eaten too much rich food and imbibed far too much island rum. A secretive smile at being free from the job and having escaped the wife who was at the spa and the teenage kids who were taking windsurfing lessons.

Check. Check. Check.

There was only one thing she hadn't yet determined. Whether he, like most of the other male tourists who parked at the bar and spent an entire afternoon trying to get into her pants, had his wedding ring stuffed into his shorts pocket, or if he actually hadn't thought that far ahead and was still dumb enough to still have it on his finger.

"So whaddya say? Doesn't that sound good?"

He wrapped his hands around his nearly empty glass. No ring. Definite tan line where one usually lived. *Check.*

She ignored the smirk. "Only if you like lots and lots of—" *sand in body cavities where sand is never supposed to go* "—vodka and peach schnapps."

His eyes glazed for a second, his smile slackening as he tried to figure out what she meant. Finally it dawned on him, but instead of allowing her to intentionally misunderstand, thereby saving himself a serious shooting down, he took his life in his hands. "Maybe I wasn't talkin' about the drink."

"That's the only thing I'm interested in hearing about."

He smirked. Which meant he wasn't giving up. What

was it about tropical sunlight, steel drums and suntan lotion that made even the most normal, probably usually nice, average Joe think he was God's gift to women?

Hmm…the rum didn't hurt. That was for sure.

"So you're not a sex-on-the-beach fan? How about screaming orgasms—do you recommend those?"

Considering she hadn't had one that didn't involve batteries in a long time, she really couldn't say.

"'Cause I could sure go for one and I'd love for you to have one, too." The guy's eyebrows literally wagged up and down. "On me."

Her jaw clenched as she sucked in a few deep, controlling breaths. Ignoring the guy for a minute, to give herself time to figure out how to deal with him, she reached for a glass. Liz made a top-shelf margarita—on the rocks, none of that frozen stuff—and slid it across the bar to Frank. He was a regular, who watched this afternoon's drama with big eyes and a broad smile.

Frank was a fan of fireworks. And he knew that with a few more words, there was going to be quite a display.

"I love screaming orgasms," the guy said. "Especially when they're shared."

Why? Why did this always happen to her?

Okay, she was tall. She was curvy. She had nice reddish-brown hair. She was maybe pretty, though she'd never call herself beautiful. And she tended bar. Did that mean every man who walked into the place had to think she wanted only one of two things—to hear his life story or to fall into his bed? Yeesh.

"Or what about a buttery nipple? A bald puss—"

"That's enough!" she snapped, cutting him off with

a sharp slap of her hand on the broad oak bar, smoothed by years of heat and the salty air that streamed in off the water. "Mister, I know you think you're being cute. But there's absolutely nothing you might have that I want, other than a polite attitude and a fair tip. There's nothing you can do to shock me, nothing you can say I haven't heard a million times before. So knock it off before I cut you off."

His smile faltered a bit, then he laughed deeply, as if she was playing hard to get.

Men's brains and bricks. There was a genetic correlation there somewhere, she was certain of it.

"Maybe you just haven't heard them from the right guy."

Rolling her eyes, she informed him, "If it was George Clooney sitting right where you are now who tried those same lines on me, *he* wouldn't be scoring, either. Now would you please just stop?"

He held up both hands, palms out. "Got it. No more drink jokes." Then, her ultimate I'm-not-interested message apparently having gone over his head, he added, "So you think I look like George Clooney, huh?"

Her hand flew and scooped up a nearby glass. But upon hearing Frank's warning throat-clearing, she dashed its contents into the small bar sink. "Go away. Would you? Just go away."

"Geez, there's no need to get testy."

Liz sighed deeply, realizing she had, indeed, been testy. He was just another sad guy trying to escape his cold and dull daily life. Only, unlike her, he had to return to it.

Fortunately he'd had the sense to call her testy and not bitchy. Testy she could handle. Bitchy would have earned him a face full of tequila, and her a trip to Trinity's office for a lecture on wasting good booze.

Liz waved a hand in the air, brushing off the whole thing. "It's okay. Let's just forget it. It's been a long day."

He nodded and she allowed herself to relax.

"Not a problem." She should have known by the sneaky tone of his voice that he was going to seriously piss her off. "I think what I really want is a comfortable screw, anyway."

Liz swung around and strode to the back corner of the bar to grab some olives and bring her blood pressure under control. She slowly counted to twenty, feeling the annoyance slide out of her. Finally, when she felt capable, she returned to the front and faced him.

Enough was enough. Time to play dirty.

She leaned across the bar, batting her eyes. Her long reddish-brown ponytail swung forward over her shoulder so that the end of it curled enticingly against her breasts.

He must have been from another planet because he'd obviously never seen a woman's breasts before. At least, that was what she read from the bug-eyed stare focused on her cleavage.

"Mmm," she said, forcing herself not to yank her scoop-neck tank top up a couple of inches, "a really comfortable one? I prefer a golden screw myself. Or, ooh, a kinky orgasm."

Down went the jaw. The mouth hung open.

"But let me tell you, you haven't had anything until you've tried a nymphomaniac."

"A nympho—"

"Maniac," she said, almost purring. "It will tear you up. You will hardly be able to walk afterward." Forcing herself not to laugh as she watched the man shifting on his seat, she leaned even closer. "You'll go back to your hotel barely able to move. Everybody will know exactly what you've been indulging in."

He gulped visibly, his Adam's apple bobbing.

"It's that potent," Liz whispered.

And finally the jerk realized he was in over his head. Remembering little wifey, apparently, he slid off the bar stool, his face redder than his burned pate. Dropping an American ten-dollar bill that didn't even cover the cost of his two drinks on the bar, he mumbled something, then spun around and headed toward the exit, not looking back even once.

Thank God. She didn't even mind making up the difference on his drinks if it spared her more of his dubious flirtation.

She watched him head out to the beach, hoping she'd scared the jerk into behaving himself. "Poor wifey," she muttered.

If she hadn't already had a firsthand lesson by way of her own cheating ex-husband, working here would have given her a dark opinion of marriage. As it was, the job simply reinforced what she already knew.

Men wanted what they couldn't have. And as soon as they had it, or thought it was within grasp, the game was over. Just like with Mr. Sex-on-the-Beach, who wouldn't even know what to *do* with a nymphomaniac. Liquid or organic.

"Guess he no' a fan of coconut rum, eh, Lizzie?" Frank said with a throaty chuckle, his lyrical, island voice soft and soothing in her ears. Every syllable spoken by the locals was a song, a story. The cadence of the language, the lilt of the voice, the island expressions and that Caribbean attitude—all made listening to a native islander's words every bit as enjoyable as getting his eventual point.

"Or peach schnapps," she said with a grin as she grabbed a rag and wiped off the counter.

"Or nymphomaniacs."

That hadn't been Frank's voice. Liz's hand stilled, her fingers tightening in the soft cotton rag. Frank sat at her right, and this deep, male comment had come from her left.

But the mere presence of another man at the bar overhearing the exchange hadn't caused her immediate tension. There was more. Her blood roared through her veins, her pulse doubled. Her breaths were deep and audible, her heartbeats so strong she felt the thud in her chest.

Something inside her recognized the voice, even before her brain processed who it belonged to. Sense memory took over. She was flooded with tension and anxiety, and even excitement, because of it.

Then she allowed her mind to catch up with what her body had known from the first syllable he'd uttered.

"Son of a bitch," she whispered, not daring to look to her left to see if she was correct.

She already knew she was. His next words confirmed it.

"Hello to you, too, Liz."

JACK BEAUMONT hadn't been sure how Liz Talbot would react to seeing him again. It had been a year and a half since he'd laid eyes on her. Eighteen months since she'd ditched her job with a major public-relations firm—not to mention ditching her cheating husband—and disappeared off the face of the earth.

Those eighteen months had treated her well. Very well. If she'd been pretty back in Boston, she was damn near stunning now. Stunning enough to cause him to watch quietly from the other side of the room, visually drinking her in for the first few minutes after his arrival.

Part of him had hoped she'd be happy when they came face-to-face. Or at least unable to hide a flash of pleasure, even if she quickly hid it behind an impersonal smile.

Wishful thinking, because he didn't even get that. No smile. No happiness. No warmth at all. Instead, as she finally turned her head and met his gaze, she looked like someone about to step on a cockroach.

"You've got to be kidding me," she muttered, speaking more to herself than to him.

Yeah. Definite dislike there.

The only question was why. An unwelcome reminder of her past life, okay. He'd been prepared for that. Personal dislike, however, hadn't even entered his mind.

After all, they'd liked each other a lot once upon a time. Neither of them had ever admitted it, considering she'd had a wedding ring on her finger and he'd been her husband's boss, but there'd been a definite spark. At least on his part. And to his knowledge, he'd never done anything to make her *dis*like him.

Unless she just hated all men after what her scumbag ex had done. Tim Talbot, the slimy little prick, was enough to make any woman swear off the opposite sex.

"Of all the rum joints in all the Caribbean, you had to walk into mine," she murmured.

"Sorry," he said with a smile. "But you can stop channeling Bogey. I'm not Ingrid Bergman and this is not Casablanca."

And they most certainly didn't have Paris. Or anything resembling a romantic relationship.

Not that he hadn't wanted one—he had. Ever since he'd first laid eyes on her, Liz had attracted him on a deep, physical level. Not merely beautiful, Liz had a smooth, throaty voice made for whispering sensual secrets, and a genuine laugh that drew the eye of every person around her. Plus, she oozed feminine self-confidence without displaying a speck of vanity.

"No, not a romantic movie like Casablanca." Her eyes—beautiful sea-green eyes—closed briefly, the sooty lashes dark against her lightly tanned cheeks. Though she quickly opened them again, they remained the tiniest bit narrowed. "This is more like *Alien vs. Predator*." Though her words were sharp, her tone was more weary than anything else.

"Ouch. Sure we can't go for *An Affair to Remember?*"

"Keep dreaming."

"Are we mortal enemies now?"

"Well, no. But we're not friends, either."

"Nice to see you, too," he said, undeterred, even as he acknowledged that she wasn't merely disinterested, she really had something against him. He just didn't know what. "Though if you're waiting for a sharp-clawed creature to erupt out of my chest, I have to say I hope you're disappointed."

"I was picturing you more as the one with the dreadlocks."

"Making you the sharp-clawed creature?"

She laughed a little before she could stop herself.

And everything suddenly felt better.

Her laugh was what he'd first noticed about Liz. It had been at a company Christmas party, four and a half years ago. Jack had taken over the company the summer before, after his father's poor health had forced him into an early retirement—and Jack into the CEO's office.

He'd been stressed, exhausted, wondering how the hell he was going to fill the shoes of a man who'd been loved and admired by all who knew him. And then he'd heard her. That light, genuine laugh—no jaded trill of amusement, no droll chuckle. Hers had been the laughter of pure holiday joy from a woman who knew how to be truly happy.

Following the sound, wanting almost to saturate himself in it, he'd spotted her standing by the tree, which was decorated with small paper ornaments. Each contained a thank-you poem from the needy kids at a local shelter—kids the company had "adopted" for the holidays. She was reading them, laughing as she lapped up the infectious excitement those kids had written about.

Seeing her, the smile, the sparkle in her green eyes, the way her hair had glimmered under the twinkling tree lights, he'd been fascinated.

Meeting her a few minutes later and learning she was the wife of his new staff writer, he'd been completely disappointed.

Yet, even knowing she was off-limits, he had still wanted to be around her. He'd wanted to know if the warmth, the laughter, were only products of holiday joy or part of a sparkling personality that outshone everyone else in the room.

She'd distracted him long after that night. And once they'd been thrown together in a working relationship, after he'd hired her firm to help him fix his reputation, he'd realized she had brains and a kind, vulnerable heart, too. The attraction had grown exponentially.

But there were some lines he wouldn't cross. The ones on a marriage certificate in particular.

"How did you find me?"

He hesitated, not sure how much to reveal. Then he stuck with a simplified version of the truth. "Coincidence, really."

"Are you saying you just walked in by chance and had no idea I was here?"

No. He hadn't said that. Just as he wasn't an adulterer, he wasn't a liar, either. Because while it had been coincidence that a former co-worker of hers had mentioned hearing Liz was living in St. Lucia, Jack had not shown up here to see her by chance. In fact, not only did he *want* to see her, he *needed* to.

The only problem was, his need would inevitably bring her more heartache. Because reliving the details of her ugly divorce wasn't going to be easy. Yet that was exactly what he wanted Liz Talbot to do.

"Does it matter?" he finally replied.

She shoved her fingers through a strand of hair that had escaped her ponytail, tucking it behind her ear. Her hair was longer now, not trendy and stylish, but instead, casual and simple. She looked younger, healthier, with color in her cheeks and no dark circles under her eyes, as he'd sometimes noted in the old days.

Island life agreed with her.

"What are you doing here, Jack?"

"Would you believe I'm on vacation?"

"I worked with you for three months, remember? You don't take vacations. You don't even take weekends."

True. In the five years since he'd taken over his father's job at the helm of Cardinal Publications, he couldn't remember going on a real, no-phones, no-interruptions vacation.

Quite a change for Bad Boy Beaumont, as the press had called him in his younger, wilder days.

The woman standing across from him was the reason it no longer did. She had done a fantastic job helping him shed the spoiled-rich-kid image he'd been carrying around since he'd been dumb enough to acquire it.

He'd been her project. Her job. In her hands, his wild-child rep had all but disappeared. The media now saw him as a smart businessman, a well-liked philanthropist and a suitable successor to his father. All thanks to her.

Liz had been one of the best, one of the brightest, one of the most successful PR execs in Boston. And here she was tending bar at a beach-front dive in the islands.

He liked that about her. A lot. The woman had more courage than just about anyone he'd ever known. A lot of people might talk about dropping out and doing something new and exciting in a strange, exotic place. She was one of the few he'd ever known to actually do it.

"Okay, you win," he admitted, realizing she was still waiting for an answer. "I'm here on business."

"I figured. Let me guess…planning to be the Rupert Murdoch of the Caribbean?"

Laughing softly, he said, "No. Just trying to open up some markets for our publications."

That was entirely true. He did want to try to increase the worldwide distribution of some of the monthly periodicals his company published, including here in the islands.

But he hadn't had to start here in St. Lucia. There had been plenty of other islands, bigger ones with more tourists and more potential distribution sites. Coming here, however, had had the advantage of bringing him face-to-face with Liz.

In truth, though, this stop hadn't been entirely about gaining his publishing business a new market. Nor was it just to see the woman he'd been so attracted to once upon a time. It had been a way to accomplish both of those objectives while also working on a third: dealing with a looming crisis that threatened his company. A crisis in the form of a potential lawsuit filed by an angry, vengeful woman.

The woman who had helped destroy Liz Talbot's marriage.

Considering they had a common enemy, Liz should be glad to help him out. But he already knew she wouldn't be.

Liz had come here to escape the past, get away from the sadness and the memories. And like some dark harbinger of evil, Jack Beaumont was about to bring that sadness and those memories right to her sunny new doorstep.

CHAPTER TWO

"So you really work here?"

Liz nodded, not trusting her voice to sound entirely normal if they got into a real conversation. She simply couldn't get used to the idea that Jack Beaumont had walked into this place. He had sat down at her bar, acting as though it was a normal, small occurrence—rather than an unbelievable, tsunami-sized one.

Maybe for him, a man used to traveling the world, meeting hundreds of people each year, it wasn't such a big deal, nor a huge surprise.

For her? Major deal. Enormous surprise.

"How'd you end up a bartender?"

Considering he knew the basics of why her marriage had fallen apart, she assumed he wasn't asking why she'd left town, but rather how she'd learned to sling drinks. "I got through college working behind a bar."

"What a coincidence. I got through college sitting in front of a bar."

Her mouth twitched, she couldn't help it. Jack had always been forthright about the mistakes he'd made in his youth; he'd never tried to hide them. She'd liked that about him.

No. No liking allowed. Given what had happened with her personal life because of him, she shouldn't have forgotten that for even a second. Because by the time she'd left Boston, she had no longer even liked one little thing about Jack Beaumont.

"I know," she said, intentionally baiting him. "I remember those pictures of you judging the wet T-shirt contest that came out in the press right before you went to your first New York stockholders meeting."

His amused expression never wavered, the zinger not piercing his confident hide. "Good thing those stockholders liked wet T-shirts."

"Who doesn't?"

Liz cast a quick glare over her shoulder, hearing Frank's low murmur. He merely offered her a cheeky wink, confirming he'd been eavesdropping.

"Sorry," he said, sounding not a bit repentant. "But it's true. Unless my Trinity's da one in a wet T-shirt and any other man is there to see." He slid off the stool. "Speakin' of which, think I'll mosey back and see where dat girl is."

Oh, wonderful. He was off to start tattling.

She'd be answering a lot of questions later. Frank, Trinity's boyfriend, would waste no time telling her everything he knew. So far that wasn't much, but it would arouse Trinity's curiosity.

Which meant… "They're going to be walking out here to check you out any minute now," she muttered, speaking more to herself than to Jack.

"Why?"

"Because Frank is telling my boss that there's a good-looking man here flirting with me and I haven't threatened to toss a drink in his face yet."

He grinned. "Good-looking?"

Remembering the jerk who'd just left, she pursed her lips and eyed him sourly. "If you ask if I think you look like a movie star, I'll have to kill you."

"I don't look like a movie star."

He was right. Jack was a hundred times better-looking, with features that needed no make-up enhancement and a tall, strong body that didn't require any special camera angles to make him appear larger than life.

He already was larger than life. And no self-respecting female bartender in the world would turn him down if he offered her a screaming orgasm.

Except this one.

Watching the door to Trinity's office, Liz said in a low voice, "If they do come out and start asking any questions, please don't let on how we know each other."

"Any particular reason?"

"My past has been off-limits since I arrived here, and I'd rather keep it that way."

He nodded once. "Understood."

"Thanks," she said, remembering how different things had been—how different *she* had been—when she'd made this island her home.

She had come with two suitcases and no real plans beyond wanting a change from her old life. Her bank account had been in good shape, thanks to several years in a high-paying job, and a reasonable judge who had refused her ex's demands for alimony. She hadn't needed to work right away. But she'd stumbled onto Trinity's place and had instantly fallen in love with both the bar and the people who worked there.

The thought of the grilling she was going to get from

those people as soon as Jack left enabled her to pull a few brain cells together. She breathed normally again—pretty much. She reminded herself to remain polite, noncommittal and uninterested.

She'd always been polite to Jack Beaumont, one of the richest men in Boston, who'd had a reputation as a womanizer and a player. He had been her husband's boss, and then her own client. So of course she'd been polite.

Noncommittal…well, while working on the campaign, trying to show the world the genuinely intelligent, hardworking man she'd come to know, she'd had to throw *noncommittal* right out. There was no way to remain only partly invested in your work in the PR biz. You either believed in the product you were selling, or you passed the job on to someone else. Because not believing it meant you'd never find the right way to pitch it.

Uninterested, though, was another matter altogether. Jack had been, probably still was, the most interesting person she had ever met.

"Are you ever going to ask me what I want?" he prompted.

"Huh?" she said, surprise widening her eyes.

"To drink."

"Oh. Sure." She swallowed, but before he opened his mouth, she stuck out an index finger in warning. "But don't ask for anything stupid. I'm not in the mood after that last guy."

The smile remained on that strong, sexy mouth, but the glitter in his eyes spoke of something other than humor. "I don't feel the need to throw out the suggestive names of drinks when I desire a woman. If I want sex on the beach, I'll take her to the beach."

Liz swallowed, her mouth going dry. The salty air washing off the warm sea suddenly seemed even hotter than a normal July day in the tropics.

Wow. He wasn't George Clooney. But that was one hell of a line.

"You know, coming from anyone else that would have sounded either arrogant or really smarmy."

He shrugged. "Sorry. Just the truth."

"I know."

Beaumont's success with women was undeniable. The man had an almost irresistible appeal. She should know. She'd spent three long months in his company.

Resisting.

Not that she'd ever considered letting anything happen between them. There had only been one cheater in her marriage, and the thought of having an affair herself had never entered her mind. Not only because she'd made a vow, but because she would never intentionally hurt someone like that. Especially someone she had loved.

No, she hadn't needed to resist the innate sexiness that enveloped the man eyeing her from across the bar. She'd needed to resist how much she had once liked him.

Rich, handsome, successful…and likable, with a quick wit, charm and a warm, genuine smile.

When heaven had bestowed its gifts, Jack Beaumont had gotten back in line for a second helping.

"What do you recommend?" he asked.

Still a little loopy-headed thinking about the way the

words "desire a woman" had sounded coming from his sensual mouth, Liz eyed him in confusion.

"My drink. Do you have a specialty?"

Get your head in the game, woman. "Uh, yeah. My margarita's pretty famous. And I make a mean rum punch."

He suddenly looked dubious. "Sounds a little frou-frou."

Ha. If he knew how much rum was in one of those things, he'd change his tune. "Two of them would put you under the bar."

"Where would they put you?" he shot back.

Liz managed to keep her smile in place. "I make them. I don't drink them."

"Fine. Rum punch it is. It's not like I have to drive."

"No, you don't. Taxis come by here all the time to scoop up tourists like you who underestimate the potency of rum and sun."

"Tourists like me, huh?" he asked, his voice soft, curious.

She knew what he meant. "I no longer consider myself a tourist."

"You've put down roots in the sand, I take it? You really are living here?"

"I have a small apartment in Castries."

Not roots, perhaps. The apartment was rented and she didn't own a car, instead getting around on a motor scooter. That, some furniture and a tiny sailboat were the only things she owned.

Still, this felt like home. As much like home as any-place else she'd lived in the past decade. And in terms of feeling safe and secure—not just physically, but emotionally—it was the best home she'd had since her parents had died when she was twenty.

"So you consider this your home now?"

"Yes," she replied as she turned away to make his drink. "I guess I do."

Working quickly and going heavy on the rum, she tried to bring her thoughts back together. Tried to figure out what he was doing here, beyond ordering a drink and looking far too good to her.

Tall, powerful, handsome enough to deaden the brain cells of even the most modern of women, he fit in anyplace. She could easily picture him in the boardroom. In a corporate jet. In a bedroom in the Playboy Mansion surrounded by bimbos.

Anywhere but sitting at her bar.

The question was why. And what, exactly, did it mean for her, other than trouble?

Trouble because, since she had last seen him, she'd been telling herself he wasn't really *that* good-looking. That his thick hair wasn't the rich, walnut shade she remembered. His eyes couldn't be the unusual mix of brown and amber that sometimes flashed into her mind whenever she poured a really good Irish whiskey. He hadn't been so tall, so broad, his smile so devastating it made her heart trip over a beat or two.

She'd convinced herself of that.

Unfortunately it was all bull. Because the man was everything she'd told herself he wasn't.

Except a good guy. He is not *a good guy, so don't start believing his act again.*

Finished mixing the drink, she nested the glass in a napkin and set it down in front of him. "You know, I pictured you more as the five-star, hedonism-resort kind of guy, with lots of rich snobs and nearly naked women. Not at a place like this."

Another lazy grin, another casual insult rolling right off him. He didn't even bother to respond, merely lifting the drink to his mouth. He sipped a little. Then deeper. When he lowered the glass, he conceded, "Not bad."

"Not too girly for you?" she asked sweetly.

"Nothing I can't handle." He might be talking about the drink, but his attention was solely on her. "Not too girly, not too sweet," he added. "Just right."

Liz hesitated, suddenly wondering if he was talking about more than the cocktail. He had that tone in his voice, that same I-get-what-I-want echo that had been there earlier. Why it should be there when he looked at her, she had no idea.

Because Jack had never wanted her. He'd never made an inappropriate gesture toward her. Sure once or twice she'd seen a sideways, appreciative glance, and she'd known he felt the same pull she did. But he'd never acted on it. So the idea of him showing up here because he had any kind of personal interest in her was ridiculous. Not least because he had to suspect she hated his guts.

Hell she didn't hate him. Couldn't possibly hate him.

But the spoiled, rich man sitting in front of her had played a part in breaking up her marriage. She had lived with his shadow for three years. Her ex had been playing a game of keeping up with Beaumont since the first day he'd gone to work for the other man. Keeping up in terms of money, style, charm and power. And, eventually, in women.

Would Tim have cheated on her if not egged on by the competition with his boss?

Maybe. But maybe not.

In the end, it hadn't come down to that competition, anyway. Beaumont had given Tim an assignment, told him to do *whatever* it took to get an interview with a reclusive, infamous author of erotic fiction.

Tim had gone to interview the woman and had done whatever it took. Many times, in any number of places and positions.

The blame was her ex-husband's. And the fault of the skanky writer who had apparently decided to act out a steal-another-woman's-husband plot for her next book. But Tim's boss had played a part and, therefore, earned more than a little of her enmity. It had never gone away, and she'd have been happy to never see any of them again.

The question therefore remained: what was he doing here? Even more important: how soon was he leaving?

"Well, I should go. I have a dinner meeting."

One question answered. Thank God.

Jack took his wallet out of his pocket and pulled out a bill that not only covered his drinks and the ones of the jerk who'd stiffed her, but probably those of all the other people in the place. "Keep the change," he said as he set the money beside his glass.

That glass was half-empty. "Too much for you?"

He laughed softly. "Not more than I can handle."

"I'll bet." She pointed toward the side exit that led to the street, rather than to the beach. "Taxis swing by every ten minutes or so. Unless you'd rather call."

Jack met her stare from across the bar, those amber eyes darkening, shining with something. Humor? Secrets?

Finally he replied, "That's not necessary." Leaning over to look out the open side of the building, he pointed toward a nearby hillside overlooking Vigie Beach. "See that white house? The one within walking distance?"

Her heart sank. She knew what he was going to say before he said it.

"It's mine for the week."

The four-letter word that almost spilled out of her mouth would have made her late mother reach for a bar of soap. Somehow Liz held it in, managing to pretend she didn't give a damn that Jack Beaumont was staying half a mile away.

"I guess that means I'll be seeing you around," he added.

Not if I see you first, buddy.

She didn't say it, of course, not wanting to let the man know he had any power over her anymore. That she cared one bit where he went or what he did.

"Suit yourself," she murmured. "Though, of course, there are a ton of other bars in the area. Maybe you'll find one that serves a weak rum punch you can actually finish."

The eyes twinkled. Was he really able to see through her snippy words and read the utter confusion she was feeling?

God, she hoped not.

He didn't pick up the drink and drain it, her words not goading him into any macho display at all. Instead, with a simple nod, he turned and walked out, leaving her staring after him until long after he'd disappeared up the beach.

CHAPTER THREE

JACK HAD ALWAYS thought being thrown into a job heading up a major international publishing firm was the biggest obstacle he would ever face. But after spending time in Liz Talbot's company yesterday, realizing she not only didn't feel particularly friendly toward him, but downright disliked him, he had begun to rethink that conclusion.

Getting around Liz's distrust was a huge obstacle.

"So why bother?" he mumbled as he drove toward his rented oceanside house the next day.

The answer was easy. Jack didn't give up on things he really wanted. Not without at least trying to get them. He'd held off before, of course, when Liz was married. He hadn't even followed her when she had taken off to heal from the divorce. Now, though, there was no reason to hold back.

And he did want her. For what and for how long, he honestly couldn't say. Right now, he only knew he wanted to be around her again, just to see if the spark he'd felt sure had been between them still existed.

Not to mention the fact that you need her.

Yeah. He did. She didn't know it yet, but she might be able to help him in a big way. Cardinal Publications was being threatened with a lawsuit by Desdemona Eros, a reclusive writer of erotic fiction, who had the money and the anger to follow through on her threats. Now that she and Liz's ex-husband had split up— another infidelity, apparently—she'd decided to take out her anger on Jack and his company. He'd received letters from her lawyers, accusing the magazine of violating her privacy by purposely insinuating Talbot into her life. And of printing libelous untruths in the subsequent article Talbot had written.

In most states, it wouldn't be an issue. But according to his own lawyers, Massachusetts had a regrettably long statute of limitations on libel actions.

All thanks to a smarmy little prick who hadn't been worth a strand of his wife's pretty hair. God, he hated to bring up that whole ugly subject with Liz, but she might be able to help. Her insights about her ex could be of use if Jack had to defend himself and his business against a lawsuit.

He only hoped Liz wouldn't hate his guts when she found out why he had really sought her out. Especially since, having seen Liz again, he'd realized his interest in her hadn't faded one bit.

Driving along the coastal road with the top down, he had to admit Liz had picked a beautiful spot to lick her wounds. He'd been to plenty of places in the world, including several other Caribbean islands. But until this week, he'd never set foot on this one. Not flat, dry and sandy like many of the other islands, St. Lucia was hilly and green. It boasted both beautiful beaches and tropical areas. Even a pair of volcanoes that were so intriguing he'd had to pull the car over this morning and just gaze at them rising above the mist.

He definitely wanted to explore, but he'd prefer to do it with a tour guide. And he had exactly the right one in mind.

Intending to go back to the house, shower and change before making his way to Trinity's Surfside Bar again, he suddenly changed his plans as he approached the establishment. From up the road, he saw someone walk out its side door. A flash of sunlight brought out the gold highlights in the head of reddish-brown hair as she strode toward a small electric scooter.

She was leaving.

Unable to resist, Jack swung the car into the tiny parking lot, packed with hard sand and bits of gravel. Liz, who had just stuck a pair of large sunglasses on her nose and held a small helmet, looked up, saw who it was and frowned.

"What are *you* doing here?" she asked as he pulled up.

The woman was seriously hard on a guy's ego. "Can't I stop in for a drink after a rough day?"

"Rough day? On vacation?"

"Working vacation," he reminded her. "Though the idea of a workday obviously doesn't mean the same thing here as it does in Boston."

Her lips widened into a smile that pulled the air right out of his lungs.

Damn, she was beautiful.

"You have no idea. The workday starts late, ends early, is cut in half by a two-hour lunch and, if the waves are good, a two-hour surfing break."

She was kidding. At least, he hoped she was. Still, considering he hadn't been able to schedule a firm meeting with the man he'd hoped to talk to, he wondered if she was right. Maybe he should have just let his assistant arrange things from a distance before jetting down here, rather than assuming people would automatically meet with him if he came calling.

"Any words of advice when it comes to business dealings?"

She cocked her head. "Go home?"

"Funny." Trying to convey how much he really could use some help, he said, "I really am a little out of my element here. I'd appreciate any insight you could give me as to how things work."

She hesitated, as if thinking about it. Considering how unfriendly she'd been last night, he knew she was torn between her innate niceness and the desire to hop on her scooter and get out of here.

"Let me guess," Liz finally said as she pushed her sunglasses onto the top of her head. "You're trying to meet with the Duke."

Confused, he merely stared up at her as she stepped closer to the side of the car. Though it took all his willpower not to allow his gaze to zone in on the soft, curvy body just a few inches from his mouth, he managed it. He kept his attention squarely on her face, wanting to hear what she had to say.

Besides, it was better for his sanity that way.

"Ray Marchand," she explained. "Everybody calls him the Duke."

"Excellent guess," he murmured. "How'd you know that?"

Interested now, though probably against her will, she leaned against the driver's-side door. She was so close he could smell the flowery scent of her perfume. "He owns the Royal Grocery chain, which is pretty much the only retail chain on the island. Not to mention a couple of luxury hotels, complete with their fancy gift shops. If you're trying to get your magazines into the local market, he'd be the place to start."

Jack tried to focus on what she was saying. He really did. But she was so close, her jean-covered hip pressed against the car. He let his eyes shift, wondering how those hips would feel in his hands. Despite her words, he found himself thinking only of how much he wanted to pull her cotton top free of the waistband and press his mouth to the soft patch of skin just inside her hipbone.

Finally, knowing he needed to remove himself from the temptation before he did something really crazy that would either scare her off or earn him a slap, he reached for the door handle.

Liz stepped out of the way, turning to lean on the hood of the car while Jack opened the door and stepped out. "The Duke is notorious for living life easy-breezy, even by island standards. He doesn't particularly like to talk business, and when he does, it's usually out on his boat."

That got his attention, and not in a good way. "His boat?"

"Yes. He's a deep-sea fisherman. Goes out just about every day on *The Regal Duchess*—that's his yacht. I see him all the time at the Rodney Bay Marina."

Deep sea. As in, far from land. Jack couldn't help it, he immediately started to feel queasy. He gripped the car door for an extra second or two before slamming it shut.

"Oh, wait, I just remembered," she said, lifting a concerned hand to her mouth. "You don't like the water, do you?"

Don't like was an understatement. Jack sometimes wondered if he'd been a sailor in a past life. Not because he was good at being at sea, but because he must have hated it so much a propensity for seasickness had been stamped into his genetic code. "Uh, not particularly."

"That's so odd."

"As I recall, you don't like mushrooms."

Her eyes flared in surprise. He couldn't tell whether it was because he thought disliking mushrooms was on par with not voluntarily setting foot on a boat or because he remembered a detail from the night they'd ordered pizza for the entire office.

He could have enlightened her. Could have told her he remembered nearly everything about the few months they'd worked together. But she was finally having a normal conversation with him, those walls down for the time being. He didn't want to say anything that might put them up again.

"I meant, it just sounds strange. Shouldn't someone with your money like to go yachting with the other gazillionaires?"

Smiling, he clarified, "Not even close. I work for the company, remember? I don't own it. And I'm not sure there's such a thing as a gazillion."

She straightened, crossing her arms in front of her and eyeing him speculatively. "What if I replaced the *g* with an *m?*"

He intentionally misunderstood. "A mazillionaire?"

Her soft laugh made the lame joke entirely worthwhile. Jack wanted to swim in it, to hear nothing but that sound and see nothing but that incredible smile.

"How your adoring fans would laugh if they knew you were a dork at heart."

"I beg your pardon?" He intentionally glowered. "I'm a widely feared and respected businessman."

"With a goofy sense of humor," she pointed out. "Don't think I've forgotten the way you started dancing like Tom Cruise in *Risky Business* the night after you gave the *Redbook* interview that made you look like a choirboy."

He threw a hand over his eyes in mock horror. "Oh, God, how much is it gonna cost me to make sure that story never comes up again?"

Dropping his hand and eyeing her again, Jack gave himself a moment to enjoy the fact that they were talking again, laughing again. He and Liz were rediscovering that same sense of warm connection they'd once shared. Her walls had fallen and she seemed to remember that they had once liked each other. A lot.

But her laughter suddenly faded. The sparkle disappeared from her eyes. Apparently she had remembered… and wasn't happy about it. The hard set of her jaw and downward tug on her mouth made it appear she'd decided she was laughing with the enemy.

Why she disliked him so much he didn't know. But he intended to find out.

"Well, then," she said, a hard note entering her voice as her defenses rose, "I guess you'd better invest in some Dramamine if you want to meet with the Duke.

Good luck not fainting and falling overboard because of your seasickness."

There hadn't been an ounce of malice in the Liz he'd known. Now she was intentionally trying to keep him away, trying to insult him. As if she wanted to make it clear that she really didn't care what he did, where he went or how he felt.

One problem. He didn't believe her.

Knowing he shouldn't, Jack couldn't resist stepping closer, leaning on the car beside her, until his arm touched hers and his trousers brushed her bare calf. He half expected her to straighten and stalk to her scooter, but she didn't. Her curvy bottom, so nicely hugged by her white jeans, stayed right where it was, pressed against the hood of the car.

Wicked, sultry images suddenly filled his head. Wild, hungry images of him lifting her by the hips to sit on the vehicle, then spreading her thighs and stepping between them.

He wondered what she had on underneath the jeans and imagined slowly tugging her zipper down to find out. Despite the road and the bar and the fact that it was broad daylight, he wanted desperately to kiss her. He wanted to explore every inch of her under the bright tropical sky, watch her beautiful skin flush from his touch and the warmth of the sun.

He wanted her in all the ways he'd thought about having her since the night they'd met.

"Jack," she whispered, his name sounding half like a warning, half like a plea on her lips.

"You really want me to fall overboard and drown?" he asked, torn between amusement and pure want.

"Because that would imply some feelings on your part."

She swallowed so hard he saw her neck quiver. "Feelings?"

He dropped his hand onto the hood, close enough for his thumb to scrape the rough jean fabric covering one hip.

"Definite feelings," he said. "You're not indifferent to me, no matter how hard you try to pretend you are."

"Keep dreaming." Her words lacked any punch whatsoever. "I feel nothing at all for you."

He ignored her, continuing to stare, trying to read her, get to the real Liz behind the shield of snarky bravado. "Not just any feelings, either. Passionate ones."

Her wide eyes narrowed with confusion and Liz's lips parted on a quick, sucked-in breath. But her surprise didn't come because he had offended her. Or even because he was wrong. In fact, she seemed almost puzzled. It was as if she honestly hadn't thought of the word *passion* in regard to herself in a long while.

Which was just about the saddest thing he'd ever heard.

He couldn't take it anymore. Without another word, he touched her face, brushing his fingers down her cheek before lifting her chin. Saying nothing, he lowered his head, pressing his mouth against hers in a soft, quiet kiss. He didn't deepen it, didn't plunge his tongue into her mouth, didn't fill his hands with that soft, feminine body.

He couldn't do *any* of those things. Because once he went down that road with Liz, there would be no turning back.

For now, it was enough just to taste her, one warm, unexpected taste to satisfy the raging hunger he'd had for her for so long.

He savored it, gave himself over to it, acknowledging one thing.

It was worth the wait. *She* was worth the wait.

Ending the kiss, giving up those beautiful lips and the breath they shared, was one of the hardest things he'd ever done. But he somehow managed it, pulling away from her with a regretful groan. He remained close enough to see the way her pulse fluttered wildly in her throat and her mouth trembled. Her eyes slowly opened, and the dreamy, sensual gleam in them almost had him diving back for another taste.

A car roared by. A door slammed. A shout rolled off the beach. He was abruptly reminded that they were in no way alone.

He stepped back altogether.

"What was that?" she whispered after a long moment.

"That was to prove you were lying."

She shook her head, jaw clenched. "I wasn't lying. I don't have feelings for you, Jack."

"I didn't say they were good feelings," he admitted, amused as she sputtered in annoyance.

"Passion…"

"Can be a very good thing. But a person can also dislike passionately. Which, I wonder, do you feel the most? Passionate dislike? Something tells me that's not it."

"You really have one hell of an ego," she said, glaring as she finally straightened and headed toward her scooter. "Now why don't you go try out that charm on some woman who's actually interested?"

He almost laughed, easily seeing the truth she was trying so hard to hide.

She'd liked the kiss. A lot.

Yanking her helmet onto her head, she snapped, "Be sure to wait until you're over shark-infested waters before falling overboard."

This time, he couldn't contain his laugh. Which only made her glare more fiercely.

"Goodbye, Jack."

Jack didn't think about it, didn't plan, he simply put his hand on the handle of her scooter. "Liz, wait."

"What?"

He wanted to say so many things. To apologize for having taken what she hadn't offered, though he'd do it again in a heartbeat if given the chance. He wanted her to know he'd liked the kiss, too, and would very much like to repeat it. Wanted to ask her how she was, really. If she liked her new life, if she ever regretted leaving her old one. He needed to understand why she was so unfriendly toward him when they had once gotten along so well.

The biggest question of all: did he have a chance with her? Either before he admitted why he'd needed to see her…or, more importantly, after?

But he didn't ask her any of those things, knowing she wouldn't answer them. So instead, he surprised even himself by saying, "I have a proposition for you."

Her shoulders stiffened and she eyed him warily.

God, the woman didn't trust him at all. Part of him wanted to grab her by the shoulders and ask her why, demand to know what he had ever done to earn the distrust he saw in her eyes. Other than stealing one little kiss.

Instead, he did the one thing he could think of that would bring her into his daily life, at least for as long as he was on the island.

"Well? What is it?"

The idea suddenly seemed like an excellent one.

"I want you to come to work for me."

CHAPTER FOUR

SHE WAS WORKING for Jack Beaumont. Again.

Of all people, of all jobs, of all places. Liz still couldn't believe she had let herself get talked into it, even now, the day after she had agreed to his crazy proposal.

Especially after that kiss. That quick, unexpected, wildly pleasurable kiss.

Get real. You took the job partly because *of that kiss.*

Taking a mental gag, Liz shoved the observation into the saucy subconscious mouth that had come up with it. Best to pretend the crazy thought had never even occurred. Jack had kissed her for one reason only—to prove a point. To make her admit she had some kind of feelings for him, good or bad. That was all. It meant nothing.

The kiss aside, part of her still wondered if she had done the right thing in saying yes. Jack was too used to getting his own way—by way of either money or charm. She had tried to refuse, despite the alluring financial offer he'd dangled in front of her. She might not need a lot of money to live here, but she had to admit the idea of building her bank balance up a bit was tempting.

But in the end, it hadn't been the salary that did the

trick. Or the kiss. He'd hit her in the one place she was vulnerable.

Her heart.

Like many other islands, St. Lucia had a strong tourist trade, but the wealth didn't always distribute itself evenly.

The tourist-resort areas were stunning and bedecked with every modern convenience. And yet, in smaller villages, many residents still lived in corrugated huts with dirt floors, and few children attended school beyond the elementary level. So for Jack to offer to fund a local group building a new secondary school specifically for low-income kids said two things.

One, he had researched the island and knew where there was need.

Two, he knew exactly how to get Liz to do what he wanted.

Which was why she was sitting beside him in his rented convertible, enjoying the unfamiliar gentleness of the early-morning sun on her face and the *whoosh* of the fresh air through her hair.

She was also forcing herself *not* to enjoy Jack's masculine scent or the exciting sizzle of energy that always seemed to surround the man. Which was easier said than done, considering every time she inhaled, she was overwhelmed by the headiness of both. And every time he parted his lips to say a single word, she was reminded of how that incredible mouth had felt pressed to her own.

"You're sure he'll be up this early?" Jack asked.

"The manager of the marina is a regular at the bar. He told me the Duke would be heading out by 8 a.m.," she said, glad he'd distracted her. Feeling any kind of attraction to Jack—to his spicy, masculine scent, or his charm or his incredible looks—was completely out of the question.

This was a job, nothing else. Not only for the kids and the money, but also, in a way, for her own peace of mind. She had been telling herself she was fine, that she'd moved on, healed after everything that had happened. That she was immune to any man's charm, could see through false promises and would never be taken in again.

Working with Jack, spending time with him, well, it was the ultimate test, wasn't it? This particular man could charm the panties off a celibate grandma.

"And you think he'll invite us along?"

"He invites me every time I see him," she said with a shrug. "I have no reason to think he won't today."

"Maybe he invites you because you're beautiful. He might not like it if you show up with me in tow."

Liz couldn't help laughing. "His wife is the most stunning woman I've ever seen. You won't even know I exist once you see her."

"I doubt any woman could make me forget you exist, Liz," he murmured.

Hearing a strange, intense note in his voice, Liz shifted uncomfortably in her seat. She shouldn't have said that, should never have put the conversation on a personal, you-and-me level.

There is no you-and-me. Never had been. Never would be.

"He invites me because he's a gregarious, fun-loving man," she explained, hoping Jack didn't hear the breathiness in her voice. "You'll see. We're almost at the marina."

Jack had picked her up at her place in Castries just after sunrise. Considering she worked until closing several nights a week, this wasn't her favorite time of day. Or her most conscious. But at least yesterday had been a day shift. Twice a week, a couple of the bigger cruise ships docked for day-long excursions, and she always worked on those afternoons. So she'd managed to roll out of bed pretty early.

That didn't mean she wouldn't pay for it later, however. She had to be back on the job at six, and would be slinging drinks until 2 or 3 a.m. Even worse, she wouldn't have a lazy, sleep-in morning to recover. Because tomorrow was the second Thursday, one of the two most profitable days of the island's month. St. Lucia was the final port of call for a Norwegian cruise lines fourteen-day itinerary. The massive ship would drop off thousands of thirsty tourists who wanted to make one more fabulous Caribbean memory before sailing back to Miami.

She was facing a long night. Followed by a longer day.

It's worth it.

For the kids' sake. And for her own peace of mind. She could do this—be with him, near him, yet remain entirely immune.

Working with him would give Liz the chance to prove something to herself before putting that part of her life out of her mind for good.

"Wow," he murmured as they came around a curve in the road and caught a glimpse of the pristine beach and the crystalline water below them. Just beyond it were the gently flapping sails of dozens of boats at Rodney Bay Marina, which presented a stunning picture. "Did you know St. Lucia was so beautiful when you decided to come here?"

"Not really."

"How'd you decide, then?"

She settled deeper against the warm, soft leather seat. "Stuck a pin in a map."

He laughed softly. The laughter faded when he realized she wasn't kidding. "You're serious?"

"Uh-huh."

"What if you'd stuck a pin in some desert? Or a frigid wasteland?"

She shrugged. "I cheated. Opened the atlas to this hemisphere and kinda peeked at the Caribbean region before covering my eyes."

"And your pin landed on tiny little St. Lucia."

"Actually, it landed in the sea, but this was the closest speck of land on the page."

He shook his head and murmured, "Follow the pin. How…"

Crazy? Reckless?

"…brave. Freeing." He glanced over, nodding at her in visible approval. "That took guts."

"Well, like I said, I did cheat a bit. No way was I going to use a globe and end up in Antarctica."

He visibly shuddered. "Or St. Petersburg."

"Russia? I've always thought that would be interesting."

"I meant Florida. That red shade of yours would definitely stand out among the blue-haired set."

She snorted a laugh, seeing the teasing grin tugging

at his mouth. "Your folks have a place there, don't they?"

"Why do you think I mentioned it? Life is so sedate there my doctor can't find my blood pressure when I come back from a visit."

"But you love them," she murmured, remembering how close Jack had been with his family. She'd liked that about him, maybe even envied it a little, not having a family of her own. Mostly she'd just thought it was pretty cool that a clan as wealthy and privileged as the Beaumonts could still get together and play killer games of Monopoly and Scrabble on weekends.

"Oh, absolutely. But I still need about ten straight cups of coffee to start my heart whenever I return from Florida," he added.

"Life is pretty quiet here, too."

He shook his head slowly. "No, I don't think so."

"The islands are known for being laid-back."

"Laid-back, yes. Catatonic, no." He hesitated, as if trying to decide how to explain, then added, "It might be slower-paced here, but there's a dramatic pulse. A low, underlying rhythm to everyday life."

She tilted her head in confusion.

"A soundtrack, I guess, that underscores life here. Where my parents live, it's a waltz. In Boston it's frenetic, high energy, lots of bass guitar and drum riffs, a cacophony of sound in a minor key."

Remembering his background, she knew why he'd chosen the analogy. "I forgot you played in a band in college. You were going to be a rock star." Hence the impromptu "Old Time Rock and Roll" dance in his office.

She had to admit it—the man could move.

His long, elegant fingers tapped out a beat on the steering wheel as he chuckled. "The closest I got was having Keith Richards on the cover of one of our men's quarterlies last year."

Understanding where he was going, she realized he was right. The islands did have a soundtrack all their own, and it wasn't just the steel-drum music so often associated with the geography. There was more. It was low and almost tribal, excitement at odds with the lazy pace.

She suddenly found herself wondering what Jack Beaumont would make of the Jump Up. The underlying beat he was describing came out in full force at the weekly street festival, where things got not only a little crazy but raucous. Hot and wild, with spicy food and spicy music, the event brought out locals and tourists alike. Inhibitions dropped as everyone gave themselves over to the seething rhythm of island life buried just below the surface. Just like he'd been talking about.

The annual carnival was even wilder. While most of South America celebrated it in February, the same time as New Orleans's infamous Mardi Gras, here in St. Lucia, Carnival was held in mid-July. It was going on right now, and next Tuesday would be the penultimate celebration.

She almost opened her mouth to ask him about it, to see if he planned to go, but that might sound too much like an offer to take him. And while she couldn't deny a surge of excitement at the thought of it, Liz was no masochist. Sitting beside him in a car, or on a boat, was going to be challenge enough.

No way did she trust herself to let down her guard

completely, dance with abandon against his hard body, share potent drinks and exotic foods.

Just the idea of it had her shifting in her seat. They hadn't touched today, hadn't exchanged a suggestive word. But the images that flooded her head had brought her to the edge of physical arousal.

One touch could push her over.

Liz wrapped her arms around herself and hunched close to the door, determined to thrust the images out of her head. And she knew exactly how to do it.

"So you're feeling all right? Sure you're up for the boat?" she asked. Before he answered, she held up a hand, palm out. "And I'm not trying to goad you, okay?"

"Meaning no more kisses?"

Heat rose in her face. "Definitely no more kisses, Mr. Beaumont, or you can find yourself another go-between to set things up with the Duke."

He didn't say anything, not agreeing to her terms, not arguing with them, either. Which, knowing Jack, could mean either he didn't care if he ever kissed her again— or he intended to do whatever the hell he wanted, whenever he wanted to do it.

She pretended not to notice the little shiver of excitement that danced up her spine at the very thought.

"You had to remind me of my problem, huh? I'd almost managed to forget where we're going. I still don't know if this is a good idea."

"It's a fine idea." She shook her head. "I love being on the water so much I have a hard time believing you don't." Sighing, she added, "I just sail and sail, letting my troubles float away."

"My troubles wouldn't be what was floating away," he snapped. "My sanity would."

"Jack, would you just trust me? The bracelet will work."

He stared at the anti-motion bracelet on his right wrist, obviously not believing her. "I've tried motion-sickness medicine before—on one of those dinner cruises in Boston Harbor."

"And?"

"It was a real struggle to get back to shore before my dinner did."

She couldn't resist laughing, though it earned her a deep frown in return.

"Nice. Laugh at a guy's weakness."

"Oh, come off it, do you have any other weaknesses? What else is there to laugh at you about?" She lifted her hand, ticking off her points. "You're rich, you're successful, you're drop-dead gorgeous."

Liz swallowed hard, wishing she hadn't pointed that one out. Hurrying on, she added, "You speak a couple of languages, give generously to charity and have a loving family that isn't the least bit dysfunctional. So forgive me for taking amusement in the fact that you have one Achilles' heel." Unable to suppress a wicked grin, she added, "Make that Achilles' stomach."

All that, and he focused exactly on what she most didn't want him to. "Drop-dead gorgeous, huh?"

"Don't make anything out of it," she shot back.

"As if I could," he muttered.

Not understanding, she shifted in her seat to stare at him. Jack's entire focus was on the road. The warm breeze blowing over the top of the windshield lifted his thick, dark hair, and her fingers suddenly tingled with an unexpected need to smooth it back. To touch it.

To touch *him*.

Liz forcefully thrust off the quick flash of heat. This was business, just business. Touching any part of Jack—from a single strand of hair to that strong build so perfectly set off in his designer shirt and tailored trousers—was out of the question. "What's that supposed to mean?"

"It means I already know you don't much care about looks."

"Repeat—what's that supposed to mean?"

Studying his handsome profile, she noted the corner of his mouth curling up, though he never glanced over. "Well, your douche-bag ex wasn't going to win any Mr. Universe contests."

Liz's jaw dropped open. He had succeeded in rendering her speechless. Not because of the commentary on Tim's looks, but because of what Jack had called him.

Not that Tim didn't deserve being called such things. He did. And she had to admit, Tim-the-toad, as she'd been thinking of him for the past year and a half, just wasn't as satisfying.

Suddenly she started to laugh. A chuckle at first, then deeper as genuine amusement flooded her.

Jack glanced over at that. "Damn, Liz, if I'd known all it took to get one of those laughs of yours was calling your ex the scumbag he is, I would have done it months ago."

Her laughter faded. Though her smile remained, it was smaller, probably a little sad. "Months ago I wasn't laughing about much of anything." She shook her head slowly. "I honestly wasn't sure I'd ever laugh again."

Jack's hand, which had been on the gearshift, rose. For a moment she thought he was going to touch her. Squeeze her hand, or her knee, offer a reassuring gesture. But he seemed to think better of it and instead, gripped the steering wheel.

His voice so quiet she almost didn't hear it above the wind whistling overhead, he said, "So you really did love him."

He didn't seem to be asking a question, just making an observation. One he didn't like, apparently, though she couldn't say why.

"Of course I did," she said, the response automatic.

Then she thought about it. She'd done a lot of that in the past eighteen months. Thinking. She'd mulled over many of the choices she had made in her life. Marrying at a pretty young age being one of them.

And she'd come to some conclusions.

Though she had no reason to confide anything in Jack Beaumont, she found herself wanting to share what she had discovered about herself. Maybe because, unlike anyone here, he'd known her in that other life.

"At least, I think I loved him when we were first together," she admitted.

"Think?"

"I was so young. I'd lost my parents a year before."

"I'm sorry," he murmured. This time, he didn't stop himself from reaching out to her. She sucked in a quick, surprised breath when his hand dropped over hers and remained there.

Her first instinct was to pull away. To keep up that wall she'd erected between herself and any man. It seemed especially important to maintain it with *this* man.

But she didn't. Maybe because she was talking about something that took a little courage to share. Or because she hadn't had much human contact in recent years, and had not realized how much she'd missed it. Perhaps it was even that the breeze had chilled her.

Or maybe you just like his hands.

She shoved that thought away. "I was young and I was alone. My parents had been madly in love. I wanted that, what they had."

"You thought you'd found it with him?"

She nodded. "Uh-huh."

"I sense there's a *but* coming."

Liz just looked at him and gave a weak smile.

"As in, *but* I quickly realized he was a weak-chinned, scum-sucking jackass?"

"Pretty much." She grinned again, liking Jack's frankness. "We were already having problems even before we moved to Boston," she admitted. "Before he…"

…decided he wanted everything you had.

God, what on earth was she doing, talking to this man, of all people, about what had happened? Beaumont had been back in her life for just a couple of days and already she was forgetting everything she'd been telling herself about him.

That he couldn't be trusted. That he was partially responsible. That he'd encouraged her husband to cheat all for the sake of a story.

She tugged her hand out from beneath his and turned her head, feeling heat rush to her cheeks. Embarrassed heat.

This wasn't how it was supposed to go. She wasn't

supposed to like him again. Period. That kiss yesterday should have been reminder enough about how good he was at getting what he wanted.

Well, he wasn't getting any more. Not from her. She couldn't afford to travel down that old road again, not now when she had finally built something new and good for herself.

Jack cleared his throat, as if he was about to say something and wasn't quite sure how it would be received. Which meant she probably didn't want to hear it.

"Liz, about what happened with Tim and the—"

"Ho-bag?" she asked with a twist of her lips.

"I was going to say 'the affair,'" he said with a chuckle. "I was just wondering if you've dealt with it. If you can talk about it."

Why he'd want to, she honestly didn't know. Yet she answered his question. "I've dealt with it. But no, I will not talk about it."

"I was hoping—"

She cut him off again. "Not going there, Jack," she said, throwing a hand up, palm out, stopping him midsentence.

"I understand," he murmured, though that thoughtful look remained.

Fortunately he didn't have the chance to try another personal topic of conversation. They suddenly rounded a curve in the windy road and spied the entrance to the marina. "We're here," she said, her manner cool, all-business. "Now let's see what we can do about getting the Duke to invite us onboard. Remember, for all intents and purposes, we're just out for a day of relaxation." She cast a quick glance over his clothes—shorts and a T-shirt. The kind of look that on anyone else would look island-casual but on Jack was just damned sexy. "You look okay."

"Gee, thanks."

"I meant," she said with a chuckle, "that while neither of us looks ready to hit a boardroom in Boston, for the Duke's yacht, bathing suits and shorts are de rigueur."

She saw the wicked gleam in his eye before he said, "Can't wait to see yours."

Damn. She really should have thought about that and worn a one-piece under her lightweight shirt and sailor pants. The bikini was fine for the yacht, probably a lot more modest than what most tourists wore on the beaches. But she didn't know if even a ski parka would have been enough to insulate her from Jack's intense gaze.

He parked the car and cut the engine, but instead of getting out, turned in his seat to face her. "About what we were discussing before, Liz… I'd really like to talk to you."

"Don't," she said, quickly shaking her head. "Please, don't."

Without giving him a chance to say another word, she reached for the door handle and stepped outside. She might be working for the man for a few days, but that didn't mean he had any right to pry into her personal life, into her feelings.

It wasn't entirely his fault. She'd started the conversation, sharing too much. But she also needed to end it, here and now. From this point on, their relationship was going to remain strictly business. No sharing, no tenderness, no laughter.

And definitely no more kissing.

CHAPTER FIVE

THE ANTI-MOTION-SICKNESS bracelet worked. At least, it worked for about an hour.

Then it stopped working.

It happened abruptly, between one heartbeat and another. One second Jack was firmly planted on two feet, watching Ray Marchand pilot his sixty-foot yacht. The next he was on his ass on a lounge chair, his head between his knees.

Why, he wondered, had ancient man ever decided to venture onto the water, when land was so blessedly still and solid?

"Hey, my friend, you're no' looking so good."

Ray Marchand, aka the Duke, sounded both concerned and a bit amused. The older man, who was probably about sixty, though his smooth face and enormous smile gave the impression of someone much younger, had been every bit the friendly, outgoing man Liz had described. And his much-younger wife was, indeed, an incredibly beautiful woman who obviously adored her husband.

Jack, on the other hand, hadn't conveyed quite as positive an impression. Liz had managed to get them an invite onto the man's yacht, but Jack had only been able to remain upright long enough for them to leave the coast.

"You're looking a little green."

A little? He could probably pass for the love child of the Jolly Green Giant and the Wicked Witch of the West. And if his stomach was still attached where it was supposed to be, and not doing loop-de-loops throughout his midsection, he'd be shocked.

Why in hell was he doing this again?

"You must really want to sell your magazines in my stores."

Oh. That.

Right now, the current circulation of every one of their periodicals sounded just fine to him. No expansion required.

"Or else you must really want to spend some time with Trinity's pretty bartender."

Jack slowly lifted his head, seeing the amused, knowing expression on the other man's face.

"Aha!" the Duke said, laughing as he slapped his thick, beefy hands together. "The things we do for love, eh, my friend?"

"Liz and I are not in love," he muttered.

"The things we do for lust, then?" the other man suggested, undeterred. "Though your seduction plan, it isn't going to work so well, I think. Not easy to woo a woman if you are looking like you drank a glass of raw eggs."

His stomach lurching, Jack closed his eyes and shook his head. The Duke's laughter only grew louder.

"I tell you what. We'll turn around, you get on dry land. This weekend, we'll get together. Me and my wife, you and your lady friend. I'll introduce you to some people. We'll talk some business."

"You're not a duke," Jack replied in a grateful whisper. "You're a prince."

Marchand laughed heartily, then waved toward the deck. "Go aft—that's toward the stern."

Jack just lifted a brow, not sure what a stern was.

Tsking, Marchand said, "You have no idea what I mean. You really have no sea legs at all, do you?"

"No."

He shook his head. "Pity. Liz likes the sea. I see her taking her small sailboat out all the time."

"I think I prefer yours," Jack replied. "Because at least if I fall overboard I'd probably be lucky enough to die."

Another belly laugh from the Duke, whose sparkling eyes and bright white smile said he knew how to enjoy life, liked surrounding himself with all the exclusive trappings. "Now, go toward the back of the boat. Sit in the center, don't lie down. Let your body roll with the ship, don't fight it. We'll be back at the dock soon." The man wagged his eyebrows. "Maybe Liz will wander back to look after you. It's nice and private back there. Great place for romance—nobody will see a thing."

"Believe me," Jack said as he lurched to his feet, "there will be nothing romantic about me if I don't get back on solid ground soon. The only thing you *could* see is me leaning over the railing. I am in no condition for romance."

"You never know. I think Liz could make you forget your troubles—and your bellyache—for a little while."

"I'm not gonna hold my breath."

Unless it helped him hold his breakfast.

Nodding his thanks, Jack did as the captain suggested. Moving slowly, carefully, he took a seat near the back railing, where the motion was much less noticeable. Though his instinct was to close his eyes and lie down, he resisted. Sitting upright, he focused on letting all his muscles relax. And gradually, as his host had promised, the tension eased, until his body began to sway along with the waves lapping against the hull.

Then he realized he was no longer alone.

"You okay?" Liz, who had been up front with Mrs. Marchand, took the seat beside him.

"Getting there," he murmured, not confident enough to risk moving his head to turn and look at her.

"You really weren't exaggerating about how hard this is for you."

"No."

"Can I do anything?"

"Distract me," he ordered, keeping his eyes straight ahead. He'd managed to find a good position and wasn't about to risk losing it. "Talk to me."

"What about?"

It really didn't matter, though he didn't tell her that. Right now, Liz seemed sympathetic. She might be more willing to open up if she thought it would help him relax. But coming right out and questioning her about the choices she'd made could also send her running in the other direction. So he decided to ease into it.

"Did you plan to work as a bartender when you came here?"

"Not really." She shifted, stretching her long legs out in front of her to sun them.

To *sun* them?

The lightweight cotton pants she'd been wearing when they'd arrived at the marina were gone, and her skin gleamed with some kind of lotion.

Though his pulse began to gush in his veins, he forced his breaths to remain normal and steady. Shifting his eyes to the left, he let his gaze travel over her. He inhaled slowly at the prettiness of her red-tinted toenails, then breathed out when he focused on her slim ankles. In again at the shapely calves. Out again at the knees. Jack fought his sudden urge to press his mouth to the warm, soft bit of skin just inside them.

Then there were no inhalations. He couldn't breathe at all, the air was stuck between his lungs and his mouth as he let his stare travel up those slender, golden thighs, so supple and smooth.

Geez. It would take days to properly explore every inch of those legs.

His perusal ended at the top of her thighs—he couldn't see farther unless he turned his head. And if he turned his head, saw the curvy hips covered in some miniscule bit of string pretending to be a bathing suit, he'd probably do one of two things.

Dive onto her in sheer lust.

Or fall out of the chair from sheer vertigo.

Either way could be very embarrassing.

He looked away, staring at a life preserver hanging from the railing, wishing someone would throw him a lifeline before he drowned in desire for the woman sitting beside him.

"I ended up at Trinity's place on a night when her old bartender had called in sick…again," she murmured with a soft, satisfied sigh, as if she was a cat curled up in a spot of sunshine on a cold day. "She desperately needed help and I jumped in to lend a hand."

Relieved to get back to normal conversation and determined not to look at her again, he asked, "And you never left?"

"Nope." Liz scooted her chair forward, enough for him to realize her bikini was fire-engine red. His heart skipped a beat. She turned so she could see his face. "Sorry, but are you purposely not looking at me? Is it the sea sickness?"

"It's safer this way," he bit out, his equilibrium thrown off now by her nearness, by the glorious sight of her nearly naked body, rather than by the motion of the water. "I should probably just try to stay still and not talk."

And not look. That was what he needed to not do. Not think, either.

He wished he could shake off the flash of lust that had turned his brain into mush, but settled, instead for pulling his sunglasses off the top of his head to cover his eyes. Which he then closed.

Liz said nothing for a moment, though he was conscious of the warmth of her leg next to his. Finally she rose from her chair.

He figured she would leave, head back to rejoin their host's wife. Which was good. Fine. Safe.

Instead, she stepped over to stand behind his chair. Before he could prepare himself, he felt those cool, soft hands touch his face. Her fingertips were at his temples, moving in small, tiny circles with just a hint of pressure.

"Good God," he said with a groan.

"Helping?"

"Oh, yeah."

She continued to stroke, as if she was easing a headache. Then she slowly moved her hands down, the pads of her fingers tracing his cheekbones, his jaw, his neck.

Her touch, meant to ease and comfort, instead brought a renewed heat and tension. Standing directly behind him, so close he could lean his head back and rest it on her full breasts, she seemed oblivious to the fire she built with every stroke. She smelled of tropical flowers and coconut, and her skin was softer than the island breeze that drifted through his open window every morning.

"You have magic in those hands," he murmured, suddenly remembering what their host had said. About this area of the yacht being so private, out of view.

"Just relax."

Funny how relaxation and tension could twist together, creating a dichotomy of responses inside him. He couldn't be more relaxed if he was reclining in the most luxurious bed ever made. But with Liz's nearly naked body just inches away, her hands doing magical things to him, the tension that came of pure, ragged longing was enough to make him shake.

Finally he couldn't take it anymore. He had to sample, had to taste.

He turned his head, his cheek brushing her inner arm, and pressed his mouth to her wrist. Though she gasped a little, she didn't pull away.

Kissing the pulse point, he slid his tongue over the vulnerable spot. He nibbled lightly, feeling her pulse grow more rapid against his lips. Moving higher, he heard the tiny catch in her breath, the sigh she couldn't contain. Her skin was hot under the sun, but so damned soft. Delicious. As he explored every inch, he couldn't help imagining how it would feel when her arms were wrapped around his neck in a close, sensual embrace.

Needing more, Jack moved his hand to hers and laced their fingers together. With a gentle tug, he brought her around the chair and down onto his lap.

He hesitated for a second, losing what sanity he had left at the sight of her beautiful body in the sexy bathing suit. Her perfect breasts were hugged by the fabric, her taut nipples jutting out in visible, blatant arousal. All from the touch of his mouth on her forearm.

What would happen if he indulged in a complete banquet of the rest of her?

"What are you doing?" she whispered, sounding a little dreamy, a little lost.

"I'm doing what I've wanted to do since I met you," he admitted as he slid a hand up to cup her head, tangling his fingers in her long hair. He drew her close, until their lips shared the same inch of morning air. Then he eliminated it, kissing her softly, all slow seduction.

She tilted her head, parting her lips on another of those soft sighs. Their tongues slid together in a slow, lazy mating. Neither took, both gave, in a sultry, shared kiss that had been years in the making.

Needing to feel her, Jack cupped her hip, then slid his hand up to caress the indentation of her waist. She arched toward his touch, silently telling him what she wanted.

As if he could resist.

He continued until he could scrape the side of his

thumb across her breast. Going slowly, giving her every chance to stop him, he toyed lightly with the sensitive peak. She jerked, groaned, then tugged his hand more fully over herself.

"Perfect," he mumbled against her mouth, taking every bit of what she offered. He slid his fingertips beneath the fabric, touching and plucking at the hard, pink nipple. Liz jerked again. He breathed deeply, inhaling the scent of beautiful, aroused woman and salty ocean air.

He wanted so much more. Wanted to tug the fabric down, move his mouth to her soft curves, suckle her deeply.

But a shout from the front of the yacht suddenly interrupted him, reminding them both of time and place. True, they were alone, Liz shielded from view by Jack's body. But the things he wanted to do with this woman required ultimate privacy. And a whole lot of time.

Not to mention a completely clear head.

Swallowing visibly, Liz pulled away, staring at him in confusion. Then, lifting her hand to her mouth, she slid off his lap and stood before him. "What was that?"

"I think it was called a kiss."

She frowned. "You're not feeling well."

"For some reason I'm feeling a lot better now." It was true. Maybe taking his focus off the roll of the waves and directing it at the incredibly sexy woman standing in front of him was all it took to combat seasickness.

"This wasn't part of the deal."

"I never said it was." He slowly rose to his feet, keeping his attention squarely on her face, ignoring the lush curves of the body he had been only moments from exploring.

"I can't do this, Jack," she insisted, shaking her head

as if to clear it. "I'm just supposed to be working for you."

"Liz, we're both adults—"

"No. This was only a job. Nothing personal, nothing intimate about it." The stiff jut of her chin said she meant it. She was erecting those barriers between them again. "If you can't agree to that, I'm afraid that when we get back to shore, we'll have to part ways."

"Impossible," he said, thrusting a frustrated hand through his hair. How the woman could be so hot in his arms one minute and so aloof the next, he honestly didn't know. "I need you."

"The Duke likes you, he told me that. You don't need me anymore."

Oh, was she wrong. So wrong. After having her in his arms, he was beginning to suspect he needed her more than he even needed to see another sunset.

He wasn't fool enough to say so. Seeing the tension in her stiff form, the self-protective way she grabbed a towel and wrapped it around her body, he knew she didn't want to hear it. He also knew he couldn't risk giving her any more reasons to back away.

Forcing a note of nonchalance he did not feel into his voice, he insisted, "Look, it was a kiss. I needed a distraction and you provided it. I feel a lot better. Thank you."

She nibbled her bottom lip, as if she wasn't quite sure she was happy getting what she'd appeared to want— an acknowledgment that their embrace hadn't meant anything.

"That doesn't mean I don't still need you." He thought quickly, wondering what limits she'd accept. "Mr. Marchand wants to get together this weekend," he said, suddenly coming up with the perfect thing. "He plans to introduce me to some other local businesspeople. I'm thinking of having a small party at the rental house, and I need your help."

Her eyes narrowed in suspicion. "To do what?"

To be by my side. To give me a chance to show you how good we can be.

He didn't admit that. "To help me with the party. I don't know anyone on the island and you do. I'll pay you extra. I'll even provide something for you to wear."

Her lips parted in surprise and her gaze shifted. She no longer met his eyes, as if his answer had taken her aback. "A uniform?"

Jack managed to hide his shock. He knew exactly what she was picturing. Black slacks, a white tuxedo shirt. Standard bartender wear.

Damn. The woman thought he wanted her to serve drinks to his guests. "Liz, you don't—"

"Fine," she snapped, cutting him off before he could explain. "I'll do it. But the donation to the school goes up by twenty-five percent."

He opened his mouth about to correct her mistaken impression then and there. Before he could do it, though, their host called from a few feet away. "We have arrived, safe and sound. Are you feeling better, my friend?"

Jack slowly turned around. "Much better," he said, surprised to realize he meant it. His seasickness had been all but forgotten during the incredible interlude he'd just shared with Liz.

"And we will find another time to meet this weekend?"

Casting a quick glance at the woman standing beside him, with her stiff shoulders and her tightly pressed lips, Jack knew what would happen if he told Liz what role he really wanted her to play at the party. She'd smile politely now, in front of Marchand, then later would back out without a moment's hesitation.

So he didn't tell her. She would figure out his intentions soon enough.

"Yes, Ray, we are looking forward to it," he said with an easy grin. "Liz and I have just been working out the arrangements. It'll be a very special night, beginning to end."

He'd make absolutely sure of it.

"SO TELL ME, girl, where is this beautiful mon of yours I been hearin' about?"

Ignoring her boss, Liz continued to wipe down the surface of the bar, taking advantage of the few minutes' respite between cruise-ship customers. Today's crowds had come into Trinity's in slow waves, rather than a great tsunami, which was a nice change.

"Louella says he's very easy on the eyes."

Louella Marchand was the Duke's much-younger wife. The woman Jack had barely given a second glance to yesterday on the boat, despite her vivid beauty.

Had he really not noticed her just because she, Liz, was around?

"No way," she mumbled, not willing to go there even in her head.

"What?" Trinity asked.

"Nothing. Just thinking out loud."

"Plus avoiding answering the question." The other woman took a seat at the bar, a knowing smile creasing her face.

Trinity was in her forties, born and raised on the island, and now ran the beach bar that had been built by her father. She often said she would marry her boyfriend, Frank, if not for the man's love of tequila, which, she claimed, would put her out of business in a year if she let him drink for free. And she had a very bad habit of minding everybody else's business—all with the best intentions, of course.

"All right," Liz admitted, knowing she would get no peace until she did. "Yes, he's very handsome."

"You know him from Boston?"

Liz shot the other woman a sidelong glance.

"My Frank. He has big ears. He said it was pretty obvious you have a past with this man."

"It's complicated."

Trinity waved a hand, setting her bangled bracelets jingling. "What is complicated about a beautiful woman and a beautiful man having a beautiful time in the bed?"

"That's out of the question."

"Why? You live like one of the nuns at St. Benedict's. It's not good for a woman to dry out like that."

Liz rolled her eyes, amused in spite of herself at Trinity's frank view of the world. "Even if I wanted to, right now I'm just working for Mr. Beaumont. I told you I'm tending bar for his private party tomorrow night."

Trinity shrugged. She hadn't been thrilled about Liz's side job—until she'd learned the terms of the deal. Her immediate family had worked hard to get where they were, but she still had relatives living in much poorer circumstances. So she'd fallen in love with Jack without ever setting eyes on him.

"After the party, you make him a special rum punch, then you have a wild celebration."

"He wants me to serve his drinks, not serve him."

He might have kissed her a couple of times, but Jack had not made any suggestion that they'd go further than that. And for a man like Jack, kissing a woman just because he felt like it was probably an everyday occurrence. It didn't mean anything.

Liar. He wanted you.

Her eyes drifted closed for a moment as heat rocketed through her. Because there had been no denying it. Yesterday, when she'd been on his lap, in his arms, when he'd touched her and driven her nearly to madness, he had been every bit as aroused. She'd felt his erection against her hip, which had just made her that much hotter.

She honestly didn't know what might have happened if the Duke hadn't called out and interrupted them. Because stopping Jack hadn't been anywhere close to the top ten things she'd wanted to do at that moment.

"Ahh…you are holding out on me," Trinity said with a disapproving wag of her finger. "Something has happened between you two."

"Didn't Louella fill you in on that, too?"

Trinity shrugged. "You mean the two of you disappearing to another part of the boat for a while? Of course she did. I meant, something happened between you in the past."

Groaning, Liz tossed the rag into the sink and dried her hands on her apron. "No. It didn't. Not ever."

That wasn't a lie. Not entirely. Because nothing had happened in the past.

Okay, there had been a night or two, maybe even just a *moment* or two, when she and Jack had been working together and their hands accidentally brushed, or they'd been standing too close and Liz held her breath in shocked anticipation. When he'd stared at her mouth and she'd studied his strong, lean body, and known they were both imagining what it would have been like to fall into each other's arms.

Maybe the exuberant hug they'd shared in his office on the day a particularly positive article had appeared in the newspaper had lasted a second too long. Had felt a bit too personal.

Maybe she had wanted him. Maybe she'd been guilty of that much.

But no more.

"Nothing happened," she repeated, talking to herself as much as to her boss.

Trinity eyed her suspiciously, then finally appeared to accept her words. She hopped off the stool. "That doesn't mean it never will."

Sure it did, at least as long as she kept reminding herself that nothing ever *should* happen between them. That it would be a bad idea to let it. Because letting Jack anywhere close—into her bed or, God forbid, into her heart—was just an invitation to heartache.

She'd gotten over her past, her lousy marriage, and even felt ready to move on. But moving on with someone she might already have deep-rooted feelings for, someone who would be jetting out of her life again in a day or two?

Bad idea, Liz.

It shouldn't be too hard to keep that in mind. She was

working for him again. Saturday night she would don the professional bartender's uniform and wait on him and his rich friends.

It was her job, what she did. So she'd had absolutely no business being a little hurt by the idea. No business at all.

And maybe it was a good thing. At least it had reminded her of just how out of her league Jack was. Keeping a professional distance was smart and right.

Even if the thought of never feeling his hands or his mouth on her again felt wrong.

Trinity's smile was knowing but gentle, with wisdom that came from years spent watching the world from behind her bar.

"Just remember, girl, the islands are a wonderful place to live your life," she said. "But nowhere on earth is the right place to hide from it."

CHAPTER SIX

LIZ ARRIVED promptly at six o'clock, an hour before the evening party was set to begin. Jack heard her chugging up the hill to the house on her little scooter several minutes before the doorbell actually rang.

The scooter was one reason he hadn't sent her outfit around to her at home. He couldn't see her driving up from Castries on that thing, not the way she was going to be dressed.

The second reason? Well, it was possible that once she saw what he'd supplied for her to wear and realized his intentions were not what she'd imagined, she might very well bolt. If he'd sent the outfit to her at home, she might never have come at all.

"Show Ms. Talbot to the second bedroom, would you?" he asked a member of the staff who looked after the house full-time. "Ask her to get ready and meet me on the terrace."

He then proceeded to wait, either for her to join him or for the sound of that scooter as it rapidly drove away.

Heading outside, he stepped to the railing of the broad patio, leaned over it and gazed out at the water. It gleamed beneath the late-afternoon sun, as if heaven itself had strewn it with a million crystals. The kind of beauty that was almost too much to see every day, and the kind Liz had wrapped herself up in completely.

Would she ever want to go back to the real world? To his world? Either with him or without him?

He didn't know. And while he hadn't been thinking along those lines when he'd flown down here to look her up, now he couldn't think of much else.

He had been telling himself all week that his presence here was to gain Liz's help with the lawsuit. And, perhaps, to see if sparks still flew between the two of them. To find out once and for all if he wanted her simply because she was the one he'd never had.

Now, he was beginning to think he had known the answer all along. With every day that passed, his attraction grew, until the thought of her—the memory of her taste, her scent, the softness of her skin—kept him up at night.

But it didn't end there. He didn't merely want her, he liked being with her. He liked her laugh and the way her mind worked. Liked her down-to-earth sense of humor, her sarcasm. Liked her courage.

God, she had actually stuck a pin in a map and followed where it led her. He didn't think he'd ever known anyone who possessed that kind of strength.

Or anyone who'd ever felt they had so little to lose by walking away from their old life.

His heart twisted, as it had when she'd first told him. Liz had left, followed her whim, because she had nothing worth staying for. Which he found not only unbearably sad, but also took as a personal challenge. He wanted to give her something to hold on to. Something to fight for. Something to stay for.

Him.

You have feelings for her.

Yeah. He did. The business, curiosity and pure physical interest hadn't been what drove him down here. Some long-denied emotion had.

He just didn't know what he was going to do about it, how he was going to let her know. Or how she was going to react.

"Ahem."

After what seemed like forever, but was in fact less than half an hour, he heard someone step outside. Not turning around, he waited for Liz's reaction. Would she tell him she was leaving? Take offense that he'd been able to guess her exact size? Ask him what the hell he thought he was doing, dressing up his bartender like she was Cinderella going to the ball?

Finally she ended his suspense, murmuring two simple words.

"It's lovely."

Jack straightened and turned around. And could only agree.

The outfit was lovely. But not nearly as lovely as the woman wearing it.

Ankle-length and silky, the dress was made to slide across the skin, to mold to the body. The jade-green fabric looked magnificent with her hair and eyes, as he'd known it would. The deep V neckline revealed the inner curves of her lush breasts. As she walked closer, the high side slit provided tantalizing glimpses of her glittering high heels, her shapely calf and one beautiful thigh.

Jack could do nothing but stare at her for a long moment, not knowing if he'd ever seen a more breathtaking sight.

"You are beautiful," he finally said.

She just smiled.

Liz had lifted most of her hair off her neck, leaving just a few long curls to brush her bare shoulders. Around her neck, she wore the emerald-and-diamond necklace he'd left for her, as well as the matching earrings. With her coloring, they looked like they'd been made for her.

"I wasn't sure you'd stay."

"I almost didn't," she admitted.

"What changed your mind?"

Liz shrugged. "I'm a sucker for silk."

Jack thought she should never wear anything else.

Actually, her not wearing anything sounded just about perfect to him right now.

"I have the feeling you don't want me serving margaritas to your guests tonight."

He slowly shook his head. "No. I want you by my side, serving only as my hostess."

A hint of wariness entered her face. "Professionally, though. Right? I mean, you just need me nearby to whisper names you forget or tell you who's who?"

Good Lord, could the woman really be so blind? Did she really think he had followed her thousands of miles just so she could act as some kind of secretary?

Then again, he hadn't told her that. Hadn't admitted anything. A mistake he needed to rectify.

Extending his arm, he led her to the railing, saying, "I didn't stumble into you by chance, you know."

"I know. You already told me you knew I was working at the bar before you showed up."

Jack let go of her arm and looked down at her. "I found out you were in St. Lucia and I came here."

Confusion creased her brow. "You...you tracked me down? You actually followed me?"

He shook his head. "Tracking you down or following you would have been a little stalkerish, don't you think?"

He'd simply waited, hoping that somehow she'd wind up back in his life one day.

"The truth is, one of your old co-workers at the agency is doing some work for us. He mentioned you had moved down here."

Liz's attention shifted to the water. "And you thought that since you had to come down here on business, you'd look me up."

"No."

"Then what?"

He lifted a hand to one long curl, smoothing it between his fingers. "I had been wondering what happened to you after you left Boston. Thinking about you." Wondering if she could hear the intensity that seemed so loud to him, he added, "I came for you, Liz. I could have sent somebody else to handle the business issues, but I came myself. Because you were here."

He didn't bring up his other reason for being there. Now, when he was finally letting her know how he felt about her, was not the time to mention her sleazy ex and his equally sleazy lover.

Hell, maybe he'd never mention them. The lawsuit

wasn't definite; it was just a possibility. And really, what more could Liz say than that Tim Talbot was as bad a husband as he'd been an employee?

Even if she could help, did he really want to put her through that? Bring pain to her now when he had finally begun to bask in those wonderful smiles and that husky laugh?

"You came just to be with me?" she asked, turning back toward him, giving him her full—surprised—attention. Her green eyes swam with confusion; her lips trembled.

Yes. No. Maybe.

I want you. I need you. But I also intended to use you.

What were the right words?

He didn't know. Nor could he find out. Because before he could respond, the door opened again. One of the servants came out, announcing their first guest. And the moment for revelations was lost.

THE EVENING WAS a great success. True to his word, Ray Marchand invited a few of his closest millionaire buddies. And some less wealthy, but equally astute ones who had their fingers in the retail pies on this island and others nearby.

Jack impressed every one of them, charmed each of their wives. He also kept Liz completely off balance for the entire evening.

She just couldn't get his words out of her head. *I came because you were here*. He hadn't been flirting, there had been no amused glint in his eye, as there might have been if he was just running a line.

He'd meant it.

Which left her wondering what she was supposed to make of that. How was she expected to feel?

He had been right in saying that intentionally tracking her down, following her, might have sounded a little like stalking. Yet somehow, his having a casual conversation with someone who knew where she was and deciding to seek her out seemed…romantic. Not stalkerish at all.

Especially since he'd waited eighteen months. Eighteen long months, during which she had recovered, moved on, rebuilt her life and her self-confidence.

It was almost as if he had been waiting for her to heal before taking his shot. And gave truth to his claim that he had been thinking about her since the time she'd left.

For a woman who'd been cheated on and had then remained alone for a long time, the idea that someone as attractive as Jack really wanted her was both heady and a little terrifying. What normal woman didn't want a man to desire her that much?

But what normal woman would ever think she could actually have him?

Besides, she wasn't entirely sure she believed it. Waiting for her, giving her time to heal and then coming after her implied altogether too much thought. Not to mention the kind of feelings—emotions—Jack Beaumont had never shown any sign of having for her. The Jack she'd worked with had been a fun, friendly, confident and slightly spoiled womanizer. If he'd had any personal interest in her, surely she would have seen some evidence of it.

Maybe you didn't want to see.

Maybe not. She'd had blinders on in so many aspects

of her life. Maybe it had just been easier to remain blind to what was happening all around her, to pretend all was well with her life, with her marriage.

To make believe she was happy even though she wasn't.

Liz puzzled over it throughout the evening even as she chatted lightly with Jack's guests, several of whom she knew from living here on the island. Not one of them made her feel out of place, despite their bank balances. That could have been because of the obviously attentive way Jack bent close to listen to her when she spoke, or the slightly possessive hand he kept on the small of her back. Considering the back of the dress was cut low, almost to her waist, she'd had a hard time even thinking when he'd touched her.

If he was seducing her, he was doing a damn good job of it. Already at a heightened level of awareness after that wildly pleasurable kiss on the boat, she was now conscious of every move of his powerful body, every brush of his hand over her skin. She kept drinking water, because every time she looked at the man, her mouth went dry.

There was no use denying it—she wanted him. Wildly. Passionately. Like she had never wanted anyone.

Liz hadn't been touched intimately by a man in a long time, and she had thought that was okay. Now she knew better. She was desperate to be touched, stroked, pleasured.

But only by one man.

The one who had just stepped out onto the patio after seeing the last of his guests to the door. Jack remained there, several feet away, backlit by soft light from inside the house, but otherwise hidden in shadow.

"I'd say that went well," he said.

Liz remained by the railing, watching him, swallowing hard as she acknowledged again just how handsome he was. When he moved, the moonlight caught glints of gold in his hair and lent an air of mystery to his shadowed face.

"Yes, I think so. I suspect you're going to get what you came here for," she replied, not intending the heavily loaded words. But once they were said, she couldn't regret them.

He obviously heard and understood, remembering what he'd said to Liz right before his guests had arrived. Approaching her slowly, Jack never took his eyes off hers. As he left the shadow of the house behind him, she saw that his expression was intense, his eyes hungry.

He stopped a few feet away, watching her, waiting for her signal. She remained still, stiff, not knowing how to proceed. She'd just essentially told this man she wanted to give herself to him. But oh, God, it had been such a long time since she'd freely given herself to anyone, Liz wasn't sure she remembered how to begin.

Fortunately Jack knew just where to start.

"Dance with me," he murmured.

He opened his arms. She smiled and stepped into them.

From somewhere up the beach, most likely Trinity's, came the lilting sounds of island music, just barely audible above the lullaby of the waves hitting the beach. Melting into Jack's body, his hard edges against her soft curves, she closed her eyes. Wordlessly, they began to sway, dancing to the music riding on the night air.

Each movement was slow and easy, filled with the slightest brushes of thigh against hip, breast against chest. One of his arms slid around her shoulders, the other around her waist. His hand flattened against the small of her back revealed by the almost backless dress. His fingers spread, the tips brushing the upper curves of her bottom, caressing her lightly but not rushing.

Not rushing at all.

Liz sighed, wrapping her arms more tightly around his neck. Wanting to taste his skin, she brushed her lips against his throat, feeling rather than hearing his low groan in response.

The movements that had been slow and lazy eased into something more. Something sensual and needful. More intense. The music itself seemed to change, until they were moving to that base, seething rhythm of the island itself that he'd been talking about the other day.

He pulled her hair down with an easy tug of the clip, letting it flow over his fingers. "Beautiful," he whispered. "I like it long."

Liz arched back, letting him tangle the strands in his hand. The position also invited him to sample her throat, to bend lower and taste her skin.

She held her breath, waiting for him to do so. And when he did, moving his mouth to the vulnerable skin below her earlobe, she shivered lightly.

His arms tightened, as if he thought she was cold. But she wasn't. The night was warm, this man's embrace incendiary.

Still swaying, she gave herself over to the magical feel of his mouth on her throat, his hand rubbing her own hair over her bare back. She nibbled at his neck, kissing her way to his jaw. He lifted his face to hers so their lips could meet, and they came together in a deep, wet kiss.

He tasted warm and spicy, like the islands, and Liz met every sultry thrust of his tongue with one of her own. She wanted to memorize his taste, experience every corner of his mouth, share every breath that left his lungs.

When he pushed the strap of Liz's dress off her shoulder, she shrugged a little to let it fall away, then dipped so the other could follow suit. The silky dress slipped down.

Jack pulled his mouth from hers and stepped back so the green fabric could drop to a puddle on the patio.

"God in heaven," he muttered, staring at her with eyes that both hungered and devoured.

Liz had never been vain, nor had she ever considered herself someone who could inspire raw lust. But right now, standing in the moonlight wearing nothing but a pair of spike-heeled shoes and flimsy thong panties, she had never been more aware of her power as a woman.

"I have never wanted anyone this much in my entire life," he admitted.

"Ditto," she said, surprising even herself. Because she hadn't thought about it until that moment. But it was entirely true.

Jack kept staring, his lips parted as he drew ragged breaths. He seemed to be struggling to keep himself in control.

She didn't want him in control. Close to losing her own, she wanted him right there with her when she gave in to the want battering every inch of her.

"Touch me," she urged, reaching for the hand still

tangled in her hair. Needing more of his touch, she drew his hand over her shoulder, to the front of her body. Their entwined fingers traveled a slow, smooth path down her clavicle, over the curve of her breast, to the taut nipple that throbbed with the need for his touch.

"Oh, yes," she hissed when he gave her the attention she craved.

He teased her, plucked at her nipple, then lifted her breast. "I have to taste you." Lowering his mouth, his warm breath gave her an instant to prepare, then his steamy mouth was on her, sucking hard and deep.

She shook, her legs going weak. Jack held her tight, supporting her as he bent her back to fully taste her, going from one breast to the other like a starving person torn between two delectable dishes.

Nearly incapable of thought, she simply thrust her fingers into his hair and held on, silently begging for more, moaning every time he gave it to her. The pleasure in her breasts sparked throughout her, shooting need directly between her shaking legs.

Kneading his thick shoulders, she reached for his collar, trying to force the buttons open. She wanted him naked. Now. And ten seconds after that, she wanted him between her thighs.

"You're a little overdressed," she said.

Jack let her go long enough to rip at his shirt. The buttons flew somewhere to the beach below.

Liz laughed, but the laughter died in her throat when she saw the shirt come off, revealing a magnificent chest and amazing shoulders. She'd had lovers before. But oh, God, none who'd ever looked like this.

"More," she demanded, reaching for his waistband.

He grabbed her hand, stopped her. "I'm hanging on by a thread here."

"Let me break it," she begged, pulling away from his hand again to reach for his belt.

The graze of her fingertips against his bulging zipper made him jerk into her hand. She cupped him through his trousers, shivering at the thought of all that male heat buried inside her.

He stepped away, unfastening his pants, letting them fall. Liz watched his every move, biting the corner of her lip in pure anticipation as he stripped off the last of his clothes.

This time, when her legs started to shake, he wasn't there to hold her up. She sank onto a lounge chair. Reaching for him, she murmured, "Now."

"No," he said as he followed her down.

He was not going to be rushed. Which both frustrated her like crazy and thrilled her beyond belief.

Kissing her again, he stroked her, toyed with her, pleasured her. He stripped her panties off, then used his hands, lips and tongue to heighten her pleasure until she felt she'd reached its very highest peak. Yet he wouldn't let her fly over it. Each time she'd get there, he would move away, refocus his efforts on another sensitive part of her body.

"Damn it," she groaned, when he once again skimmed his lips down her belly, only to move back up rather than giving her the deep, intimate kiss she needed.

This time, he took pity. Without warning, he changed direction and moved his mouth to the curls between her thighs. With long, slow strokes of his tongue, he sent her catapulting over the top. She came in a hot rush, spasming in delight, unable to control her body's wild rocking.

Before she had even recovered, he moved between her legs, spreading them so both her feet touched the ground.

Making room for himself.

Liz sucked in a breath, for some reason a little nervous. It had been a long time.

"It's been a while," Liz admitted, hearing the trepidation in her voice.

He seemed to hear it, too. Kissing her sweetly, Jack murmured, "Slow and steady then?" He moved away for a moment, grabbing a condom from the pocket of his discarded trousers.

Some intelligent woman *she* was. She hadn't even considered that little detail.

The brief interruption gave her a second to pull herself together, to shake off the last lingering worries, the hint of nervousness.

This was going to be good. Very, very good.

"Now, Jack," she begged again.

This time, he didn't refuse. Instead, he moved closer, his lean hips brushing her inner thighs. Coaxing her slick folds with his fingers to make sure she was ready for him, he groaned in anticipation, then slid into her.

Liz wrapped her arms around his neck, bringing his mouth to hers for another deep kiss. With every inch of her body that he claimed, they shared a tender breath, a gentle stroke. Until finally, with a few whispered words she couldn't make out, he plunged deep, filling her entirely.

She cried out once. And again. Each time, her cries

quickly dissipated, swallowed by the night air, the steady pulse of the island and the endlessly churning surf. And as Jack thrust into her, filling and emptying her again and again, the only thing she could hear was the raging beat of her own heart.

Until, finally, when he'd wrung from her every last molecule of pleasure her body was capable of experiencing and joined her in a shattering orgasm, she heard one more thing.

His voice.

"All those years of waiting, wondering…this was worth every one of them."

CHAPTER SEVEN

THOUGH LIZ HAD SPENT the night with him Saturday, filling his bed with her scent, not to mention utter carnal pleasure, she'd had to leave on Sunday. Jack hadn't wanted her to and had tried to bribe her into being his tour guide on the island, but she'd been insistent. Her boss had given her the previous day off to prepare for the party and she didn't want to ask for another.

Jack spent the day working, sending e-mails to his staff back in Boston about yesterday's meetings. When he was finished, he considered going down to the bar to try another of her potent rum drinks, but decided against it. Liz had made it clear she didn't want to answer questions about her old life from the people in her new one. He had to respect that.

He wondered if she would ever be willing to answer questions about her old life in private.

"Damn you, Tim," he muttered, wishing like hell the ugly issue of the lawsuit wasn't hanging over his head. He'd like nothing more than to proceed directly and honestly with Liz, let their relationship develop and grow into whatever it was going to be.

That couldn't happen, however, if he went through

with his plans to reopen the wounds caused by her divorce.

Though he'd been thinking about it all day, Jack honestly couldn't decide how to proceed. All he could think about was how much he wanted to see Liz again. Which was why, when she got off work at 2 a.m., he was waiting for her outside.

"Hi," he said as she walked out.

Though she appeared happy to see him, her smile was wan, fatigue etched in her face and made her shoulders droop. "Hi, yourself."

"Long night?"

"Very," she replied. As if they greeted each other this way every night, she stepped into his open arms and wrapped hers around his shoulders. "I think you might have to carry me to my scooter."

She was joking. But that didn't stop him from reaching for her bottom and lifting her completely off the ground.

"Hey!" she said with a surprised laugh.

"Ask and you shall receive." He turned toward the beach.

"I'm parked over there," she said, nodding toward the small lot.

"Let's walk."

"Where?" She held on as he headed around the side of the building. Her long legs wrapped more tightly around his hips, driving him mad.

"To the nearest private flat surface," he growled.

Liz nibbled his earlobe, whispering, "Sex on the beach?"

"For a start."

She shivered in anticipation, which made Jack pick up the pace. The lights from the bar had flipped off one by one, and nearby buildings and homes were also dark. Moonlight washed the sand, but didn't banish every shadow. He had spotted any number of nice, intimate places when he'd walked up here on his way to meet Liz.

But where he most wanted her was in the water. The Caribbean surf was gentle, the sea warm. Lying at the water's edge, feeling it flow over their entwined limbs as he buried himself inside her sounded like heaven on earth.

"Hurry," she said, her legs still gripping him.

"Five minutes," he replied. Then they should be out of sight of any night owls who might still be eyeing the beach.

Good thing. He was already rock-hard.

"Your legs hurting, honey?" a voice called just as Jack was about to step off the cement walkway onto the sand. "Too much physical activity?"

Jack froze and Liz stiffened against him.

"Trinity," she muttered. "My boss."

He turned around slowly. Though Liz wriggled, he didn't put her down, just kept holding her curvy bottom, keeping her right where he wanted her. Leaping apart like they'd been doing something wrong wouldn't make it any easier for Liz to face her co-workers tomorrow.

"Hello," Jack said with a smile. The attractive, dark-skinned woman wearing a long, loose skirt and brightly colored blouse approached from the door of the bar. Her smile was wicked, her eyes sparkling with amusement.

"Poor girl," she said with an exaggerated tsk, "she must be so overworked to need such physical assistance."

Liz turned her head and looked at her boss over her shoulder. "Say it and go away."

The other woman laughed.

"I mean it. Tell me I told you so, then go home and laugh all night about how right you were."

"Okay. I told you so. Now I'll go home and laugh and you can get on with whatever *you're* going to be doing all night."

She wagged her brows a little, then her smile faded. Eyeing Jack, she stuck out an index finger. "You be careful. Don't go breakin' her heart again, not now when it's finally all patched up."

"I wouldn't dream of it," he told her.

He meant it. Breaking Liz's heart was the last thing he would ever do. He wanted to fill it completely. If only she'd let him. Their physical relationship seemed like a step in the right direction.

While questioning her about the past, asking her to relive it, was a hugely wrong one.

"'Night you two," said Trinity, waving before she turned and walked away.

Jack made sure they were truly alone, then turned and carried Liz down to the beach.

"I'll never live this down," she said, though she didn't sound rueful or resigned. Instead, as she settled her head on his shoulder, her face buried in the crook of his neck, she sounded pleased.

"Do you care?"

"Not really."

He gave her a squeeze. "I didn't mean to put you in the position of having to answer questions you don't want to answer."

Her lips scraped his neck, her tongue flicking out against the pulse point. "Well, what position do you want to put me in?" she asked in a throaty whisper.

Heat rushed back to his groin, and she answered it by rubbing against him, as if taking the pressure where she needed it most. His groan of pleasure was drowned out by hers.

"I can think of one or two," he admitted as they escaped the last hints of light, nearing ultimate privacy.

"That's funny. I can think of thirty or forty."

"Okay. I'll get right to work on that."

ON THE DAY when Jack had first shown up at Trinity's bar, he had told Liz he'd rented the beach house for a week. That had been over seven days ago.

Yet he was still here.

He didn't seem in a hurry to leave St. Lucia and, to her knowledge, hadn't yet packed a single bag or made any travel reservations. Liz assumed it was because of his work. The party Saturday night had opened a lot of doors to him, and he'd spent all day Monday going to meetings.

A part of her, however, couldn't help wondering if she was another reason he stayed.

She didn't ask him, of course. Talking about his plans was just about as off-limits as talking about what had happened back in Boston. There was only now. This time, this place, this wild, sensual affair that had taken her completely by surprise.

She knew she should probably already be feeling some regret. The old Liz might already be worrying what it would be like when he left, taking with him all the excitement and raw passion she'd been feeling. Yet those thoughts seldom came to mind. Because what was happening between them here and now was not only washing away any remnants of darkness that had remained in her heart, but also filling it with light that would last a long time into the future.

"Is there any chance we'll find a parking place in town?" Jack asked doubtfully as he maneuvered his rented convertible into the town of Castries on Tuesday morning.

A few short days ago, Liz had wondered what it might be like to experience the true beat of the island at one of the wild and sultry street festivals.

She was about to find out.

Carnival Tuesday was one of the wildest days of the year. The party started at dawn and continued all day, with concerts, pageants, parades. Every food vendor on the island would set up shop, any musician who owned an instrument could find an audience. Trinity had shut down the bar because everyone would be here on this day.

"Just park at my building," Liz replied, already leaning forward in her seat, staring wide-eyed at the brightly costumed revelers. "I have a reserved spot."

"Scooter-size? I'm afraid I might just be too big to fit."

"It's amazing how easy it is to squeeze into tight places if you're motivated enough."

He grabbed her hand from the seat and lifted it to his mouth. Pressing a kiss on her knuckles, he whispered, "I am very well motivated."

"At least three times last night and twice the night before."

Lord, she had never in her life had so much sex in such a short time. And yet she still craved it, still went wet and tender with want just thinking about the wild, incredible things he had done to her over the past few nights.

"Enough," she said, pulling her hand away. "Or I'm going to have to run up to my apartment and change my underwear."

"I don't know what you mean." The self-satisfied expression made a liar out of him. He knew exactly how he affected her. "Your underwear looked perfectly fine to me when I ripped them off you two seconds after you put them on this morning."

Her thighs tightened. "Stop it or I'll get even."

"Maybe we should detour up to your apartment."

"Maybe we should go get a big, cold drink to cool off. I have the feeling if we go up, we'll miss the parade completely. Not to mention the rest of the day."

He pulled the car into her parking lot, right into the spot she pointed him toward. "I'd sure as hell hope so."

As he cut the engine, Liz asked, "Are you serious? Do you really want to skip today? Because we don't have to…"

"I want to go," he told her as he got out of the car. "I can't wait to dance with you again."

She licked her lips. "Carnival's pretty wild. But we will have to keep our clothes on while we dance this time."

"Aww, hell."

Hand in hand, they walked out of the parking lot and were almost immediately absorbed into the street party. Performers had already drawn large crowds. The air was redolent with island scents—spicy jerk chicken, simmering black beans, fruity rum drinks—and they tried a little of everything.

Beneath it all, that seething, hungry beat thrummed

on. The island had a pulse, a vibrancy that demanded life be lived in full measure, no holding back. They walked to that beat, swayed to it, danced to it in the street, along with thousands of others. Jack might have seduced her slowly with the dance on the patio the other night, but today, as they spun and thrust and gyrated against one another, pure, wanton lust was the name of the game.

As she'd remembered, he was an excellent dancer, natural and smooth, and more than one woman had shuffled between them.

Liz didn't mind. Today was about being wild, free and joyful.

Besides. She'd be going home with the man.

"You're loving this," he said, speaking loudly to be heard over the music and the writhing crowd.

Out of breath, Liz merely nodded. She lifted her hands to her hair, tugging it off her hot, sweaty body and holding it out of the way. Jack's eyes followed her every move, telling her without words that he wanted to taste the salty sheen of her skin.

"Let's get out of here!" she snapped, suddenly unable to wait. The entire afternoon had been filled with intense foreplay. Now she wanted the payoff.

He didn't need to be asked twice. Grabbing her hand, he pulled her with him as he worked his way through the crowd. They were quite a few blocks from her place now, and Liz didn't relish the long walk. Neither, apparently, did Jack. He led her to a side street, then flagged one of the many taxis waiting to pick up partyers who'd had a little too much liquid fun.

"That was fantastic," Jack said as they settled into the back seat and gave the driver the address.

"I know." She breathed deeply, trying to slow her still-racing heart. "I never got that good a workout after a grueling step-aerobics class."

Wanting to pull her hair into a ponytail to get it off her face, Liz unzipped the fanny pack she'd worn over her capris. Preferring not to carry a purse at the festival, she'd tucked a few necessities into it.

As she grabbed a ponytail holder, she noticed her cell phone. The message symbol was lit. No way would she have heard it ring over the noise of the crowd.

Though normally she would ignore it, she decided to check the message. Though Carnival Tuesday was wildly fun, it could also be dangerous. She didn't want to think anyone she knew was in trouble, but since she so seldom received calls on the cell, she couldn't rule it out.

"Let me check this, okay?" she told Jack.

Nodding, he reached into his back pocket for his wallet. They were almost at her place.

Dialing, Liz waited for the recording. The tiniest bit anxious, she waited to make sure there was no emergency.

Then she heard the voice on the other end. Tension didn't begin to describe it. Full-fledged shock flooded her. And the heart that had been gradually slowing its pace seemed to come to a dead stop for a few seconds.

"Liz, it's me. Tim."

Her ex-husband hadn't tried to call her once since the divorce had been finalized more than a year ago. She'd gone on her merry way thinking she'd never have to listen to his voice again. So hearing that casual greeting yanked the proverbial rug out from under her, big time.

"I need to talk to you, to tell you something," he said. There was a slight slur to his words. Liz didn't think there was a time difference between here and Boston, so it was certainly not late enough for him to be drunk on a weekday.

"I got a call from one of hotshot Jack Beaumont's lawyers about what's going on with the company." His voice dripped dislike when he said Jack's name. "I hear he's down there trying to get your help."

She didn't follow at first, wondering why he would think she'd care what was going on at Jack's company.

"It's all bull, you know. He's using this lawsuit as an excuse to do what he's wanted to do since he met you—get in your pants."

Liz reached for the button to shut the phone off. Damn Tim to hell. He had no right to do this to her, no business contacting her at all or making such snide remarks.

Before she ended the call, though, she heard him say one more thing: "He's the reason we broke up, you know."

She hesitated.

"He wanted you from the get-go and he did every-thing he could to come between us. Set up that inter-view, told Desi I'd do whatever she wanted me to do."

Desi. The ho-bag herself, Desdemona Eros.

"He even encouraged me to have sex with her so the story would have a real authentic note. So his high-priced lawyers better cover my ass in this lawsuit, too. It's all his—"

The phone beeped, signaling that Tim had run out of time to finish delivering his ugly words.

Turned out he hadn't needed any more time. She had gotten the message loud and clear.

The world seemed to be spinning, pressing in on her with enormous weight. Jack, the man sitting beside her, had intentionally broken up her marriage? It was crazy. Utterly ridiculous. He had never made an inappropriate move toward her.

And yet….

He'd admitted he came here for her. He'd pursued her relentlessly since his arrival.

But had he come here *just* for her? Had he really? Or was it for some other reason? A business reason, involving this mysterious lawsuit Tim had mentioned.

Had she once again been completely fooled by a man she'd developed deep feelings for?

"God, no," she whispered, slowly putting the phone back into her fanny pack.

"What?"

She swallowed, not knowing where to start. With the accusation that Jack had manipulated things to free her up for his own pursuit, or that he'd come here not to seduce her, but to use her?

"Here you go, brother. Glad to hear you like our island's little party," the driver said.

Liz watched, still stunned into silence, while Jack pulled money out of his wallet and handed it to the driver. But before Jack could refold the wallet and put it away, Liz caught sight of something inside.

It was one of those plastic sleeves, used for holding pictures of loved ones. And in the split second's glance she'd had of it, she saw a face that completely shocked her. Her own.

"Let me see that," she said, reaching for the wallet and pulling it out of his hand.

Jack said nothing, watching her as she opened the

fine leather and flipped to the photograph. "It's me," she murmured.

Liz as she'd looked several years ago. Her hair was short, and she stood beside a Christmas tree. She was smiling, laughing really, and the photograph had been taken from somewhere across the room—she hadn't been posing.

"The first night I ever saw you," Jack admitted.

Ignoring the driver, who tapped the steering wheel impatiently, she looked into Jack's eyes. "You took this?"

He shook his head, which gave her a moment of relief.

"I found it in a bunch taken by someone else at the party and kept a copy."

"Has it been here in your wallet ever since?"

"No," he admitted, his voice throbbing with intensity. As if he wanted to make sure she understood. "I haven't been pining away, and I haven't been celibate since the night we met. But once I stumbled across this picture and realized I was going to be seeing you again, I couldn't help…remembering."

"Remembering what?" she whispered.

He gave a helpless shrug. "How I felt about you from the minute I laid eyes on you."

Liz's throat closed and she had a hard time breathing. Such an admission might have seemed incredibly romantic in another time, under other circumstances. Now, with Tim's words echoing in her head, it was almost painful to hear.

"How did you feel?"

With a helpless half smile, he admitted the truth. "I wanted you from the very first. And working with you made me realize it wasn't just *want*—I liked you more than any woman I'd ever met. Truth is, I'm crazy about you, Liz."

Closing her eyes briefly, she let the truth of it wash over her. He'd seen her. Wanted her. Kept his distance because she was married—at least until, with his help, she was no longer married. Then he had eventually followed her to her new life.

All so the rich, charming Bad Boy Beaumont could get what he wanted.

He didn't hold a gun to Tim's head. Nobody had forced her ex to drop his pants. He'd cheated all on his own. And, she suspected, the affair that ended their marriage had not been his first one.

The thought calmed her a little. But there was still too much she didn't understand. She had to know for sure. Find out if the rest of the ugly accusations were true.

"So when you said you came here for me, you really meant it. This talk about opening new markets for the company, that was just a small part of it. You really flew to this island to explore your attraction to me, right? And for *no* other reason?"

She held her breath. Confusion still whirled in her brain, doubt thrusting daggers into her heart. Liz honestly wasn't even sure how she wanted him to respond.

Which was worse? The idea that the man beside her had hoped for her marriage to break up, perhaps even helped it along, then pursued her to get her into his bed? Or that he was here because of some damned lawsuit, and having her was merely a side benefit?

"Well? Answer me, Jack. Why did you really come to this island?"

His silence continued, and his mouth opened, then closed, as if he didn't know what to say.

Which said it all, really.

Liz didn't think, didn't plan, didn't say one word. She simply reached for the handle, opened the door and jumped out.

And then she walked away, intentionally disappearing into the crowd.

CHAPTER EIGHT

JACK HADN'T BEEN sure how Liz would react when she learned how he felt about her. Considering even he himself hadn't known the depth of his feelings until recently, he'd imagined she would react with anything from skepticism to amusement.

As it turned out, he hadn't had time to tell her much at all. Nor to even answer her question. Just the news that he'd wanted her for such a long time had been enough to send her running.

Jackass.

He'd been so focused on trying to find the words to admit that one of his reasons for coming here was to ask for her help in dealing with his legal troubles, he hadn't even noticed how upset she truly was.

It had just suddenly seemed so ridiculous. The idea that Liz should have to talk about the condition of her marriage—Tim's other infidelities, anything she knew about the affair with Desdemona—just to save his company a few bucks, was out of the question. Yet he had to admit the truth to her, clear the air about it, even though he had no intention of following through.

She hadn't stuck around long enough to listen. And

her mood hadn't been skeptical and it hadn't been amused. It had been pure, raw anger he'd seen in her eyes, combined with a flash of utter sadness.

He just didn't know why.

Though he'd quickly gotten out of the car and hurried after her, she'd been impossible to locate in the dense crowd. He'd searched fruitlessly for an hour, then realizing she might simply have doubled back and gone home, he went to her place. She didn't answer the door, and the windows were dark and shuttered.

"Damn it, Liz," he muttered, unable to understand. Okay, it hadn't exactly been the most romantic time and place. And he had played it a little safe, telling her he was crazy about her rather than admitting he was head over heels in love with her.

But he didn't think that was it. Liz had run, but she wasn't a coward. Something had spooked her, big time. She was troubled.

He suddenly thought of something she'd said last week. About where she went to let her troubles float away.

To her sailboat.

"Oh, God, please, anything but that," he said. With no other ideas, though, he had to at least check.

Not even considering driving through the madness surrounding her building, he cut to another street and flagged down a taxi. This time he asked to be taken to the marina.

"No action up there," the driver said. "All the ladies are in town tonight. Things are just heating up."

"I think I've had as much heat as I can handle," he replied. Liz was as much as he ever *wanted* to handle.

As they drove away from Castries, the traffic all but disappeared. What few cars were on the road were heading into town, not out of it. He wondered for a second if he was making a serious mistake. Liz had friends on the island. She could easily have gone to see one of them.

But something told him she hadn't. Whatever was bothering her, it cut deep. Her expression had told him that much. And if she truly was angry with him, thinking he was some kind of stalker for having an old picture of her in his wallet, she might have sought out the one place she knew he wouldn't follow: the sea.

When he arrived at the marina and saw the empty slip where her small sailboat had been docked the other day, he knew he'd been right.

"Hey, Jack!" a voice called.

He looked up to see the Duke, with his beautiful wife on his arm and another couple beside them. "Ray."

"You look miserable, my friend. Too much fun at Carnival?"

"Not exactly."

"It can be a bit much. That's why we're going out for a sunset cruise." The other man laughed. "I would invite you to join us, but…"

"Thanks. I'll just wait here."

Marchand walked closer, gazing at the empty slip. "She set sail about half an hour ago. She can't have gotten too far."

"You saw Liz?"

The man nodded. "She didn't look too happy. In fact, I'd say her face was almost as sad as yours is right now."

"I've got to talk to her. Find out what's wrong."

Marchand looked at the sky. "Long summer day, hours till sunset. You could be here awhile."

Jack thought about it, pictured Liz out there for hours, letting her troubles—including whatever feelings she had for him—disappear on the waves. He couldn't stand the thought of it.

"That trick—sitting still in the back of the boat," he said. "It worked pretty well last week."

Throwing back his head, Marchand let out a deep belly laugh. "I told you," he called back to his wife. "Men do crazy things for the women they love." Putting a hand on Jack's shoulder, he added, "Come, my friend. For you, I will make sure my ship sails as smoothly as a child's toy in a bathtub."

LOWERING THE SAILS once she was well offshore, northeast of the island, Liz turned to watch the sun dropping lower in the western sky. It would be a few hours yet before the great blue sea opened its yawning mouth and devoured it. A few hours before she would have to head in and deal with the problem she'd come here to escape.

You shouldn't have run.

No, she shouldn't have. She was no damned coward. If Jack really had messed up her life for his own selfish purposes and then come here to use her, to boot, she should have stayed right there and told him exactly where he could go.

But what if he hadn't?

Back in the cab, fresh off the wild day, the dancing, the heat and that insidious voice on the phone, Liz's emotions had been swinging wildly. She knew better than anyone that her ex was a world-class liar when it suited his purpose. She also knew he'd relish the chance both to screw with her life and deprive Jack of something he might want.

That photograph in Jack's wallet, his acknowledgment that he'd wanted her from the moment he'd met her and his silence about why he'd come to the island had all combined to fill her with confusion.

The evidence was circumstantial. But oh, it was damning.

Maybe if she'd been a little stronger, she would have given him the benefit of the doubt. Or at least questioned him further and waited for his answers. In recent days, however, as she'd begun to open up her heart, to think she might actually be capable of giving it to someone again, she'd almost been waiting for the rug to be pulled out from under her feet. As if Jack hurting her was inevitable.

And she was hurt. Badly. Not just because of the idea that he'd manipulated her, but the thought that she'd lost what she'd only started to realize she had.

Love. She had been falling more deeply in love with Jack by the minute. It had probably started that first night at the bar when he'd refused to down that rum punch despite her snarky provocation. It had grown ever since. From his embarrassed admission about his seasickness to the way he'd danced with her in the moonlight, had carried her on the beach, had danced with her at Carnival…each moment spent with him had built on the foundation that she suspected had been there for a long time. Her walls had crumbled and he'd stormed past them, right into her heart.

"Ahoy, there!"

Startled by a voice out here in the middle of beautiful nothingness, Liz swiveled her head. She'd been so lost in thought she hadn't even noticed the Duke's massive yacht cruising closer and closer.

"I've got someone here who wants to talk to you!"

Confused, Liz merely watched and waited. A figure left the deck, descending a side ladder onto a platform where two Jet Skis were lashed down. It took her a few seconds to process that that someone was Jack.

"Oh, my God," she whispered.

He'd come after her? Followed her? *Again?*

For some reason, perhaps because she had been sitting here thinking about how much she loved the man, the realization that he was actively pursuing her again didn't upset her. Not at all. In fact, she found it so heartbreakingly sweet, she melted a little right on the spot.

Even from twenty yards away, she could see the paleness of Jack's face. But he didn't slow down, instead, he just stripped off his shirt, kicked off his shoes and dove into the sea.

Liz immediately moved to raise the sails, worried about the distance. She needn't have, though. His powerful arms cut through the water smoothly, his strong legs scissoring. Stroke after stroke he eliminated the distance between them, until he was within a few feet of her small sailboat.

There he stopped, treading water and looking up at her.

"Are you crazy?"

He shook his head.

"What on earth possessed you to do that?"

"What, swim over here? I'm a good swimmer. Much better in the water than on it."

"I meant, why did you hitch a ride on *The Regal Duchess?* After the last time, I didn't think you'd ever leave land again, unless it was in the first class cabin of a jet liner."

"I needed to talk to you," he said nonchalantly, as if the occurrence was an everyday one for him, rather than the ordeal she suspected it had been.

"So talk."

"It's a little hard looking up at you like this."

"You asking if you can come aboard?"

"Nope." He reached for her, wrapping a hand around her ankle. "You come down here."

She could have resisted, he didn't grip tightly and his tug wasn't too hard. But she let herself go, let Jack drag her into the gentle water. They faced one another, each holding on to the side of the boat.

"That's better."

"You're crazy. You do know you're going to have to get onboard to get back to shore. Unless I tie you to the back and keel-haul you." She pursed her lips. "Which, to be honest, sounds pretty tempting right now."

He lifted a hand and brushed a long strand of wet hair back from her face. "Why, Liz? What happened? What went wrong?"

She didn't explain right away. She couldn't. What was happening was between her and Jack. It had everything to do with whether she could trust him, let herself love him. Bringing her sleazy ex-husband into the conversation sent the wrong message.

Yet she had to know the truth.

"I need to ask you something. A few somethings, actually."

"Go ahead."

"You said you've wanted me since the night we met."

He simply nodded.

"Was I just oblivious? I mean, did you send signals I never saw?"

"No. You were off-limits and I knew it."

He'd gone exactly where she needed him to, and she would not have to mention her ex's name at all.

"So you let it go. You would never have acted on it."

His eyes twinkled. "I'm not a saint, Liz. I can't guarantee I never would have flirted with you or taken advantage of some random mistletoe if I'd ever found you beneath it." The amusement faded. "Beyond that, no. I was content to wait."

"Wait for what?"

"This might be painful to hear," he warned.

"I can take it. There's not much I don't know."

"Okay, then. I was willing to wait until you finally realized you were married to a manipulative, adulterous bastard and shook him off like the leech he was."

She swallowed hard. "You knew that would happen?"

"I'm so sorry, Liz. Everybody knew. His affairs were so well-known it was only a matter of time."

"Affairs?" she asked, though she had already suspected. "Plural?"

The color fell out of his face. "Jesus, Liz, you said you knew."

"Never mind." She waved an unconcerned hand, her reaction probably surprising herself more than him.

Because, while disappointing and more than a little re-volting, that news no longer had the power to hurt her.

Jack grabbed her shoulder, squeezing, forcing her to meet his eyes to gauge the sincerity there. "I am sorry. I would *never* have hurt you like that if I'd realized you didn't know."

He was telling the truth. About everything. She knew it by the hitch in his voice, the sadness in his eyes, the twist of his mouth. He hurt for her, hated being the one to bring the painful news. Because he cared about her.

She knew it. Had no doubt about it anymore. He cared.

Maybe he even loved her.

"You really waited, didn't you? You sat back, not doing a thing to interfere…"

"Like what?" he asked, appearing genuinely confused.

"It doesn't matter." And it didn't. She realized now that Jack had nothing to do with her marriage ending. That her ex's infidelities could be blamed on nobody but the douche bag himself.

Liz began to laugh a little, liking Jack's influence on her. But the laughter didn't last, because the other part of Tim's accusation came to mind.

"Is there something about a lawsuit that I should be aware of?" she asked, not wanting to play around anymore but to get to the bottom of things. An hour or so ago, when she had doubted Jack's feelings for her, the idea had stung. But now, seeing the light of warmth shining in this man's amazing eyes, not much had the capacity to bother her.

Jack's jaw fell open. "How did you know that?"

"I had a phone message from a very unpleasant little birdy and he made some ugly insinuations."

"That bastard. I'll—"

She waved a hand. "He's not worth it. But I want to hear the truth."

"About why I came here?"

"Yes. Why you came. You know, beyond the stuff about how much you wanted me, blah blah. Get to the other part."

His lips twitched in amusement. "Blah blah? My feelings for you are summed up with the words *blah blah?*"

Feelings. *Love?* She smiled a little, but pressed on. "What's the lawsuit about?"

Jack immediately explained, and Liz fell silent, listening intently. Somehow, she could muster no surprise that the erotica writer was the vengeful type, nor that she, too, had been betrayed.

"I'd say it served her right, if I gave a damn, which I don't," she said when he'd finished speaking.

"Liz, I might have had the vague idea that you could help with this, but believe me, opening up all this garbage is the last thing I want to do to you. We'll deal with Ms. Eros and her lawyers. I know a few good ones myself." He moved a little closer, his handsome face blocking out the sun hanging low in the sky behind him, until his dark hair became a halo of fading daylight. "I'm sorry. So sorry that I didn't tell you exactly why I came here. The truth is, after one day in your company, I knew I would never do anything to cause you that kind of pain again."

His words rang with sincerity and his expression was

so loving she melted a little more, right there in the cool waters of the open sea. The amazing man treading water in front of her, having set sail knowing it would make him utterly miserable, felt the same way about her as she did about him. She knew it, deep down in her soul, the way her mother must have known her father would be the love of her life until the day they died together.

It only remained to say the words. And to hear them.

"I love you, Jack," she said simply, no longer having any walls to hide behind or any reason to seek them out.

"I love you, too, Liz."

They didn't melt into each other's arms, didn't sink into deep, hungry kisses. Instead, they simply savored the moment, there by the boat, staring into each other's eyes. The sound of the water lapping gently against their bodies was only slightly louder than the echo of the words they'd both just said.

I love you.

Finally moving closer, until their legs brushed and entwined beneath the surface, she whispered, "Thanks for coming out here for me. And for coming so far to find me again."

He ran the pad of his thumb along her lower lip. "I'll always come for you, Liz."

His mouth finally lowered to hers in a long, tender kiss. For the longest time, they rocked on the water, touching, kissing, loving.

Not letting go, not ever wanting to let go.

Until finally the sun began to drop and she knew it was time to head in.

"I hate to do this to you, but it's a hell of a long swim," she murmured as she pulled herself back up on deck. She extended a hand to help him, though he didn't need it, easily hoisting himself up to sit beside her.

"If it gets bad, I'll just jump in the water."

"As long as you jump back out," she said.

"Deal."

Liz raised the sails, knowing Jack was watching every move she made. So far, he didn't look too green. She took care in steering, trying to avoid any waves, which the Caribbean seldom had, anyway.

"Doing okay?"

He didn't speak, he merely nodded. Which made her suspect he was going to need to take a swim soon. Thinking about it, she had to chuckle. "I don't think your solution of jumping in and swimming every so often will help much on a Boston Harbor dinner cruise."

Instead of laughing with her, he asked, "Does that mean you think we might see Boston Harbor again?"

She knew what he was saying. What he was offering. The incredible man was willing to do anything, give up his entire world, to be with her.

Funny, though. She suddenly realized she was ready to do exactly the same thing for him.

"I do miss snow at Christmastime," she mused.

He understood. "And I'll bet the islands don't have anything to compare with opening day at Fenway Park."

"Crisp fall days."

"Summer concerts in the park."

They were within sight of shore now. The masts of the boats docked at the marina shone brightly against the tropical greens and blues of the beautiful island.

With an appreciative sigh, he admitted, "But this is good, too."

"No doubt," she said with a laugh.

"Okay, then. It's settled."

"What's settled?"

"We'll be bi-continental. The house is for sale, you know."

Her jaw dropped. "The house? *That* house? The one you're renting?"

"Sure. I might not be a gazillionaire, but I can afford it. We'll come as often as possible, at least until the kids are old enough to be in school. Then we'll have to work something out for summers and holidays."

She didn't think it was possible for her jaw to drop any farther, yet it did.

"Oh, come on, you don't seriously think I'm going to risk letting you get away again, do you?"

Tears rose to her eyes at the look of pure, unrestrained love on his face. Though the boat swayed beneath him, he dropped to one knee and took her hand. "Will you marry me, Liz?"

She couldn't answer, couldn't make her voice work. All she could do was blink away her tears and nod.

"I'd stand up again to seal it with a kiss," he said. "But considering the way my head is spinning, I think you'd better come down here."

She sank down to face him, her sweet, funny, sexy man. "I'm not laughing at you, but I have to say, I'm glad you have that one single weakness. It makes you that much more adorable."

He shook his head slowly. "Oh, no, darlin', you're wrong about that. I've got two."

Moving closer, he pressed his lips to her forehead,

her cheekbones, then finally her mouth, each tender caress telling her what his second weakness was.

Her.

"I love you, Jack," she said, needing to say it again, knowing she would say it thousands and thousands of times over the next several decades.

He sat down, pulling Liz with him so she could settle onto his lap. Wrapping his arms around her waist, Jack kissed her temple and held her loosely so their bodies gently rocked together on the waves.

They stayed that way for a moment, bathed in each other's nearness, as well as in the warmth of the last golden rays of tropical sun.

And with his arms tight around her and his love filling all the empty places in her heart, Liz smiled as they sailed into the sunset.

* * * * *

FEVERED

Lori Wilde

To Bill, my rock, I love you.

CHAPTER ONE

MACY GATWICK fine-tuned the focus on her high-powered field binoculars and scanned the tropical forest, ostensibly searching for the rare, red-throated Costa Rican swallow like the rest of her bird-watching group.

"You gettin' anything?" asked Amelia Pettigrew, the spry older woman beside her.

Amelia was dressed in camouflage cargo shorts, hiking boots and water-resistant knee socks. Her short, gray curls were tucked up inside a New York Yankees baseball cap. Macy had met Amelia and her traveling companion, Harry Longley, in the San José airport the previous day when they'd all ended up on the bus to El Marro Lindo.

"Nope, not getting anything at all." Macy grimaced, recognizing ironically how the conversation mirrored the sad state of her sex life.

"Shh," cautioned their guide, Stratford Kingman, from the Coronado Bed and Breakfast where the group was staying. Not counting Stratford and Macy, every single member of the tour was over the age of fifty.

Stratford was around Macy's age, but he stood a

good four inches shorter than her five-foot-seven-inch height. He had a thin, sharp nose, intense brown eyes burning behind thick, black-framed glasses and from what she could tell, a near rabid fascination with tropical birds. "The red-throated Costa Rican swallow is quite shy."

Macy rolled her eyes. If she hoped to achieve her real objective she was going to have to shake off these bird enthusiasts ASAP.

"However, they are highly passionate birds. Their courtship ritual is sudden and intense, but once they mate, they're mated for life," Stratford continued.

"So if you're a red-throated Costa Rican swallow the moral of that story is be careful who you mate with because you'll be stuck with them for life?" someone in the group joked.

"Sounds more like grand passion leads to great love to me." Harry winked at Amelia, who coyly smiled and lowered her lashes.

"This way," Stratford whispered and tiptoed through the pond fronds. "And keep your eyes peeled. Often the thing you seek most is hiding right under your nose."

I'm going to find a runaway chemical engineer hiding under a palm frond? Who knew?

One by one the group fell in line behind Stratford, leaving Harry, Amelia and Macy bringing up the rear.

"Oh, darn." Macy shoved a hand through her rapidly frizzing curls.

"Do you have a problem, dear?" Amelia asked.

"I forgot my camera," she lied smoothly.

"What's that hanging out of your backpack?" Harry asked, cocking one bushy eyebrow up on his forehead.

"Umm—" Macy stuffed her Canon Rebel deeper into the knapsack "—it's broken. I forgot my good camera. I'm just gonna go—" she jerked a thumb behind her "—back to the B and B and get it."

"Shouldn't you tell Stratford," Amelia murmured, "in case you get lost?"

"Will you tell him for me?" Macy asked. "I've got my compass." She patted her jeans. "I'll catch up with you guys later."

"Well…," Amelia said, but Macy didn't give her time to voice her objection.

She turned and hurried back the way they'd come, but once she was out of sight of the group, she veered off the path and plunged into the vegetation, snatching the map from her back pocket as she went. She headed north toward the banana plantations, batting aside broad-leaved plants, her hiking boots sinking into the soft mossy earth, the binoculars around her neck bouncing against her chest.

Forty minutes later, hair bushing out from her head courtesy of the ninety-percent humidity, pulse strumming from the strenuous climb up the sloping terrain, she paused to take a break. Macy plopped down on a lichen-covered rock and fished out a bottle of water and a protein bar from her knapsack.

As a freelance investigative journalist, Macy was prepared for the unexpected. Besides food and water, she also carried a first-aid kit, flashlights, flares, a small tarp, a satellite cell phone and extra clothing. Prepared yes, but the heavy knapsack was slowing her down, big time.

She finished off the protein bar, capped the water bottle and then checked the map. She should be getting close, but in the lush green maze of tropical plants it was easy to lose her bearings.

As she was packing up to continue on her way, the cell phone rang. Gotta love technology. She was never out of touch, not even in a tropical rain forest.

Without even looking at the caller ID she knew who it was. "What's up, Greg?"

"You find the young corporate hotshot who went all Tarzan in the jungle?"

"Not yet."

"Well, hurry. I want to put your interview in next week's edition." Greg Winston published *Gotcha,* a popular online magazine devoted to uncovering scandals, scams and corporate misconduct. He was eager because Macy was sitting on a potential bombshell of a story.

She was pretty darned eager herself. What Greg didn't know, and she wasn't about to tell him, was that this exposé—if she didn't mess it up—was exactly the ticket she needed to land her a long-coveted job at Alliance News Network. From the time she was a young girl scribbling in her diary and penning the neighborhood newsletter, she'd wanted nothing more than to write for the crème de la crème. She'd had several interviews at ANN and she was getting close. The last time they'd told her, "Blow the lid off something big and you're in."

Macy had spent the past six months searching for her "something big" and finally she believed she'd found it. She could almost taste the story, could feel the undercurrent of scandal strumming through her blood. But it wasn't cheap. The trip to Costa Rica was on her own dime. If she came up bust, she'd be eating nothing but ramen noodles for a month.

"You still there?" Greg asked.

"Once I find Cutler, you'll get your story. He's been dodging reporters. Hence the Costa Rican hideaway. No one's been able to get an interview. Rumor has it he's living in a remote cabin in the rain forest and working on his uncle's banana plantation."

Macy was determined to get to the bottom of why the brilliant chemical engineer Armando Cutler had unexpectedly exited his position as fourth vice president of Hollister Chemicals. After earning three lucrative patents for the company, he'd been a shining star on the fast track being groomed to one day take over as CEO, plus he'd been working on a much ballyhooed project having something to do with a revolutionary new fuel additive.

Then without warning, he'd resigned and taken off for Costa Rica while Hollister's top competitor, Bond and Martin, announced they were conducting trials for a fuel additive rumored to boost engine performance to the point where cars would get up to a hundred miles a gallon.

Coincidence?

Macy thought not. Her instincts told her there was much more to the story.

Had Bond and Martin stolen Cutler's formula? If so, why had he thrown in the towel? Why not file a lawsuit? From what she'd gleaned, Armando was a scrapper from childhood, having grown up in a rough neighborhood without a father. He wasn't the kind of guy who walked away from trouble.

And yet he had.

Why?

Curiosity—the thing that had gotten her into so much trouble as a kid, but now completely defined her as an adult—gnawed at Macy. She'd tried to get an interview with Cutler, but he'd refused to answer his phone or return her calls. His evasiveness had fueled her suspicions. That was when she'd decided to fly to Costa Rica and pretend to be a bird-watcher. Her plan was to find him, gain his trust and then tell him she was a reporter interested only in the truth.

Okay, okay, so lying to get an interview isn't exactly honest, but I'm not above a little deception in order to crack a big story.

"So you won't have the article in by next week?" Greg sounded disappointed.

"I'm guessing not."

Greg muttered a curse. "Call me as soon as you get the scoop."

"You'll be the first to know."

Her boss grunted and hung up.

Macy stuck the phone back in her knapsack and started walking again. Birds flitted through the trees. Critters rustled in the undergrowth. Insects buzzed.

It took a lot to unnerve Macy, but she was unaccustomed to the exotic sounds of the rain forest. Not to mention that the verdant cloak of foliage blocking out the noonday sun cast suspicious shadows over the forest floor.

"Buck up, keep going. This is it. Everything you've ever dreamed of is in the palm of your hand," she said out loud.

Macy trudged through humidity so heavy it felt as if she was pushing against an invisible revolving door.

Sweat pearled at the hollow of her throat. Her legs felt as if she had ten-pound weights strapped to her ankles. Why had she thought coming out here under the facade of a bird aficionado was such a stellar idea?

And then she heard it. The thing she was searching for.

Heady rushing.

The San Pablo Waterfall.

The local landmark signaled that she was on the right course. She parted two large palm fronds and spied the waterfall in the distance. Supposedly Armando Cutler's cabin was near San Pablo.

Macy raised the binoculars for a closer look at the waterfall. A flutter of wings, a flash of red. Was that the red-throated Costa Rican swallow?

What do you care? You're not here to bird-watch.

Still, she couldn't help tracking the swallow's flight as it soared and dipped around the waterfall, playing in the spray. And then she spied something that made her forget all about rare birds.

A man.

Underneath the waterfall.

Totally naked.

Spontaneously, Macy sucked in her breath and felt a thick lump of unexpected pure animal lust clog up her throat. She brought the binoculars to her eyes. Her gaze raked down his body, starting at the top of his dark head and sliding over the sharp angles and honed muscles of his exquisite frame.

As a reporter she was trained to notice details, and notice she did. His shoulders were as broad and straight as an ironing board, the control of his rigid posture belying his freewheeling nudity. An enigma. Immediately Macy was intrigued.

Who was this guy? Could it be Cutler?

She crouched, shifted her knapsack off her shoulders and searched inside for her camera. She found it, flipped off the cover, attached the zoom lens and peered through the viewfinder.

Her heart thundered, galloping faster as she studied the planes of his broad, sinewy back only slightly veiled by the curtain of falling water.

He was tall and ripped—nothing about him was soft. He was a rock, rooted in place, untouched by the blasting force of water.

The evidence of his physical strength and power caused a shiver to blister down her spine. He had his head dipped. Dark strands of sleek, midnight-black hair plastered against his neck.

Torn between desire and guilt over spying on the guy, Macy pulled her bottom lip up between her teeth and let out a long, slow sigh. Her blood boiled. Her stomach churned.

And when her gaze strayed to the curve of his bare butt, Macy lost all capacity to breathe. She'd never been one of those women who openly ogled good-looking guys, but by gosh, she was ogling now.

Who wouldn't? Who couldn't? With a physique like his on display, all wet and shiny?

Compelled and hungry to get a closer look, Macy tiptoed through the thicket of greenery, escalating excitement making her pulse skitter.

She trod a thin path along the soft ground. The gurgling water grew louder. She stepped into a clearing, spied a small wooden footbridge, drenched in spray, leading to the falls. As she tread cautiously, she let her camera fall around her neck and pulled out her binoculars.

He moved beneath the waterfall and she simply couldn't drag her gaze away.

Magnificent, exquisite, divine—there weren't enough superlatives in the English language to describe him.

Then, head still down, he turned and she caught a full-frontal view of the man in all his glory and she almost lost her footing.

What in hell was the matter with her?

Macy shook her head, trying desperately to scatter the spell he'd woven on her. She shouldn't be, couldn't be, feeling like this. It was unprofessional. She had work to do and she refused to be distracted by a compelling sideshow. Besides, she'd sworn off gorgeous men. They were far more trouble than they were worth.

"Once bitten, twice shy," she muttered, but still, she didn't glance away. She couldn't help noticing this man had been blessed in ways her ex-husband had not.

Then he raised his head and she saw his face clearly for the first time.

It was the man she'd been searching for.

ARMANDO CUTLER stood beneath the splashing waterfall trying desperately to wash away his sins.

But in spite of the breathtaking beauty of his Costa Rican hideaway, he couldn't cleanse the dirt from his soul. Over and over again, he mentally replayed the pivotal moment when everything in his life had changed.

And not for the better.

He'd been overly confident and blind to his own weaknesses. Arrogant, some might say. His intentions had been good, but the cost of his hubris ran high.

Wincing, Armando closed his eyes, braced his forearms against the rocky outcropping and ducked his head. The water sluiced over him with a power fueled by the recent summer rains.

It took all the strength in his muscular runner's thighs to hold him in place against the tumbling onslaught. Truth was, he wouldn't be all that distressed if the water shoved him headlong off the twenty-foot drop and into the turbulent green pool below.

Underneath his breath, he cursed himself, both for his spectacular failure and his inability to shake the guilt knocking around his brain.

You gotta stop feeling sorry for yourself.

He tossed his head, sending strands of wet hair—which three months ago had been clipped into an appropriate corporate style—slapping against his face.

A year ago he'd been on the cover of *D* magazine, lauded at twenty-nine as the heir apparent to the CEO position at Hollister Chemicals. Now he was lying low, licking his wounds in a tropical mountain cabin near his uncle's San Pablo banana plantation and struggling to get his life back on track.

And all because he'd gotten involved with the wrong woman.

Sucker.

Armando snorted, tilted back his head and let the water blast his face. He was glad his mother wasn't around to see her only child's downfall. It would have broken her heart.

At the thought of his late mother, Armando's gut pinched tight. It had been just six months since he'd lost her to cancer, and the wound was still achingly fresh. In fact, his deathbed promise to her was what prompted him to let down his guard with Jennifer Kemp. Under normal circumstances he wouldn't have jumped into a relationship so quickly.

I promise, Mom. I'll get married. Settle down, have children.

He'd been hurting and looking for someone to help him keep his promise. He'd been stupidly vulnerable when he'd met Jennifer at work. He'd never dreamed his sexy colleague was a corporate spy when he'd allowed her to seduce him that night in his corner office, which overlooked downtown Houston.

Jennifer had appeared in his doorway wearing a come-hither smile and a skimpy blue dress, the light shining through the filmy material, her long, blond hair curling down her shoulders, her magnificent cleavage on display. He'd fallen for the bait. A dumb catfish swallowing a shiny lure.

"Armando." She'd called his name in a sultry voice that shot darts of desire straight to his groin.

Stupidly, unforgivably, he'd gotten to his feet, neglecting to log out on his secure computer before crossing the room to pull Jennifer into his arms. Lust drove him. Ego blinded him. When she suggested they make love on the rooftop, he'd carried her up the stairs. Never once thinking about leaving his computer completely vulnerable, never guessing she had an accomplice waiting in the wings.

He'd been the world's biggest fool.

Forget it.

But he could not. He'd been trying to do just that for three months.

Armando clenched his jaw and let out a breath of pent-up frustration. He might not know what to do about his sunken career, but there was one important lesson he'd learned from this mess—*stay far away from beautiful, deceptive females.*

Regret burned his gut. Shame sat on his shoulders.

All at once, Armando felt a strange prickly sensation at the back of his neck and he froze.

Instinct had him cocking his head, listening. Toeing the rocky ledge, he stepped from beneath the falls. He peered out across the forest and saw a slight rustle of fronds beside the pool below.

He paused, frowning. Nothing more than the normal rain-forest sights and sounds surrounded him.

"Probably some animal," he muttered under his breath.

And yet he couldn't shake the feeling he was being watched.

CHAPTER TWO

MACY GULPED, lowered the binoculars and pulled back into the tropical thicket. Had he seen her?

You wanted to get close to him. That was the point. Yes, but now that she was here and had seen firsthand how incredibly gorgeous he was, she suddenly felt fifteen and tongue-tied. *Get over it. You have a job to do. Get out there and pretend to be taking pictures of that swallow.*

But he was naked. That definitely put a kink in things. She was just going to wait right here until he finished his nature shower and then—

She heard rustling in the bushes in front of her. It sounded like something big. A puma? A jaguar? A panther? Her pulse leapt into her throat. Did they even have pumas or jaguars or panthers in Costa Rica? Dammit, she should have done more research on the place before blithely jumping into the tropical forest alone. Macy stepped back, moving deeper into the lush foliage, feeling distinctly like prey.

More rustling as the furtive creature came closer and closer. Her blood pounded in her ears, boom, boom, boom, until she could hear nothing else. She couldn't see anything either except thick, wet, slick greenery. The plants in front of her trembled. Fear wrapped around her thick as the humidity.

If she screamed for Cutler would he hear her above the sound of the waterfall?

You're freaking yourself out. Calm down.

Good advice, but she was out of her element and totally unprepared for the dangers lurking in the rain forest. She took a deep breath, but it got stuck half way into her lungs as the plants around her vibrated with movement. Something big was most definitely coming straight toward her.

Get to Cutler. Who cares if he's naked?

She turned to run but her rubber-soled hiking boots sank in the damp soil and she stumbled. Instinctively her fingers curled around her camera. Snap the photo of her attacker before she died so when the search party found her body they'd know what was responsible for her demise.

The fronds parted.

Macy raised her camera, spied sleek black hair. *Panther,* was her first thought. *How did Cutler get down off that waterfall so fast?* was her second. Her mind barely had time to register that his tanned, long-limbed, muscular body was even more delicious up close and personal than it had been at a distance, before her finger clicked off the shot.

"Who the hell are you?" Cutler growled. "And why are you trespassing?"

ARMANDO SCOWLED DOWN at the slender brunette crouched among the vegetation, camera clutched in her hand—correction, make that a *dazzling* brunette looking at him with Bambi eyes and a feisty stare.

"Oh," she said in a smoky, torch-singer voice, "I wasn't aware this was private property."

"Well, it is," he growled.

"I apologize. I didn't mean to disturb your sanctuary."

He fixed on the camera and he took a step closer. He'd had his fill of cameras and nosy reporters. "Were you taking pictures of me?"

Her eyes widened. "You? Why would I be taking pictures of you?"

"Don't deny it. I know you snapped a shot of me as I came through the bushes. I heard the click. Now give me your camera." He held out his palm.

She stepped back, held her camera behind her. "What is your problem?"

"I'm going to delete that shot you took of me."

Her gaze flicked over him. Armando was suddenly aware that the only thing he had on was a pair of swim trunks he'd managed to pull on. He was also aware of just how adventuresome she looked in her Banana Republic attire of khaki cargo pants, hiking boots, green T-shirt and red bandanna.

"Okay, dude, I'll agree, you're hot and all, but seriously, you've got some ego. I took your picture because I thought you were a panther coming to eat me."

Armando glowered. "Panther?"

"Or puma or jaguar or whatever you guys call predatory cats down here."

"Why would you think I was a jaguar?"

"Hey, the palm fronds were moving and I knew

something big was coming my way and I thought, this is it, I'm gonna die, so I might as well take a picture of my killer." She shrugged. "I snapped you, instead."

"You sound disappointed."

She laughed. The sound was so compelling he wanted her to keep doing it.

"While it would have been sweet to get a picture of a jaguar, believe me, I'm quite relieved to live to take pictures another day."

He took another step toward her. She backed up again. He narrowed his gaze. "Are you a reporter?"

"A reporter? What on earth makes you ask that?"

Armando scrutinized her. She looked innocent enough—well, except for those full, sensuous lips, which didn't look the least bit innocent—but then, Jennifer had looked innocent, as well. "You have a camera."

"And reporters are the only people in the world who are allowed to have cameras? Why would you even assume that? Is there some breaking news story in the middle of the rain forest that I should know about?"

He ignored that last part. "If you're not a reporter, what are you doing out here?"

"I'm here," she said, "for the swallow."

He raised his eyebrows. "Swallow?"

She held up her camera. "The rare, red-throated Costa Rican swallow. I'm an avid bird-watcher."

Hmm, not what he expected from a woman who looked like she could double for a cover model, but he'd been surprised by women before. "Red-throated, huh?"

Her face lit up. "Have you seen one? Because I

thought I saw one. Which is how I got separated from my bird-watching group. I wanted to be the first one to get it on camera, so I struck out on my own and didn't tell the rest of the group where I was going."

"I didn't know bird-watching was so competitive."

"You have no idea."

"Well, San Pablo waterfall is the best place to look. And dusk is the best time."

"That's what I read on the Internet. It sounds as if you know a thing or two about bird-watching yourself." She gave him a dazzling smile.

"I know the falls." He cocked his head and studied her, suspicion still prodding the back of his brain. "You don't look like a bird-watcher."

"What? Bird-watchers can only be little old ladies or nerdy guys in safari hats? That's insulting."

"That's not what I meant."

"What did you mean?"

"You look like you'd be more comfortable on the arm of a dignitary at some kind of celebrity ball." Armando knew this because he'd been one of those dignitaries and she would have been exactly the kind of woman he'd have latched on his arm—smart, beautiful, confident. "Bird-watching seems too sedate a pastime for someone like you."

Her smile enchanted him. She was forgiving him for being rude. "It calms me. My grandfather used to take me bird-watching. He taught me bird calls, too."

"A woman of many talents." Armando kept his tone light, but there was something dangerous about the way she was making him feel. Her T-shirt, damp from the humid air, had molded itself around her full breasts. And the V-neck exposing just a hint of cleavage kicked his libido out of the cold freeze he'd shoved it into after that mess with Jennifer.

"So what are you doing here?" She canted her head, lowered her eyelashes in a seductive expression. "Looking all Tarzan?"

"I live here."

"In the jungle? So you really are Tarzan?"

His tongue stuck to the roof of his mouth. He wasn't about to tell her how he'd ended up here. Instead, he nodded. "Yeah, that's me. Tarzan."

"Well," she said, "I better see if I can find my bird-watching group. I'm sure they're wondering where I got to."

"Where are you staying?"

"The Coronado Bed and Breakfast in El Marro Lindo," she said.

"Do you know how to get back to the main path?"

"I don't," she admitted with a playful grin. "Would you mind showing me?"

Armando hesitated, struggling to resist the effect her smile was having on his body. Not to mention those emerald-green eyes. Captivating. The woman was lithe and toned. His groin tightened and he involuntarily licked his lips.

An image of Jennifer popped into his head. Letting his hormones rule had gotten him into this fix. He wasn't about to do it again. Leading this woman back to the main road wasn't smart. Best to just send her on her way and forget he'd ever met her.

"Got a pen and paper?" he asked. "I'll draw you a map."

"Oh, yeah, sure."

Was it his imagination or did she looked disappointed?

She dug around in her impossibly large knapsack and finally came up with a pencil and a small spiral notepad. "Okay."

"You do have a compass, right?"

She patted the left side pocket of her cargo pants. "Check."

He reached for the pencil and paper and their fingers brushed in the transfer. A hot flush blasted up Armando's neck and he found himself slowly blowing out his breath through pursed lips. *Hicarumba*, what was this feeling she stirred inside him?

Quickly he drew a map for her, complete with compass points. "Here's how you get back to the main path," he said.

She leaned close to get a better look at the map and he caught a whiff of her scent. She smelled like daisies. Fresh and sweet and all girl-next-door. Something else about her that was unexpected.

He cleared his throat and used the pencil to point out landmarks on the map he'd drawn. "Here's the way to the main path, but just in case you don't meet up with your group, I've added direction back to El Marro Lindo and the Coronado."

"That's so kind of you." Her appreciation appeared as twin dimples in her right cheek.

"You better get a move on. It's a four-mile hike back and when the sun sets in the jungle, it sets quickly," he advised. "Then you really will have to worry about jaguars."

"Thanks for the warning." She took his map and

stuck it into her back pocket, tucked the pencil behind her ear and shouldered her knapsack.

He couldn't stop himself from watching her push her way through the vegetation, admitting that it wasn't often a woman aroused him the way this one had. He noted with a sense of disquiet that she looked every bit as good walking away as she had from the front. Luckily, the forest swallowed up the sexy bird-watcher after just a few steps, and all that remained of her was the sound of her feet tromping through the brush.

"GOODNESS," AMELIA Pettigrew exclaimed when Macy accidentally caught up with the bird-watching group. Her plan had been to circle around, end up back at the waterfall and pretend she was hopeless at reading a map so she would have an excuse to interact with Cutler again. Instead, she'd run smack-dab into the bird-watchers. "Are you okay?"

"Fine." Macy forced a smile. "I'm fine."

"You don't look fine," Harry put in. "You look—"

"Flushed," Amelia interrupted. "You look all hot and flushed and flustered. Like you've been running." Amelia narrowed her eyes and scrutinized Macy's face. "On second thought, you look the way I felt when I first met Harry in the rec room at the Robson Ranch Retirement Center. Definitely hot and flushed and flustered."

Harry blushed.

"See?" Amelia crowed to Macy as she pointed at Harry's reddened cheeks. "That's how you look."

Macy raised a hand to her forehead. She did feel a

bit overheated. "It's the humidity," she explained. It had nothing at all to do with brushing up against Tarzan.

"People, people," Stratford Kingman said. "We don't have much daylight left. This is your last chance today for a glimpse of the red-throated Costa Rican swallow. I suggest you close your mouths and put your binoculars to your eyes. We're heading back to the B and B in twenty minutes."

Yay! Now all she had to do was slip away from the group again and scurry back to the waterfall to find Cutler.

"Come on," Amelia motioned her to follow them.

"Um…" No excuse popped into her head. "I'm not going to stay with the group."

Amelia looked alarmed. "It's getting dark. You can't stay out here alone. It's too dangerous. I'm going to have to tell Stratford."

"Please don't." Macy put out a hand to stop her.

"He's responsible for us."

"Just tell him I'm staying with a friend and not to worry about me," Macy said.

Amelia's eyes widened. "You met someone in the jungle? You modern young women are so daring."

"No more daring than you," Harry said, slipping his arm around her waist. "I remember what we did—"

"Shh." This time it was Amelia's turn to blush.

"It's not that daring," Macy confessed. "I came here to find him."

"Reconnecting with an ex-lover?" Harry guessed.

"Something along those lines," Macy hedged. "So you don't have to worry about me. Have fun with the swallows."

"You go on, dear," Amelia said, looking gleeful to be

serving as matchmaker. "We'll make sure Stratford doesn't get alarmed and come searching for you."

"Thanks so much." Macy smiled back at Amelia, and then slipped into the forest again.

CHAPTER THREE

It took Macy less time to find the falls again, but when she got there, Cutler was gone.

What? You expected him to spend the entire day taking a shower?

The shadows deepened and the sounds of forest creatures grew louder.

Okay, don't panic. His cabin has got to be around here somewhere.

In the daylight hours it was not a daunting prospect. But in the gathering twilight, visions of predatory animals danced in her head. She thought of Dorothy's chant from *The Wizard of Oz* and changed it a bit to suit her situation. *Pumas and jaguars and panthers, oh my.*

What direction should she go? She took her compass from her cargo pants to ascertain north. But what good did that do when she had no idea in what direction Cutler's cabin lay?

Dumb plan. Dumb, dumb, dumb. Pressing a palm to her forehead, she looked up.

And that's when she saw him.

Tarzan in all his half-naked glory, performing yoga on the cliff above and to the right of the waterfall, the remaining daylight bathing his body in a bronze glow. He was in the middle of the warrior pose, arms outstretched, body perfectly straight and still.

Macy's stomach fluttered the way it always did when she was about to unearth a great story.

He shifted his pose and in that moment he looked down and their gazes connected. His steady, black-eyed stare stole her breath and told her those butterflies in her stomach had very little to do with the unfolding story and everything to do with the enigmatic man himself.

Feigning air-headedness, she smiled, raised a hand and waved. "Yoo-hoo!"

He shook his head, and then gracefully jackknifed off the edge of the cliff into the mossy green pool below. He hit the water smooth as a missile. Small droplets spattered her skin.

Seconds later, he broke the surface, floating on his back and giving her a laconic smile. "You're back."

She shrugged. "I got lost."

"You can't read a map?"

"I get my directions mixed up."

"What about your compass?"

She had the compass still clutched in her palm. She put her hand behind her and dropped the compass on the ground. "Lost it."

He climbed out of the swimming hole, slinging water from his hair in the process with a provocative movement and then he slowly sauntered toward her. Her heart pounded, her mouth went dry. She tried not to stare at his chest, but damn, it was so honed and ripped and tanned she couldn't help herself.

"It's too late to send you back out into the forest alone."

"Yes," she agreed.

He stood peering at her with such a suspicious look in his eyes that for the longest moment she thought he'd figured out who she was and what she was doing there.

But finally he stuck out his hand. "Armando Cutler," he said.

"Macy…um…Mason," she said, using her ex-husband's last name so she wasn't telling a total lie. "It's a pleasure to meet you, Armando."

"I figured since I have little choice but to take you home for the night, we may as well know each other's names."

"Take me home?" She laughed nervously, even though this invitation was exactly what she'd been angling for when she'd concocted her scheme.

"It'll be completely dark out here in twenty minutes. The Coronado is over an hour's walk away and I'm not wearing my hiking shoes. The rain forest is not some-where you want to be unprepared at night."

"No," she whispered.

With that, Armando stepped over to a nearby rock, picked up the gray T-shirt she hadn't seen lying there and wrestled it over his head. He jammed his feet into a pair of thick-soled, black flip-flops and turned back to her. "Come with me."

For a split second, Macy hesitated. Why was she hesitating? This was exactly what she'd been aiming for. But something about Cutler was raising red flags all over the place. Why did he so readily offer to take her back to his place? Did he have seduction on his mind?

She thought of the dossier she'd built on him. He'd

been something of a ladies' man at one point in his life, but his mother's battle with cancer seemed to have changed him. Or maybe not. Maybe a woman was behind the secret scandal that had sent him into hiding in Costa Rica. Macy suspected as much.

Cutler held out his hand again, this time to help her over the rocks surrounding the pool. He looked her squarely in the eyes. Macy touched him and a blistering wildfire of sensation blazed up her forearm. To regain her composure, she lowered her lashes, averted her gaze from the sexy man beside her and focused her concentration on picking her way over the rocks.

She gulped, struggling to combat the way his nearness affected her. He smelled so good. Like rain forest and tropical fruit and masculine musk. Macy couldn't recall the last time a man had made her feel this way. Her ex-husband had never made her feel like this—so aware. So attuned. So aroused.

"Give me your knapsack," he said.

"Wh-what for?" she stammered, thinking about the press badge and passport she had tucked away inside.

"Because it looks heavy."

"Oh."

"You're not accustomed to men being chivalrous?"

She forced a laugh and handed him her knapsack. "I'm too independent."

"So, Macy-who's-not-used-to-chivalrous men," he said, shouldering her knapsack and escorting her through the thickening dusk, "since we're going to be spending the night together, I'm thinking maybe we should get better acquainted."

Ulp. Just what did he mean by spending the night together?

"What do you do when you're not bird-watching and getting lost?" he asked.

"Online business," she said, hoping that was vague enough. And it was true. *Gotcha* was an online magazine.

"What? Selling stuff on eBay?"

"Something like that. How about you? What do you do when you're not splashing around in waterfalls?" she asked, eager to shift the conversation away from her.

"I'm between careers right now."

"Oh?"

"Midlife crisis," he said.

"Aren't you a little young for that?"

He shrugged. "You're never too young to reevaluate your life."

"I guess that's true."

"Where you from?" he asked, leading her around the falls.

"Oklahoma. Ever been there?"

"Sure," he said. "I'm a Texan. Been up to Turner Falls many times when I was a kid. I'm originally from Austin. Went to the University of Texas. Go Longhorns."

"No, no, go Sooners," she said, referring to the fierce rivalry between the Universities of Texas and Oklahoma. "I'm an OU alumna. School of—" She almost said journalism, but quickly bit it off and finished with, "business."

He looked over at her and grinned. His teeth flashing white in the darkness. It was the first time she'd seen him genuinely smile.

"Did you move to Costa Rica?" she asked. "Or is this just a vacation?"

"I've taken a sabbatical. That early-midlife-crisis thing. I still have my condo in Houston, but I'm not sure I'm keeping it."

"No? I thought Houston was booming these days with all the drilling for natural gas," she said, tiptoeing around the subject. She had to be careful. It was a fine balance, eliciting information from him without giving herself away.

"It is. That's what makes it a perfect time to sell."

"You're not in the oil business?" She held her breath, hoping she wasn't pushing too far.

"Not anymore," Armando muttered, then said, "Up you go."

She raised her head, surprised to see a set of stone stairs leading upward. The foliage around the steps was so thick and the darkness so deep she couldn't see how far up they went.

"You go first," Armando said. "I'm right behind you."

She grabbed hold of the metal railing and started up, acutely aware of the man behind her. Low-hanging branches brushed her face, sending shivers down her spine. This place was damned spooky. She would hate to be out here by herself at night.

"This forest could do with a trim," she grumbled.

"It'd just grow back the next day."

"Seriously?"

"It is a rain forest. Sometimes when I'm lying in bed at night I swear I can hear it growing."

Macy had a sudden image of Armando in bed at

night, lying naked under crisp white sheets, the sultry summer breeze blowing in through his open window. She felt herself flush hot all over.

They climbed the rest of the way in silence and it seemed like an hour, but it was actually less than a minute by the time they reached the top.

And then she saw the cabin, set on a mossy bank of rocks and soil. It was made of stone and couldn't have been more than six hundred square feet total.

It had a wraparound porch, also made of stone. On the porch sat a rocking chair and two or three camp chairs. A whimsical windsock flew from the roof, and wind chimes tinkled gently in the surrounding jacaranda trees.

While she stood taking it all in, Armando walked around her, headed for the door. Once he reached the porch, he stopped, looked back. "You coming?"

SHE JUST NEEDED a place to crash for the night, Armando rationalized as he stood aside and let her cross the threshold into his stone bungalow. That's all this was. Jungle hospitality. He was just being kind to a ditzy bird-watcher who'd lost her way.

A lost, ditzy bird-watcher who also happened to be one of the sexiest brunettes he'd ever clamped eyes on. Showing off a pair of world-class legs that made even cargo pants look good. And smelling of hothouse flowers, rich volcanic Costa Rican soil and heady, feminine musk.

Briefly, he closed his eyes and bit down on his tongue to keep from groaning out loud.

"Armando?"

"Uh-huh?"

"Are you all right?"

"Never better." He lied smoothly.

"You look like you're in pain."

"Muscle cramp." He lifted his left leg and rubbed his calf.

"Please, let me." She crouched on the floor beside him and reached for him.

Armando lowered his leg. The minute her soft fingertips sank into his skin, he knew he was in over his head. She kneaded him like an expert masseuse, digging into his calf with accomplished motions. He hadn't realized how tense his muscles were until she started the clockwise technique.

This time he did groan.

He dropped her knapsack and it fell to the floor with a solid plop.

"Better?" she asked.

Hell no. The desire tugging at him was much worse now.

"Better," he croaked and reached his hand down to help her to her feet.

Alarm butted against the inside of his chest. What was going on here? How could he be so strongly and completely engrossed with this woman? The last time he'd been instantly attracted…well, it was *Jennifer*.

Why had he invited Macy to stay at his cabin? What had he been thinking?

You were thinking she could end up as jaguar prey if she spent the night alone in the forest. Never mind that she'd be utterly terrified.

He was too soft. This kind of misguided chivalry was how he ended up here in the first place. If he hadn't stopped to change Jennifer's tire in the employees' parking lot that very first time they met, he might never have noticed her, and he'd be on the fast track to becoming CEO of Hollister Chemicals. It would be *his* patent making the headlines, not Bond and Martin's. Of course, he realized now it had all been a setup.

All because you didn't know when to keep your pants zipped. Can't you be chivalrous without being stupid?

Then again, how much lower could he sink? He was out of a job, hiding out in Costa Rica licking his wounds. What else could she take away from him?

Privacy. Her very presence here had already stolen that.

"You hungry?" he asked, desperate to keep busy and not think about how dumb he'd been to bring her into his tropical hideaway.

"Starved." She placed a palm to her stomach.

"Grilled mahimahi?"

"Sounds excellent. How can I help?"

The cabin was one big room—bed in the middle, stove in the far corner. No living room. No couch. No television. Just a few camp chairs, a bookcase, the kitchen table and a battered old refrigerator. When he'd walked into the place he'd seen the sparseness as a godsend. Now, looking at it through her eyes, he was aware of how bare the place was. Definitely not built with the fairer sex in mind.

"Grill's outback," he said, grabbing a bottle of chardonnay off the kitchen counter and two glasses from the cabinet. He handed them to her, along with plates and cutlery. "You take these and I'll grab the fish."

She waited while he took the fish from the fridge. He'd caught the mahimahi the previous evening when he'd gone fishing with his uncle.

Armando led her out the back entrance to a stone

patio covered by a rattan awning. High on the bluff, the backyard overlooked his uncle's banana plantation in the valley below. But in the darkness, all that could be seen of the plantation were a few lights dotting the landscape.

"It smells so good out here." She took a deep breath. "Like hothouse flowers."

"That's jasmine," he said, naming the flowers that grew in abundance along the side of the cabin.

Armando set the fish on the sideboard and fired up the propane grill. Once it was going, he stepped back to light the tiki torches lining the patio. The flames flickered in the breeze.

The evening air smelled heavy. Armando's nose twitched. More rain was on the way. Hopefully, not before he got his bird-watching tourist out of here the next morning.

He finished with the tiki torches and turned back to see Macy seated on the patio, a glass of wine in her hand, another one sitting on the table waiting for him.

He sat down across from her. She tilted her head back, stared up at the sky. "Look at all those stars. You don't see stars like that back in the States."

"You don't," he agreed.

The pale, rising moon gave him hope that the heavy rains were still a day or more away.

Macy's face glimmered in the moonlight and he found himself sliding frequent glances in her direction. He studied the shape of her narrow nose, the bow of her mouth, the high cheekbones.

The wine tasted sweetly tart on his tongue. The smell of grilling fish mingling with the scent of jasmine teased his nose. The sound of the waterfall was carried even up here, a soft, soothing rushing in the darkness. He never realized how romantic this place was. It had a guy thinking thoughts he shouldn't be thinking about an errant tourist.

"What shall we have to go with the fish?" Macy took a sip of wine and eyed him over the rim of her glass.

"Grilled fruit?" He nodded at the bowl of fruit on the picnic table between them—bananas, pineapple, mangos, passion fruit.

"Mmm, sounds delicious."

The way she said "mmm" strummed a response inside him like vibrating guitar strings. He took a small knife from the pocket of his swim trunks and went to work carving up the fruit.

While he tended to the food, Macy got up and strolled around the patio. In the light from the tiki torches, he noticed she'd taken off her hiking boots and socks and that her toenails were painted a glistening shade of pearly pink.

She tilted her head back, eyes on the sky, wineglass clutched in her hand, and slowly spun around. "Isn't this just the most perfect thing on earth?"

Bedazzled, Armando stared. The breeze tousled her hair, mussing it about her shoulders. Her T-shirt hugged her breasts so closely he could make out the hard pebbles of her nipples showing through her thin bra. The little ties at the hem of her cargo pants dangled provocatively against her knees, moving with her, swaying against her smooth, taut skin.

"Yeah," he murmured, trying to ignore the lump in his throat. "Perfect."

"A toast," she said, raising her glass and sauntering closer.

"To…?"

"The perfect tropical hideaway." She clinked the rim of her glass against his.

"The perfect tropical hideaway," he echoed, and took a big swallow of wine, praying the alcohol would soothe his frayed nerves.

She set down her glass and picked up the plates. "Dish up the grub." She smiled and extended a plate. "The food smells ready."

"It smells ready?"

"That's how I cook," she said. "With my nose."

She seemed so earnest he laughed. "Okay."

He flipped the food from the grill and onto the waiting plates. He turned off the propane and sat down at the table. She plunked down next to him—not across from him as he would have preferred. This way she was far too close.

"Omigosh, this is sooo good." She made a soft little moaning sound of pleasure.

Armando picked up his fork, forcing himself to focus on the delicious tidbits on his plate, instead of the delicious tidbit beside him.

She was right. The night was perfect. The taste of the tropical feast, the restful sound of the waterfall, the shimmering moonlight, the air rich with the smell of flowers, volcanic soil and intoxicating woman. Being with her like this made him forget that the rest of the world existed, which was exactly what he'd been aiming for when he'd come to Costa Rica.

The redemption of forgetfulness.

"Penny," she said.

"What?" He blinked at her.

She had her head angled toward him, a pensive expression on her face, the tines of her fork resting against the tip of her little pink tongue. "Penny for your thoughts. You looked a thousand miles away."

He shook his head. "Nothing. Never mind."

"Anything you want to discuss?"

He shrugged.

"Sometimes it's easier to talk to a stranger than someone you know. I'm a good listener."

He laughed because he didn't know what else to do. "I don't have any deep, dark secrets."

"No?"

"You don't believe me?"

"Everyone has secrets." Macy picked up a grilled pineapple ring with her fingers and took a bite.

"Do you?"

"I do."

He leaned in closer, mesmerized by the impish twinkle in her eyes. "You can whisper it into my ear. No one else ever need know."

She giggled and the sound had a dizzying effect on him. Or maybe it was the wine. He'd drained his glass.

"If I told you, it wouldn't be a secret, would it."

That comment spiked his curiosity. The woman intrigued him, no doubt about it. She sure didn't seem like a bird-watcher. Maybe *that* was her secret. She wasn't really here to watch birds.

"You tell me one of your secrets and I'll tell you one of mine," he said as an enticement.

She pursed her lips as if she was considering his proposition.

"Well?" he said. Why was he pushing this? Did he really have a secret desire to unburden himself to a stranger?

"I have a tattoo," she said.

"What's secret about that?"

Her grin grew sly. "The location of the tattoo."

"Hmm, now you've piqued my interest. What's the tattoo of?"

"That's another part of the secret."

"How do I find out more?" He inched closer and she didn't move away. His heart pounded. Her little game was driving him crazy and she knew it.

"You gotta give to get," she teased.

He liked her more with every passing moment. When was the last time he'd experienced such an instant rapport with anyone? Sure, he'd been sexually attracted to Jennifer from the moment he'd met her, and while that had been hot, there hadn't been this…this…what *was* this?

The chemistry was undeniable, but it went beyond that. Armando felt as if an invisible string connected them. It was a bizarre sensation, and while he didn't want to feel it, he didn't want it to go away, either.

"Your turn," she murmured.

"Huh?"

"You owe me a secret."

"You only gave me a hint of a secret. So I only owe you a hint."

"Fair enough," she said. "What's your hint of a secret?"

"I'm hiding from something. That's why I'm here," Armando said, amazed at how easily the admission fell out of him.

"Ooh." She didn't seem the least bit intimidated by his confession, but rather intrigued. "Are you an outlaw on the run from justice?"

"Nothing that colorful."

She leaned in, touching her shoulder against his. "What are you hiding from?"

"You tell me where your tattoo is located and I might be persuaded to share that information."

"Guess." Her smile was wicked.

He arched an eyebrow. "Your breast?"

She shook her head.

Heat arrowed straight through him. Armando gulped. "Your belly?"

Again, she shook her head.

Okay, he wasn't going to guess again. He wasn't going to say what was popping into his head. It was too...*dangerous*.

She pressed her lips to his ear and whispered huskily, "Lower."

"You like to tease."

"A little," she admitted with a flutter of her eyelids, but something in her gaze told him it was all bravado. She liked to act brazenly, but underneath it ran a streak of shyness.

The paradox of her captivated him. His body was so hard he could barely draw in air. His every primal instinct was telling him to kiss her, but he knew it was wrong. Somehow he managed to hold on to his control.

"Some secrets," he murmured, "are better kept buried."

CHAPTER FOUR

MACY LET OUT a pent-up breath. For a split second there she thought he was going to kiss her, and she had a sneaking suspicion that being kissed by Armando Cutler would be like getting shaken by an earthquake. Involuntarily Macy reached up to finger her lips, as if she could feel the impact.

Great, now he was backing out of the game, just when she was getting somewhere with her investigation. "Don't you want to know what and where my tattoo is?"

He got up from the table, began collecting cutlery and plates. "Not tonight."

"If not tonight, then when?"

"Some fantasies are better left to the imagination," he said.

"You're pretty philosophical."

"Recently I've had a lot of time to think, and I've decided prudence is underrated and acting on instinct is overrated."

"Now we're back to secrets again," she said lightly, but her stomach was crammed with nervous, fluttering butterflies.

"You're probably tired and will want to make an

early start of it back to the Coronado tomorrow. The cabin doesn't have a shower, but you can take a bath if you want before you hit the sack." He was talking like an auctioneer, fast and sharp.

Had she tipped her hand somehow? Given herself away?

Her head spun from the romantic atmosphere, the wine and, most of all, him.

He wasn't looking at her, just standing there with the dirty dishes in his hand. "Could you open the back door?"

"Yeah sure." Macy knew she wasn't going to get anything more from him tonight. But there was still tomorrow. Perhaps he'd leave her alone in the cabin and she'd have time to do a little snooping.

She got up from the picnic table and sauntered toward the screen door. She opened it and stood aside as Armando brushed past. His hip accidentally grazed hers.

Simultaneously they sucked in audible breaths and then both tried to act like it had never happened, Armando heading for the sink, Macy skittering across the room to where her knapsack lay. She picked it up, fished around inside and came up with a change of clothes—a white, baby-doll muscle shirt with an OU logo on it and a pair of gray flannel short shorts.

"I think I'll take you up on that offer of a bath," she said. "Spending the day searching for the red-throated swallow has left me feeling a bit grimy."

He nodded.

She paused a moment outside the bathroom door as

it occurred to her that there was only one bed in the cabin. There was two of them and no couch in sight. "Um, what are the sleeping arrangements?"

He grinned and wet his lips.

Their gazes locked.

The air vibrated between them. She wanted the story. Wanted it badly. But not like this. Cutler made her feel too out of control.

"Hammock," he said.

"What?"

"You take the bed. I'll take the hammock in the backyard."

"Oh." She hadn't seen a hammock in the backyard, but then again, she hadn't been looking for one. "Listen, I could take the hammock. I don't want to throw you out of your own bed."

"You're the guest," he said. "Besides, how would that look? Making you sleep in a hammock?"

"Gallant of you," she said, "but honestly, I've slept in worse places than a hammock. I don't mind."

"I do. You take the bed. End of discussion."

All rightee then. "Fine," she said, hand on the doorknob, clothes tucked under her arm. "I'll take the bed. So good night."

"Good night," Armando echoed. "I hope you get that photo."

"Photo?" For a moment she didn't know what he was talking about.

"The red-throated swallow."

Oh, yes, the bird had flown right out of her mind. "I'm sure I will," she said, her pulse quickening and her stomach tightening. Great, now she was feeling guilty about lying to him.

Drop the guilt. You're only doing what you have to do to land your dream job.

So why did she feel like such a Benedict Arnold?

Macy locked the bathroom door behind her. Sitting on the side of the tub, she adjusted the faucets to the right temperature and let the water flow. What had happened to her tonight? Why was she having so many conflicting feelings? What was this unexpected chemistry between herself and Cutler? And most important of all, why was she letting it get to her?

When the tub was filled, she stripped off her clothes and sank into the warm, inviting water. A bar of sandalwood soap rested in the soap dish on the side of the old claw-foot tub. She picked it up, held it to her nose. It smelled of him. Clean and masculine. Tarzan in all his treetop glory.

She laid her head back against the cool porcelain. Closing her eyes, she luxuriated in the moment.

Suddenly a deliciously erotic fantasy overtook her.

Against the back of her eyelids, she saw Armando, the dark-eyed stranger she'd come here to betray. *"Macy,"* she imagined him whispering her name in his sultry, velvet-smooth voice. It sent shivers down her spine.

Her heart slammed against her rib cage at the thought of Armando stepping cockily into the bathtub with her. Her nipples hardened and her breasts swelled. Heat pooled deep inside her.

She envisioned Armando's hands, broad and flat and gentle, caressing her skin, skimming down her throat, cupping her naked breasts, moving lower, circling her naval, teasing her mercilessly.

Just thinking about him made Macy feel achy and wet and hot. She slid her fingertips over her tender skin.

In her mind's eye, his hand dipped between her legs, caressing, rubbing her swollen sex. He drew small circles against her inner thigh with his thumb.

She pictured him in the bath with her—his caress, his hand kneading the delicate bud, dangling her on the edge of pleasure. She envisioned his mouth covering hers, his tongue tasting, exploring. Her heart raced and her mind spun out of control.

In her daydream he looked at her with ravenous eyes as he stood naked over her in the tub. His manhood pushing against her wet flesh, taking her, claiming her.

Stop it! What are you doing?

She shook her head, dispelling the fantasy. The bathroom was steamy hot, but inside she was hotter. She wanted him. More than she'd ever wanted anyone. The sizzling sexual desire shook her to her core. Just what on earth had she gotten herself into?

WHILE MACY TOOK a bath, Armando paced the patio. The moon had disappeared behind a bank of clouds and the darkness was so deep he felt as if he'd been absorbed by it. His throbbing, achy body melted into the humid night. He thought of Macy, naked in his bathtub, and he groaned out loud.

The truth was, she'd gotten to him, slipped under his radar. That realization scared him.

And it took every ounce of strength he possessed not

to march into that bathroom, scoop her out of his tub and make love to her all night long.

Armando fisted his hands. He couldn't, he wouldn't act on impulse. But his erection was so hard he could barely draw in air. Dammit, he wanted her.

She'd done this to him. Made him desire her in a way he'd never desired another. Torture. Wanting her was pure torture.

He tried to think of Jennifer to remember how lust had gotten him into trouble before. But this felt like so much more than just lust. This felt like…*destiny*.

Idiotic, that thought. He didn't even know her.

And yet, he couldn't stop thinking about her. He imagined her touch. The vision caused every nerve ending in his body to jolt with electrical awareness as he imagined the feel of her soft lips, the sweet taste of her tongue. He visualized her long, silken curls tickling his bare skin. He saw her full, pink mouth tip up in a beguiling grin.

He closed his eyes and took in a deep breath. *Stop thinking about her.*

Resolutely, he shoved all thoughts of her from his head and collapsed into the hammock. The wind had picked up, rocking the rope swing. He could hear the rushing waterfall, taste the black, mysterious night. He inhaled it—the night—smelling thickly of overripe fruit and impending rain.

The jungle hideaway had given him solace when he needed it. Escape. It brought him back to his family's roots, reminded him of his departed mother. It felt familiar and real. More real than his condo back in Houston. More real than the career he'd ruined. But he'd come here to get his life back on track, to figure out his next move. Instead, fate had delivered him an unexpected complication—a sexy brunette who'd shown up out of nowhere to mess up his best-laid plans.

And that's when the heavens opened up and the monsoon began.

THE SOUND OF THUNDER pulled Macy from a light sleep. She opened her eyes in the darkness, blinked, momentarily disoriented.

Where was she?

Lightning flashed, bathing the little stone cabin in the rain forest with one vivid stab of hot, white illumination. In that moment she saw him standing in the doorway—tall, imposing, soaked to the skin, his wet hair plastered against his face.

The thrill of fear shot its way through her blood, infecting her with blinding, driving, primal need. Her fingers curled around the crisp white sheet as blackness descended as quickly as the light had come.

More rumbling shook the cabin.

Nervously she drew her knees to her chest. She was in an isolated mountain getaway with a total stranger. Yes, she knew a bit about him from her research. By all accounts, he'd been an honorable, upstanding, intelligent man. But Macy knew from firsthand experience you could love someone and never really know what was in their hearts.

"Armando," she whispered.

"Don't be frightened, *querida*."

Querida.

A Spanish word for sweetheart. Her stomach jumped. "What's happening?"

"The rains have hit."

"And you got soaked out of the hammock."

"Yes."

The air was thick with the sound of their breathing. Every muscle in her body tensed. Lightning flashed again. Armando had moved from the doorway to the middle of the room.

"There's nowhere else for you to sleep," she murmured.

"I'll get blankets from the cupboard," he said, "build a pallet on the floor."

"The floor is made of stone."

"It will do."

"I've slept on stone," she said, recalling a story she'd covered in a wartorn country in the Middle East and the night she'd spent in a bombed-out government building. "It's not comfortable."

"A woman like you?" He sounded skeptical. "You should only sleep on the plushest of mattresses."

"Right back at you." She threw aside the sheet. "Get in."

"You're inviting me to share your bed?"

"Hey, it's your bed. Turnabout is fair play. But don't get any funny ideas. This is all about comfort and warmth. No hanky-panky."

"I can promise I won't touch," he said. "But I can't promise I won't think about touching."

Macy inhaled audibly. "Honesty is an honorable quality."

She felt his big body sink onto the mattress and felt her own body immediately heat up. Her muscles tensed. Her mouth grew dry. She lay on her back staring up at the ceiling, completely aware of the man beside her—his scent, his warm dampness, the sound of his ragged breathing.

What had she gotten herself into? Armando might be able to keep *his* hands to himself, but the question was, could she?

CHAPTER FIVE

UNABLE TO SLEEP, Armando arose at dawn, even though the torrential rains drowned out the sun. Lying that close to Macy all night, aching to touch her but knowing it was not a smart thing to do had been pure torture.

But once he was up, he had nowhere to go and nothing to do. He sat in a camp chair for a while watching her sleep, trying to sort out the feelings rushing through him.

Looking at her, he was walloped by an impact that possessed all the power and sizzle of a lightning strike. All common sense, all rational thought leaked from Armando's brain and puddled at his feet.

Macy lay curled on her side, her fan of hair dark against the white pillow case. Everything about her intrigued him. She was a paradox, at once feminine and beautiful, but at the same time tomboyish and adventuresome. She was the embodiment of the girl next door but with an unexpectedly elegant twist.

Armando shook his head. What the hell was happening to him? He'd never felt like this. But this feeling…it seemed so *right*. Yet at the same time, he was afraid to trust his own judgment.

He'd been in Costa Rica for three months trying to put his life back together, and just when he thought he was ready to face the world again, along came Macy, pulling the rug out from under him.

This is crazy. You don't even know her.

He'd told himself that very thing a hundred times during his sleepless night, but no matter how he tried, he could not shake the bizarre sensation that they shared an unbreakable bond. It was foolish, but there it was.

He prowled the cabin, pacing to the back window to stare glumly out at the driving rain. He needed to get out of here, away from her so he could think without sexual desire gumming up his brain. But a steady stream of high-intensity water sluiced from the sky. Neither one of them was going anywhere today.

"Armando."

He turned to see Macy standing halfway between him and the bed wearing nothing but a white, oversize University of Oklahoma T-shirt and a pair of gray flannel shorts that showed off a mile of long, lean, tanned legs. Her hair was mussed, her cheek sheet-creased and *that smile*.

Her smile smacked him like a sucker punch to the gut.

"Good morning," she greeted him with a yawn and stretched her arms over her head.

He couldn't help noticing how her shirt rode up with the gesture revealing just the slightest flash of bare skin on her belly. "Good morning."

"I'm starving. What's for breakfast?" She padded across the stone floor in her sock feet headed for the refrigerator. She looked completely at ease and he admired her self-confidence.

He was headed down a treacherous path and he knew it, but what was he going to do? They were trapped here. Together. Alone.

She cocked her head and studied him. "Is everything all right? Did you sleep well?"

"Yeah," he lied.

"Me, too." She turned back to the refrigerator. "You've got eggs and cheese. How about an omelet?"

"Sounds good."

"How long do you think it's going to rain?" she asked, cradling the carton of eggs in the crook of one elbow, balancing a stick of butter on top of it and grabbing a hunk of cheddar with her other hand. She used her hip to bump the refrigerator door closed. "Got an omelet pan?"

"We're not that sophisticated in the jungle. Why don't you let me do that?" he offered. "I make a mean omelet, if I do say so myself, and you're my guest."

"I thought you'd never ask." She grinned. "I'm not much of a cook and I never really got the wrist action down for omelets. I usually just end up with scrambled eggs."

He took a skillet from beneath the cabinet, set it on the stove and fired up the burner.

"Here," she said, "I'll crack the eggs. Breaking things I'm good at."

"Oh, yeah?" Armando sliced two pats of butter into the skillet. "What have you broken?"

"My marriage, for one thing."

"You're divorced?"

"Happily. For two years now."

"What happened?" he asked, acutely aware of her standing at his elbow, cracking eggs and sliding them into a bowl while he moved the pan, guiding the butter around the side of the skillet as it melted. "Or is that too nosy?"

"My ex decided he preferred blondes."

"He cheated on you."

"Uh-huh." She seemed very okay with it, breaking the last egg and tossing the shells into the trash can. He admired her laid-back attitude. He wished he could be as philosophical about life.

"So how is it your fault that the marriage broke up?" he asked.

"I didn't believe in hair dye." She laughed at her own joke. "No, seriously, it was my fault because I couldn't see what was right under my own nose. Doug was always a charmer, but feckless. I thought he'd change. He didn't." She shrugged.

"Do you miss being married?"

"Not to Doug," she said enthusiastically, and leaned her back against the counter. "But sometimes I wonder what it would be like to have a husband who's a real partner, not just a glorified roommate, and a family of my own. How about you? Ever been married?"

He shook his head, whisked the eggs with a fork.

"Why not?" she asked. "Handsome man like you."

"Too ambitious, I suppose. Never had the time for a long-term relationship."

Macy looked around the room. "This is the pinnacle of your ambition?"

He snorted. "It's a long story. Could you slice some of that cheese for me?"

"Sure." She picked up the knife and started slicing, dropping the thin strips of cheddar into the eggs.

He was hyperaware of her. How well they worked together, cooking side by side. "My mother was ill for a long time," he said, not knowing why he was telling her this. "I was an only child and between her and my work, I guess I just didn't make time for relationships. She died six months ago," he said.

"Oh, Armando, I'm so sorry. I—"

"It's okay. It still hurts and I miss her a lot, but she's out of pain and that's the important thing."

Macy touched his shoulder and gave him a squeeze of sympathy so sincere he had to swallow hard to hold back his emotions. She said nothing else, but her hand slipped to his waist and she held it there, standing beside him while he flipped the omelet in the pan.

"How about you?" he asked. "Are your parents living?"

"Yes, I'm blessed," she said. "Both my parents are healthy and still working. Mom's a high-school algebra teacher, Dad works for the post office. They've been married thirty-nine years and are still madly in love. They hold hands like teenagers. Mom says Dad is her greatest passion and Dad says she is his one grand love. They're adorable."

"It sounds nice."

"What about your dad?" Macy asked. "Is he still around?"

"He took off when I was five. I don't really have much contact with him."

"That's such a shame."

"Any brothers or sisters?" he asked, shifting the topic of conversation away from himself again.

"Two sisters, three brothers."

"Wow, big family."

Macy nodded. "Both my parents were only children and they wanted lots of kids."

"What's your birth placement?"

"Third oldest."

"You must have gotten lost in the shuffle."

Macy started to say that her place in a large brood had a lot to do with her adventuresome nature and her passionate drive for success as an investigative journalist. She'd always felt a need to prove herself, to compete with her older siblings for attention. But then she remembered that Armando was a subject, that she was investigating him and that she'd lied to him about who she really was.

How could she have forgotten about that? How had she lost sight of her goal?

She slid a surreptitious glance his way. He finished the first omelet, flipped it onto a plate and started in on the second one.

When he finished, they took their plates to the table. Outside, water tumbled over the eaves of the cabin, obscuring the view from the window. All Macy could see was a heavy blur of green beyond the rain. They were wrapped in a verdant cocoon, warm and safe from the raging summer storm.

But that meant there was nothing to look at except the handsome man sitting across from her. She noticed the way his ebony hair curled around his ear, how the muscles in his forearms moved, how thick and sturdy his wrists were. Her gaze slid over the expanse of his broad shoulders underneath his orange University of Texas T-shirt. Sooners and Longhorns. Natural rivals.

A sense of foreboding came over Macy. She liked

Armando too much, and she was getting too emotionally invested in him. Highly unprofessional.

That's when she realized that no matter how she played this thing, it wasn't going to end well between them.

AFTER BREAKFAST Armando filled the sink with water to wash dishes, while Macy picked up a cup towel, preparing to dry. He squeezed too much soap into the running water and tiny soap bubbles immediately rose into the air.

Macy giggled as a cloud of froth floated around her head.

"Hang on, you've got bubbles in your hair," Armando said, and reached up to gently brush his fingers through her bangs.

Their gazes met and Macy couldn't look away from his soulful brown eyes. Immediately her muscles tightened and her mouth went dry. She put out the tip of her tongue to moisten her lips.

He seemed as mesmerized as she, his hand still at her forehead, his attention trained on her.

She ducked her head. "My hair's a mess. Tropical rain forests and wavy hair do not go together. Normally, I iron my hair straight but…" She knew she was babbling but she couldn't seem to stop herself.

"I love curly hair."

"Got a Shirley Temple complex, do you?" she teased. Humor was her default defense mechanism when she was feeling totally out of her element.

"I have a Macy Mason complex."

She gulped. Hearing him call her by her ex-husband's last name had her stomach balling up tight. "Um, Armando…," she began, but got no further.

He slid his fingers up her neck, cupped the back of her head in his palm and pulled her closer. He was going to kiss her and she wasn't going to do a thing to stop him.

His lips closed over her mouth.

Macy moaned softly and wrapped her arms around his neck. They were chest to chest, pelvis to pelvis, the firm thrust of his erection leaving no doubt in her mind about how much he wanted her.

Armando pulled his mouth from her lips and kissed her chin. She tossed her head back, letting him explore, relishing the feel of his tongue gliding down the length of her throat. His hands were just as busy, one traveling down to cup her buttocks, the other slipping underneath the hem of her T-shirt, his knuckles grazing her bare belly.

She could have stopped him. She should have stopped him. But she didn't want to. Aching need swamped her body with delicious heat. When his hand reached her breasts, she breathed in a heartfelt sigh of desire.

Macy touched him, stroking him through his jeans. He exhaled a groan. The rough, masculine sound escalated her hunger. Her nipples beaded up hard against her bra.

But what was her excuse? She was a willing partner.

Both his hands were cupping her breasts now, his thumbs kneading her tender nipples through the material of her bra, shooting sparks of sensation through her nerve endings.

This was too much, too soon. She was responding

so eagerly simply because she hadn't been with a man since her divorce. This was unprofessional behavior. Never mind that she was deceiving him.

Macy put a hand to his chest and stepped back.

He lifted his head, met her eyes. "I…I'm…," he stammered. "That was out of line. I shouldn't have… you don't deserve to be pawed like that. I have no excuse except you're just so damned irresistible."

"It's okay," she said, her voice husky, even though it was anything but okay. Her hands were trembling, but she tried her best to hide it from him.

"No, no, it's my fault. I crossed the line. I should have more self-control."

"It's the rain," she said. "And the forced proximity."

"And the chemistry."

"There is that." She smiled.

"Pretty amazing chemistry."

Yes, and she'd intended to take advantage of that chemistry to get an interview from him. Suddenly she felt lower than a sea slug.

"I don't want to…we don't even know each other," she said.

"I understand. You're a woman of integrity."

"I like to take relationships slow. Since my divorce… I haven't…I'm just not ready."

"I understand completely. Sex complicates things."

"Yes."

He raised his palms. "From now on, it's strictly hands-off."

"Yes," she murmured, but at the same time she felt utterly disappointed.

What she hadn't counted on was being unable to

control this wildfire attraction that made her forget why she was there. When she looked into those compelling brown eyes, she forgot her own name.

"I'm going to go put on some more clothes," she said.

"Good idea," he croaked. "I'll finish up these dishes."

YOU'RE LOSING IT, Cutler.

Armando scrubbed the dishes with far more vigor than was required. The bathroom door closed and he couldn't stop himself from picturing Macy in there changing clothes. He imagined her naked body, and a shiver of desire passed through his body. He could still taste her on his tongue. He could still smell her scent in his nostrils. He could still feel the imprint of her firm, feminine body pressed against him.

What a woman!

Hell, he was in serious trouble.

Gloomily he stared out at the torrential rain, watching the onslaught of water gouge rivulets into the bank of earth outside the cabin.

Armando had dated a lot of women in his life. Beautiful women, intelligent women, accomplished women and, yet, none of them had ever stirred him in quite the same way Macy had. There was something different about her. She seemed to embody all the qualities he'd ever wanted in a mate—attractive, smart, witty, adventuresome.

Honestly, he never acted this impulsively. Not even when he'd allowed Jennifer to seduce him. They'd already been seeing each other for a few weeks when she showed up at his office with espionage on her mind. But this thing with Macy was so powerful it caused him to act in a completely inappropriate manner, and he had no idea what to do about it. He couldn't get away from her. The rain had seen to that.

He couldn't run, he couldn't hide. So he'd have to face the attraction and fight his way through it. All he needed was a distraction, something to keep their minds off the strong sexual pull.

Resolutely, he tugged the drain stopper from the sink to let the dishwater out, then he turned and went for the closet.

CHAPTER SIX

"BACKGAMMON, CHESS, cards or Monopoly?"

"Huh?" Macy emerged from the bathroom, dressed in blue jeans, a red sleeveless shirt and hiking boots. She was doing everything she could to combat the urge to tumble into bed with Armando. The more clothing she had to take off, the better.

"Backgammon, chess, cards or Monopoly?" Armando stood in front of a closet filled with camping supplies and board games.

"You want to play a game?" she asked.

He gestured at the window. She turned to look at the rain. It was as if someone had turned on a water spigot. "No television. No leaving the cabin in this rain. Backgammon, chess, cards or Monopoly?"

"Cards," she said.

"Cards, it is." He plucked up a deck of cards from the shelf and closed the closet door. "What game?"

"Poker."

"You're not messing around."

"What did you take me for?" She grinned. "The kind of girl who plays Old Maid?"

"You?" He shook his head. "Never."

"What will we play for?" She rubbed her palms together.

They looked at each other and she saw in his eyes the same thing she was thinking. *Let's play strip poker.* But that's not what he said.

What he said was, "Cookies."

"Cookies?"

"Oreos." He went to the kitchen cabinet, pulled out a package of cookies.

"Oreos, it is," she said with equal parts disappointment and relief that he hadn't said clothing. What in hell was wrong with her? Did she *want* to wreck her life?

They sat down at the table. Armando divided the cookies into two equal piles, while Macy shuffled the cards. "Five card stud," she said. "Nothing wild."

"You deal those cards like you know what you're doing."

"Six kids in the family. We played a lot of games. I won my share of allowance money off my siblings."

"Now she tells me," Armando muttered.

"Kiss your Oreos goodbye."

"Good at the bluff, are you?"

"You have no idea." Macy grinned and dealt the cards. "One cookie ante."

"How long have you been interested in bird-watching?" he asked as he glanced at his cards and then discarded four.

She looked at her hand. Pair of twos. She doled out four new cards for Armando, took three for herself.

"It's a relatively new hobby," she said, not wanting to tell him any more fibs than she had to in order to achieve her objective.

"Why the fascination with the red-throated Costa Rican swallow?" he asked.

An uneasy sensation prickled her skin. Macy shrugged. Was he getting suspicious of her? But how? She thought of her press badge in the knapsack and her stomach churned. Had Armando been snooping in her things?

"It's not a fascination," she said. "I've just always wanted to visit Costa Rica and my bird-watching book said it was a great place to come if you wanted to locate several species of rare tropical birds."

"So you really don't know much about the red-throated swallow?" he asked.

"Not much," she said, squinting at her poker hand. It consisted of the pair of twos, an ace, a five and a seven. "I raise you a cookie."

"I see your raise and I raise you two Oreos."

She peeked at him. His face was impassive, his cards held against his chest. Was he bluffing? She added two more cookies to the middle of the table. "Have you ever seen a red-throated swallow?"

"I have. They're indigenous to the San Pablo water-fall."

"I know. That's why I'm here." She added two more cookies to the middle of the table. "Call."

They lay their cards down faceup. Armando had nothing.

"Bluffer," she grinned, and pulled the pile of cookies to her side of the table.

Armando picked up the cards, shuffled the deck for his turn to deal.

"Do you think you could guide me to find the

swallows?" she asked, trying to keep up her cover story. "You know, when the rain stops."

"Sure," he said. "Do you know why the red-throated swallows are so rare?"

She shook her head.

"The red-throated swallows are monogamous. They mate for life," he said. "But they're plagued by the bigger, promiscuous black-chested swallows that steal the red-throated swallow's nests and throw out their eggs before they can hatch."

"I don't like the sound of those black-chested swallows."

"Unpleasant creatures," he agreed.

They played out the hand. Macy won again. She shuffled, dealt for the third hand.

Armando stared at his cards and scowled.

"How many cards do you want?" she asked.

He tossed his cards on the table. "I fold."

"Don't give up so easily," she said.

"These cards were worthless."

"You never know what you could make with a fresh start."

"If you start singing a song about ants and a rubber tree plant, I'm leaving, storm or no storm," he teased.

"I'm just saying, you never know what's around the next corner. Maybe the next five cards are a royal flush."

"The odds of that happening are like a million to one."

"Still, there is that one. I know a lot of people give up too soon when if they'd just stuck things out, they'd have achieved their goals," she said.

"And my goal is…?"

"Oreos."

"I had all the Oreos to begin with."

"And now you've lost eight of them. You want to lose more?"

"Okay, deal me five new cards."

"Is that why you're here?" Macy asked, doling out the cards. "You gave up on something that was once important to you?"

"I didn't give up," he said. "I screwed up. Royally."

"Oh?" she said, trying to sound indifferent. Was he on the verge of telling her what had happened? Was she within seconds of getting her interview? Macy put on her best poker face. "Sounds like there's a story behind that."

He waved a hand. "It's a long one."

"Hey, it's not like we're going anywhere, but you know, if it's too personal, hey…" She shrugged. "Just tell me it's none of my business."

Please tell me, please tell me, please tell me.

Macy tensed, waiting. She could almost taste the peaches grown in red Georgia soil that would come with that job at ANN.

"I'll raise you three cookies," he said.

She studied his face. "You're bluffing again."

"Am I?"

"What do you do for a living, Armando Cutler?"

"Trying to ascertain if I'm as good at bluffing as you are?" he asked.

Nervousness tripped down her spine. *Had* he looked into her knapsack? *Did* he know she was a journalist? Was he just toying with her? Macy bit her bottom lip. "Are you?"

"I am…was…a chemical engineer."

"Hmm," she said, trying to appear nonchalant. "Sounds mathematical."

"I work…worked for Hollister Chemicals. Ever heard of them?"

Be cool, be cool, be cool.

"I'll meet your bet." She dropped three cookies into the pile in the middle of the table. "I think I've heard of Hollister. Weren't they the company touting a fuel additive that would allow vehicles to get a hundred miles to the gallon or something?"

"Yes."

Perspiration dampened the back of her neck and she had to remind herself to keep breathing. "Did you work on that project?"

"I did. In fact, I headed the project."

"So when does the additive hit the market?"

"You'll have to ask Bond and Martin about that."

She blinked, pretending to be confused. "Who are Bond and Martin?"

"They're the ones working on the fuel additive now."

"I don't understand."

"Like black-chested Costa Rican swallows, they stole the formula from Hollister."

"Ouch." Macy sucked in her breath through clenched teeth. "How does something like that happen? I mean, aren't there strict security measures in place to prevent corporate espionage?"

"There are."

"So…I'm guessing this is something you really don't want to talk about." *Please don't stop talking.*

"I raise you three more cookies."

"You're bluffing."

"Maybe…" His eyes darkened and she couldn't help feeling that she was walking on eggshells. "You willing to take that risk?"

"You're bluffing."

"Could be. You'll never know if you fold."

"Hollister didn't want to spend the money on security? Is that it?" she dared to ask. "I find this corporate espionage fascinating."

He paused for so long she thought she'd gone too far. "There were strict security measures."

"Then how did the black-chested swallow steal your eggs, so to speak?"

Their gazes were locked. Neither one of them looked away.

"Through seduction." Armando's voice was brittle.

"I'm not following you."

"Let's just say, I let my heart rule my head and it was my downfall."

"Ah," she said, excitement pumping blood through her veins in a rapid rush of adrenaline. Now they were getting down to the nitty-gritty. This was what she'd come to Costa Rica to uncover. "Bond and Martin sent a femme fatale and you fell for her wiles."

"Guilty as charged," he said. "It's your turn."

Macy gulped and pushed her entire pile of Oreos into the middle of table. "I'm all in."

"You sure you want to do that?"

"No gain without a little risk, right?"

"Turn 'em over," he said.

She showed him her cards. "Ace high."

Armando laid down the five fresh cards she'd dealt

after she'd talked him into not giving up. His grin was wicked. "I'm glad I took your advice and didn't give up."

Macy looked down at the cards and her pulse leaped. One in a million indeed.

He'd had a royal flush.

RAIN BUFFETED the cabin for the next two days and nights, and it felt as if the little stone bungalow was situated directly under the San Pablo Waterfalls.

To pass the time and to keep from acting on their rapidly escalating attraction, Armando and Macy cooked and ate and played games. They popped popcorn and sipped hot chocolate. They made sugar cookies and decorated them with icing. Armando proved to be a very talented artist in the cookie-decorating department. She beat him at backgammon, he trounced her at chess. They both won two games apiece of Monopoly. And when they tired of eating and games, they talked.

They talked for hours—about their childhoods, about movies and books and sports. They shared the stories of their lives. The big defining moments. There was the day when Armando was five and his father never came to pick him up at the arcade where he'd left him. For Macy there was the time she fractured her leg while in-line skating and came to understand that her childhood dream of becoming a prima ballerina was over. And the small, but important turning points—when they first realized there was no such thing as Santa, their first kisses, first day of high school.

The more they talked, the stronger the bond between them grew, and then on the third day, as they lay on the bed, side by side in the darkness of early morning, completely aware of each other's bodies, but doing their best not to touch each other, Armando began to talk about the details of what had ruined him at Hollister Chemicals. Macy held her breath as she learned how he'd let grief and lust lead him down the path to destruction after his mother's death.

As he talked, anger gripped her. Anger aimed at that corporate spy Jennifer Kemp. She had a strong urge to hunt the woman down and slap her silly for hurting Armando. The intensity of that urge took her by surprise. How could she have such contempt for a woman she didn't even know?

You're no better than she is, taking advantage of Armando for your own gain, whispered her conscience.

She pushed the thought aside, but the tightness knotting up her chest did not abate.

"Macy," he said.

"Yes?" She could feel the heat from his big body radiating through the thin cotton sheet.

"What possessed you to get a tattoo?"

She chuckled. It wasn't what she'd been expecting. "College. Girls' night out got out of hand."

"Drinks were involved, I'm guessing."

"Tequila shots, to be exact."

"Ouch."

"Honestly, I don't even remember getting the tattoo."

"Are you ever going to show it to me?"

"You sure you really want to see it?"

"Absolutely."

"Okay," she said.

He reached over and flipped on the bedside lamp, his eyes widening with interest.

"You're going to be disappointed," she said.

"Why's that?"

"It's not located anywhere risqué."

"No?"

Feeling sheepish, she tossed back the covers and brought her left foot up to rest on her right knee.

"It's on your foot?"

"The sole of my foot," she said.

He tilted his head. "It's not artwork."

"No, it's my favorite quote," she said. "By Denis Diderot."

He leaned in closer. She could feel his warm breath on her toes. "'Only passions, great passions, can elevate the soul to great things,'" he read aloud.

"Apparently I'm quite profound when blitzed out of my skull on tequila," she said.

Armando laughed and lifted his head. "I think it's perfect."

"Perfect?"

"It fits you to a T."

"You think?"

"I know. You're just like that tattoo. Fun-loving, adventurous, passionate, soulful, literary. I can't begin to tell you how much knowing you has helped me."

"Really? How's that?"

"I came to Costa Rica full of rage and remorse. I was humbled and shamed. I'd hit rock bottom. Even after three months here, I still couldn't shake my anger over being betrayed by someone I trusted. I couldn't see a way to pick up the pieces of my life."

"No?" she breathed.

"Not until I met you." Then Armando picked up her hand and squeezed it.

One touch was all it took to unravel her completely. Every ounce of resolve she possessed flew out the window. Any thoughts of her career disappeared. Her mind was focused on one thing and one thing only.

Armando.

Apparently he was just as lost as she. With a groan of pure desire, he reached for her at the same time she rolled into his arms.

Their lips met in an electrical charge of energy that rivaled the heated lightning flickering at the window. Macy had never in her life wanted a man more than she wanted Armando.

The misgivings she'd been having disappeared in the onslaught of sensation. His mouth consumed hers and she gave as good as she got, kissing him with a fever so hot she felt as if she'd been seared from the inside out.

Without another word, they undressed each other. His hands roved over her body—touching her breasts, her waist, her hips. Her tongue licked his bare skin and she reveled in the salty taste of him. Savagely he kissed her, and Macy's body came alive, strumming with the heady rush of hormones. Her flesh tingled with anticipation, her muscles tensed, eager for more attention.

Armando threaded his fingers through her hair, held her head still while he blazed more kisses over her forehead, her eyelids, her cheekbones, the tip of her nose.

Then when he lowered his mouth to capture first one

nipple and then the other, Macy let out a low, soft moan of intense pleasure. Her body caught fire.

"I have to have you," she whispered. "Do you have any protection?"

He groaned. "Damn. You were driving me so wild I totally forgot about protection."

"Do you…please tell me you have a condom, because I don't and I need you so badly," she whimpered. "I can't stand it."

"I came up here to be alone. I didn't expect company."

"No!"

He laughed.

"It's not funny."

"Don't worry." He kissed her. "I think I have an emergency condom tucked away in my wallet."

"You just have one?"

"Greedy, greedy." He chuckled and reached into the bedside table for his wallet.

A minute later, with the condom in place, Armando slipped his hands under her buttocks and rolled her over until Macy was straddling him, her knees on either side of his waist.

A flash of lightning flooded the room in split-second illumination, emphasizing the intensity of what was happening between them. Myriad sensations pelted her. The sound of his ragged breathing. The heat of his flesh. The scrape of his beard stubble as he claimed her mouth in another kiss.

A maelstrom of wicked delight swept her away, increasing the sexual drive that had been building since she'd first spied him underneath that waterfall.

He tasted robust and masculine. Their tongues played. Gliding in and around and over each other.

The burning urge to stroke him, to travel the tempting terrain of his body compelled her hand lower. She ran her fingertips over his belly, exalting in the way his taut stomach muscles quivered at her touch. His low groan of pleasure lit her up inside.

She tracked her hand lower and excitement stirred her blood.

"I gotta have you now, babe," he crooned.

Gleefully, Macy sank onto him, gasping as he filled her up completely. A groan tore from his lips as she ground her pelvis against him.

Armando couldn't breathe. The sensation of being inside her was that incredible.

She rose and then lowered herself on him again. He wrapped his hands around her waist, guiding the rhythm of her moves, watching her with fascination. She was gorgeous. Each stroke brought him closer and closer to bliss.

He fought the urge to come. It was a fierce battle. The way she was contracting around him was almost more than he could bear. He had to clench his jaw and close his eyes and concentrate on making sure her pleasure was as great as his. He lightly pinched her nipples between his thumb and forefinger and she went wild, thrashing and calling his name.

"Macy," he breathed, and it felt as if he hadn't really lived until this very moment.

"Armando…I'm about to…I…"

"That's it, *querida,* come for me. Let go."

It was all the permission she needed. Climax overtook

them both, their bodies merging in a crashing frenzy. Together they clung and called out each other's name, catapulted into the sweetest orgasm he'd ever experienced.

SOMETIME LATER Macy awoke to the now habitual sound of rain striking the roof and the feel of Armando still inside her. They'd never separated. She'd collapsed on his chest in the aftermath of their exquisite crescendo and had apparently dozed. She felt him grow harder and instantly, she was excited all over again.

And within seconds she was off and flying. She moaned softly.

Armando reached up a hand to thread his fingers through her hair and guide her face down to his so he could capture her lips in a fierce kiss. Then he carefully flipped their bodies over so they didn't disconnect. He was on top now and she happily relinquished control. His mouth captured hers as he thrust into her. Pushing harder and faster until the bed slammed noisily against the wall.

Dear heavens, she was already on the verge of coming again. She clung to him, grabbed his buttocks, pulling him in deeper.

And then there she was, enveloped in a wave of sensation even more potent than the first orgasm. She shuddered in his arms, moaning soft and low. Her body spasmed around him. He came along with her, his sound purely masculine as his release shattered into hers.

CHAPTER SEVEN

IT WAS SEVERAL HOURS later when Armando awoke from a deep, sated slumber to find Macy's sweet butt tucked tightly against his pelvis. He had his arm thrown around her, cinching her to him.

He wanted to make love to her all over again, but they were out of condoms. Still, there were other ways two people who were as sexually compatible as they were could satisfy each other.

He lay there, smelling the floral scent of her dark, wavy hair and marveled at the feeling burrowing deep into his heart. Being with Macy felt so natural, so easy, so perfect. She'd made him laugh again and when he was with her, hope filled his heart. For the first time in three months he believed he had a future, and he wanted to share it with her.

The only downside to their relationship as far as he could see was that his insatiable hunger for her sapped his vigor.

You don't even really know her. Sure, you've spent three days together spilling all your dark secrets, but is that enough? Are you sure you can trust her?

She turned in his arms, murmuring something he

couldn't make out, and buried her face against his chest. Groaning, he tightened his arms around her and claimed her lips.

He might not have known her long, but he felt as if he'd been waiting for her his entire life. And sometimes a guy just had to take a leap of faith. Armando decided he would take his chances and let the chips fall where they may.

AFTER HOURS SPENT pleasuring each other in as many creative ways as they could dream up while the rainstorm continued to shake the cabin, hunger and thirst finally pushed Macy and Armando from the blissful cocoon of their bed.

As Macy watched Armando pull on his T-shirt, she had to admit a disturbing truth to herself. She was falling for him and that significantly complicated the plans she'd made for her life.

Aside from the fact that she'd come here under false pretenses, she wasn't sure she was ready for another relationship. Divorce had soured her on marriage and she didn't know if she'd ever want to try again.

Marriage?

Where had that thought come from? No one was talking marriage. Sure, she admired and respected Armando. They definitely had fun together. And the sex? Groundbreaking, phenomenal, the best she'd ever had.

But here she was, crazily, illogically, jumping the gun, thinking that admiration, respect, fun and great sex meant anything beyond a good time.

Most of all, she couldn't forget her goal. The one

thing she'd worked for her entire adult life—becoming an investigative reporter for ANN. And she knew that the story she'd gleaned from Armando about lust, greed and corporate espionage was her ticket to achieving this long-held dream.

Macy padded to the bathroom, racked by guilt and indecision. She stared at her reflection in the mirror and was shocked by what she saw. Her hair was a wild tumble about her face. Her chin was reddened from the friction between it and Armando's beard stubble. Her lips were swollen from his kisses. And her eyes glowed with a light she'd never seen there. Unsettled, she ran a brush through her hair.

Armando's knuckles rapped against the bathroom door. "Macy," he said. "You've got to come see this."

She opened the door to find him standing there, his own eyes glowing with excitement. "What is it?"

"Get your camera and come with me."

His enthusiasm infected her. Macy went to her knapsack, sitting on the chest of drawers, and dug out her camera. He took her hand and led her to the back door. Warm rain blew across her skin when he opened the door.

Armando draped one arm around her shoulders, leaned in close. "Look there." He pointed. "Can you see them underneath the shelter of the jacaranda?"

Macy squinted through the driving downpour. "What am I looking for?"

"What did you come here to find?"

You. A story. Something to further my career.

But she'd found much more than she'd bargained for and it scared her.

Then she saw it. The small, twin slashes of red on a low-hanging branch of the tree. The vibrant scarlet throats of two, otherwise brown, little birds huddled together against nature's onslaught.

It was a rare pair of red-throated Costa Rican swallows. She breathed deeply and automatically reached for the telephoto lens and attached it to her camera, as if these birds really were the reason she had come here.

Armando's arm slipped from her shoulders to her waist as she snapped the pictures. It felt good to have him hug her against him. Too good. She didn't appreciate this glimpse into what things could be like between them if they'd met under different circumstances, if she hadn't been deceiving him.

As his now familiar exciting scent met her nostrils, Macy tried to imagine what his reaction would be if she told him the truth.

What would he say if she told him her name was Macy Gatwick, not Macy Mason? And that she had no real interest in the red-throated Costa Rican swallow? That bird-watching was just a ruse to meet him, because she wrote exposés for an online magazine and his story of sexual betrayal was her ticket to stardom?

Her stomach churned. What was wrong with her? When had she lost her moral compass?

Armando swore under his breath and for one bizarre moment, Macy thought he'd read her mind and now knew everything about her, including the fact that she'd lied to him to further her career.

Just like Jennifer Kemp, who'd hurt him so badly.

"Where are your binoculars?" he asked.

"They're in my knapsack," she said, alarmed by his grim expression. "What's wrong?"

"From here it looks like the west slope is about to break off."

She lowered her camera, the swallows forgotten in the wake of his sudden mood change. "What does that mean?"

"Mudslide," he muttered, turning and stalking toward the chest of drawers.

She stood in the doorway trying to see what he'd seen through the curtain of rain. She could barely even make out that there was a valley in the far distance. "Mudslide?"

"It'll wash out the main road to San Pablo and El Marro Lindo."

She looked over her shoulder at him. "What does that mean?"

"We could be stuck here for weeks." Armando grabbed her knapsack.

"I can't be stuck here for weeks," she muttered. "Three days in this cabin is bad enough."

His head came up and she realized how insensitive that sounded.

"I…that's not what I meant…"

"I know what you meant," he said, but his voice was so neutral she couldn't read him. "That's why I need the binoculars, to see if we have enough time to get you out of here before the road goes."

She turned back to peer out the door at the deluge. "We're leaving? In this rain?"

"It's now or never."

She drew in a deep breath. Anxiety crept down her spine. She felt Armando come up behind her. "I can't even see the road."

"What is this?" he asked in a flinty voice.

Macy swiveled around.

Armando stood in front of her, his face as impassive as a rock cliff, her press badge dangling from his finger, her satellite phone clutched in his hand.

"I CAN EXPLAIN."

Armando stared at her, unable to believe this was happening to him again.

No! It couldn't be true. He didn't want it to be true. But he could tell from the shamed expression on her face that it was. He thought their time together had been special. What an idiot. She must have been secretly laughing at him while she'd knowingly betrayed his trust.

Just like Jennifer.

But this was a thousand times worse. For one thing, with Jennifer, he'd had a hand in his own downfall, but not in this instance. Here, he'd been minding his own business, trying to get his life together. Trying to figure out how he'd screwed up his career so badly. But this…this was all Macy's doing. She hunted him down. She'd conned him into bringing her into his cabin, letting down his guard and foolishly telling her everything about his past.

For another thing—and this was what hurt so damned much—he'd fallen in love with her.

Macy had broken his heart.

"That's okay." He held up his palm. "I don't need to hear any more of your lies."

"This looks bad, I know but—"

"Let me see if I've gotten any of it wrong," he said. "According to this press badge, your real name is Macy

Gatwick and you write for *Gotcha* magazine. The name seems self-explanatory. Anything about that not true?"

Macy shook her head as misery saturated her. He looked so utterly wounded her heart shriveled. "Armando, please, I—"

"You came here to find out what had happened to my career at Hollister Chemicals and why Bond and Martin were suddenly developing the fuel additive that should have belonged to me," he interrupted her again.

She deserved to be cut off. She knew it. But it killed her that he wouldn't listen to what she had to say. He was hurting, she understood that, but she needed to let him know how much she'd changed. How being with him had changed her, in just three short days.

"You came here," he continued, "to betray me."

The angry look in his eyes took her breath away. He hated her. He wasn't interested in hearing anything she had to say.

She was still standing in the open doorway, the wind blowing rain over her feet. She felt as if she was sinking, drowning in the emotions flickering in his eyes— outrage, hurt, bewilderment, humiliation, scorn.

"This was all a ploy. A scheme you cooked up to get to me. You had no interest in red-throated swallows and you had no interest in me, beyond getting my story."

Wretchedly, she nodded. "I've been trying my whole career to get a job as an investigative reporter for ANN. It's my lifelong dream. Your story was supposed to be my big break."

"Then you got what you came for, didn't you?" He spit out the words in obvious disgust. "Let me just help you on your way." He punched a number into her satellite phone. When someone answered on the other end, he said abruptly, "This is Armando. I have an American tourist stranded in my cabin. The main road to El Marro Lindo is about to wash out. She needs rescue."

He hung up and tossed her the phone. Then he put on the rain slicker and rubber boots parked at the back door.

"Where are you going?" she cried.

He threw her a look that chilled her to the bone. "As far away from you as I can get," he said, then turned and plunged into the rain-soaked jungle.

CHAPTER EIGHT

"So?" MACY'S BOSS, Greg Winston, stood in the doorway of the communal office at *Gotcha* magazine, hands on his hips, a scowl on his plump, ruddy face. "Where's the piece on Armando Cutler?"

Macy exhaled wistfully and pulled her attention from the photograph of two red-throated Costa Rican swallows huddled together under the rain-soaked jacaranda tree that she'd propped against her coffee mug. She'd been dreading this showdown with Greg ever since she'd arrived at the office. She might be a lot of things, but a coward wasn't one of them.

Splaying her palms on the desk, she pushed herself to her feet and met his glare. "I'm not turning in the piece."

Greg's scowl deepened. "Does this have anything to do with the assistant producer from ANN sitting in our lobby?"

Macy blinked. "What?"

"Don't play dumb—it doesn't suit you," Greg said. "He's asked for you by name."

"Seriously?"

"I don't want to lose you, Macy," Greg said. "You're

the best reporter I've got, but I know your dreams are bigger than *Gotcha* magazine. Just please do me a favor and take your job interview elsewhere."

Stunned, Macy slipped the photo of the swallows into her pocket and then wandered into the lobby to find Tom Sternon, the assistant producer with whom she'd had a past interview, sitting beside the window. He stood and extended his hand. "Macy Gatwick, it's good to see you again."

She shook his hand. "Yes, nice to see you, too."

"We heard about your rescue from San Pablo in Costa Rica. It's our understanding you spent time with Armando Cutler. We tried for weeks to get an interview with him after Bond and Martin scooped his fuel additive."

"Mr. Sternon," she said. "Could we have this conversation in the coffee shop next door?"

"Certainly."

Once they were ensconced at a bistro table in the Latte Café, cups of coffee in their hands, Sternon began his pitch again. "Have you given Cutler's story to *Gotcha?*"

"I have not."

"Smart woman." Sternon smiled and steepled his fingers. "We have a win-win proposition. Give us your exclusive interview with Armando Cutler and we have a job waiting for you at ANN."

Macy listened to Tom Sternon say the words she'd wanted to hear more than anything since she was an eighteen-year-old journalism student at the University of Oklahoma. She'd worked hard for this, had dreamed of it for years, but now that it had come to pass, it felt...

Empty.

She reached into her pocket, felt the edges of the photograph. She thought about Armando and those hot, wet nights they'd shared in that little jungle cabin.

She could not forget how she'd behaved—lying to him to get a story, worming her way into his confidence. Was she going to take that last step and issue the blow of ultimate betrayal in order to get what she wanted?

A crossroads.

She was staring at a crossroads and her decision would affect the rest of her life. Was she like those black-chested swallows stealing nests from the red-throated swallows? Was she any different from Jennifer Kemp?

"Well?" Tom Sternon prompted.

Macy looked into his eyes and did something she never dreamed she'd do. "Thank you for the offer, Mr. Sternon, but I don't think ANN is the place for me."

"WE WANT YOU to come back to work for us."

At the pleading tone in his former boss's voice, Armando smiled.

When he'd opened the door of his Houston condo to find Charles Barrington, the CEO of Hollister Chemicals, standing in his hallway, this was the last thing he'd expected to hear. They were now in Armando's living room, Barrington perched on the edge of the sofa, briefcase in hand.

Armando had been back in Houston for two weeks and he'd been bracing for the fallout that was sure to erupt when Macy's exposé hit the media. He'd come home to face the music, having realized he'd accomplished nothing by hiding out, only to discover nothing had happened.

Until now.

And the twist was so surprising he didn't know how to react to Barrington's request.

"Excuse me?" Armando said, completely puzzled by this turn of events. "I let a corporate spy get her hands on our most promising formula and you want me to come back to work for you?"

Barrington nodded.

"Why?"

Barrington grinned. "Bond and Martin couldn't make the formula work. We want you to take another stab at it."

"What makes you think I can?"

"Because you already hold three similar patents for us. You've got the magic touch, Cutler. They might have gotten hold of your formula, but without you, they can't make it work."

Understanding dawned. "I get it," Armando said. "You're terrified Bond and Martin are going to hire me."

"Um…er…," Barrington stammered. "Yes, that's true, but—"

"Let me save you the spiel. I don't want to come back."

Barrington's face blanched. "They've already hired you."

"No."

Relief flashed over his ex-boss's features. "We'll double your previous salary."

"Simply to keep me from working for Bond and

Martin?" Armando shook his head. Laughable that the biggest mistake he'd ever made in his life was ending up being the most lucrative.

Scratch that.

The biggest mistake of his life was trusting and falling for Macy Gatwick.

Get over it. Time to stop licking your wounds and accept responsibility for your sexual indiscretions.

But chiding himself didn't stop him from feeling like an idiot. How could he have believed she was falling for him the way he'd fallen for her? Though her sexual feelings had seemed real enough, they'd differed in the emotional bond. He'd felt it, but clearly she had not. She'd been looking for a story, and sex had been nothing more than a means to an end.

You don't really believe that, insisted a hopeful voice in the back of him mind. *If you were nothing more than a story to her, why hasn't the story broken?*

How he wanted to think that he'd been as special to her as she'd been to him! But he was afraid to believe. Afraid to trust.

"I'll do whatever it takes," Barrington said, taking a contract from his briefcase. "We want you back. Along with the raise, you'll get a promotion."

"I think you'd regret the offer if I accepted," Armando said, and then he told Barrington about Macy Gatwick.

"You spilled your guts to a reporter?" Barrington exclaimed.

"I didn't know she was a reporter."

"This is…I can't believe…what is it with you and women?" Barrington got to his feet, stuffed the sheaf of papers back into his briefcase.

"I guess I'm just a fool for love."

"You've got to find out when she intends to break this story. We have to get our ducks in a row. Hire a spin doctor to do serious damage control."

"I take it the job offer is off the table?"

"Hell, yes, you're a serious liability," Barrington said. "Even Bond and Martin won't hire you after this hits the fan. Now call that woman and find out what's going on."

Armando realized Barrington was right. He couldn't keep walking around with his breath bated. He had to know when Macy's exposé on him would surface, for his own sake as much as for Hollister Chemicals.

He looked up the number for *Gotcha* magazine and placed the call with sweaty palms. When the receptionist answered, he asked for Macy.

"Ms. Gatwick isn't in. May I take a message?"

"Could I speak to the managing editor, please?"

"Who may I ask is calling?"

"Armando Cutler."

A minute later, the managing editor was on the line. "Greg Winston here."

Armando introduced himself and said, "I need to know when you're going to run Macy's article about me."

There was a long moment of silence and then Winston said, "We're not."

"What do you mean?"

"We're not running the story."

Hope bloomed in his heart and then something else occurred to him and all hope vanished. With a story like this one, Macy had the opportunity to end up on television. "She took the story elsewhere," he said flatly.

"A representative from ANN came to see her last week," Winston confirmed.

Armando hadn't thought he could feel any worse about this than he already did, but he was wrong. "She's given them the exclusive."

"No," Winston said, sounding jovial. "She refused them, too."

The roller coaster of hope was back. "What do you mean? Did she get a better offer?"

"She's burying the story. I gotta tell you, Cutler, I don't know what hold you have over her, but it's a powerful one. You've turned my most cutthroat reporter into a lovesick puppy."

Hope morphed into excitement. "Can you tell me where she is?" he asked. "I need to speak to her."

"You don't know?"

"Just tell me," Armando commanded.

"Macy went back to Costa Rica," Winston said, "to find you."

CHAPTER NINE

"YOU CAME BACK after Tarzan," Amelia Pettigrew had just greeted Macy in the lobby of the Coronado Bed and Breakfast.

"I did," Macy confirmed.

Amelia looked over at Harry, who was busy cleaning the lenses of his binoculars. "I told you she was in love."

"You did at that." Harry smiled.

"You guys haven't left yet?" Macy said, surprised to find the elderly couple still in Costa Rica.

"We decided to move here," Amelia said. "In fact, we're meeting with a real-estate agent in twenty minutes."

"And after that," Harry said, putting the strap of the binoculars around his neck and then slipping his arm around Amelia's waist, "we have an appointment with a local chaplan."

"You're getting married!"

Amelia blushed as Harry kissed her cheek. "We are. Next week, here at the Coronado."

"And you and Tarzan are invited," Harry added.

"That's wonderful! Congratulations. I'd love to come to the wedding, but I can't speak for Tarzan."

"You haven't told him that you love him yet, have you?" Amelia nodded.

Macy caught her breath. "That's what I'm here for."

"The main road to San Pablo is still washed out." Harry shook his head. "That was one hell of a mudslide."

"I don't care if I have to hack my way through the jungle," Macy declared. "I must get back to the cabin."

"Go get your man," Amelia and Harry said in unison.

THREE MISERABLE HOURS later, Macy finally reached the San Pablo Waterfalls, but once there she was hit with indecision and disappointment. She didn't know what she expected to find. Armando showering under the falls as he'd been the very first time she'd laid eyes on him?

She tilted her head up in the direction of the cabin, trying to see it through the thick overgrowth of trees, but she couldn't from where she stood. Dejected, she plunked down on a boulder, swiped the sweat from her forehead and pulled a bottle of water from her knapsack. Had coming back here been a huge mistake? Was Armando still furious? Could she convince him to forgive her and give her a second chance?

"You look like you could use a cold shower."

Macy jerked her head around and gasped to see Armando standing behind her, wearing swim trunks and a University of Texas T-shirt. She'd never seen a more beautiful sight.

"How did you know I was here?"

"A cute elderly couple at the Coronado told me."

Her pulse skittered. He'd been looking for her. "You went to the Coronado?"

"It was my first stop after the airport."

"Airport?"

"I just flew in from Houston."

"You've been to the States?"

Armando nodded. "I also know you didn't publish that story. And I know you turned down a job offer from ANN."

She swallowed hard. "You do?"

"Why, Macy?"

"I realized I'd been acting like a black-chested swallow," she said.

Armando laughed and the sound filled her with joy. "I came to tell you that I don't blame you for doing your job, but I needed to know…" He paused, gulped.

"Yes?"

"I need to know why you didn't release the story. Is it because you feel this…this…"

"Passion," she supplied. "The grandest passion I've ever felt. I'm more passionate for you than I am for journalism and that's saying something. Until now, being an investigative reporter was my greatest love."

"And now?" he murmured, moving ever closer through the palm fronds.

Her hands were trembling. "I turned down ANN to prove my love for you."

"Ah, *querida*," he breathed, and gathered her into his arms. "I've never felt this grand passion before, either."

She looked deeply into his eyes. "It all happened so quickly."

"Like a lightning bolt," he agreed. "But when it's right, it's right."

"You know," she said. "I can be a writer from anywhere in the world."

"Even Costa Rica?"

"Especially Costa Rica."

"That's good," he said, "because I've been thinking that maybe I'd like to start my own company. A green company seeking alternative sources to fossil fuel."

"Costa Rica is big into ecology."

"Now, about that shower," he said, reaching out to take her hand. "Have you ever made love underneath a waterfall?"

"I can't say that I have," she murmured, rapture spreading through her heart.

Armando took her by the hand and led her up the rocky steps to the waterfall, and there behind the tropical waters, they made love while the red-throated swallows flitted happily through the trees.

* * * * *

*Celebrate 60 years of pure reading pleasure
with Harlequin!*

To commemorate the event, Harlequin Intrigue® is thrilled to invite you to the wedding of The Colby Agency's J. T. Baxley and his bride, Eve Mattson.

That is, of course, if J.T. can find the woman who left him at the altar. Considering he's a private investigator for one of the top agencies in the country—the best of the best—that shouldn't be a problem. The real setback is that his bride isn't who she appears to be…and her mysterious past has put them both in danger.

Enjoy an exclusive glimpse of Debra Webb's latest addition to
THE COLBY AGENCY:
ELITE RECONNAISSANCE DIVISION

THE BRIDE'S SECRETS

Available August 2009 from Harlequin Intrigue®.

The dark figures on the dock were still firing. The bullets cutting through the surface of the water without the warning boom of shots told Eve they were using silencers.

That was to her benefit. Silencers decreased the accuracy of every shot and lessened the range.

She grabbed for the rocks. Scrambled through the darkness. Bumped her knee on a boulder. Cursed.

Burrowing into the waist-deep grass, she kept low and crawled forward. Faster. Pushed harder. Needed as much distance as possible.

Shots pinged on the rocks.

J.T. scrambled alongside her.

He was breathing hard.

They had to stay close to the ground until they reached the next row of warehouses. Even though she was relatively certain they were out of range at this point, she wasn't taking any risks. And she wasn't slowing down.

J.T. had to keep up.

The splat of a bullet hitting the ground next to Eve had her rolling left. Maybe they weren't completely out of range.

She bumped J.T. He grunted.

His injured arm. Dammit. She could apologize later.

Half a dozen more yards.

Almost in the clear.

As she reached the cover of the alley between the first two warehouses she tensed.

Silence.

No pings or splats.

She glanced back at the dock. Deserted.

Time to run.

Her car was parked another block down.

Pushing to her feet, she sprinted forward. The wet bag dragged at her shoulder. She ignored it.

By the time she reached the lot where her car was parked, she had dug the keys from her pocket and hit the fob. Six seconds later she was behind the wheel. She hit the ignition as J.T. collapsed into the passenger seat. Tires squealed as she spun out of the slot.

"What the hell did you do to me?"

From the corner of her eye she watched him shake his head in an attempt to clear it.

He would be pissed when she told him about the tranquilizer.

She'd needed him cooperative until she formulated a plan. A drug-induced state of unconsciousness had been the fastest and most efficient method to ensure his continued solidarity.

"I can't really talk right now." Eve weaved into the right lane as the street widened to four lanes. What she needed was traffic. It was Saturday night—shouldn't be that difficult to find as soon as they were out of the old warehouse district.

A glance in the rearview mirror warned that their unwanted company had caught up.

Sensing her tension, J.T. turned to peer over his left shoulder.

"I hope you have a plan B."

She shot him a look. "There's always plan G." Then she pulled the Glock out of her waistband.

Cutting the steering wheel left, she slid between two vehicles. Another veer to the right and she'd put several cars between hers and the enemy.

She was betting they wouldn't pull out the firepower in the open like this, but a girl could never be too sure when it came to an unknown enemy.

Deep blending was the way to go.

Two traffic lights ahead the marquis of a movie theater provided exactly the opportunity she was looking for.

The digital numbers on the dash indicated it was just past midnight. Perfect timing. The late movie would be purging its audience into the crowd of teenagers who liked hanging out in the parking lot.

She took a hard right onto the property that sported a twelve-screen theater, numerous fast-food hot spots and a chain superstore. Speeding across the lot, she selected a lane of parking slots. Pulling in as close to the theater entrance as possible, she shut off the engine and reached for her door.

"Let's go."

Thankfully he didn't argue.

Rounding the hood of her car, she shoved the Glock into her bag, then wrapped her arm around J.T.'s and merged into the crowd.

With her free hand she finger-combed her long hair.

It was soaked, as were her clothes. The kids she bumped into noticed, gave her death-ray glares.

They just didn't know.

As she and J.T. moved in closer to the building, she grabbed a baseball cap from an innocent bystander. The crowd made it easy. The kid who owned the cap had made it even easier by stuffing the cap bill-first into his waistband at the small of his back.

Pushing through the loitering crowd, she made her way to the side of the building next to the main entrance. She pushed J.T. against the wall and dropped her bag to the ground. Peeled off her tee and let it fall.

His gaze instantly zeroed in on her breasts, where the cami she wore had glued to her skin like an extra layer. A zing of desire shot through her veins.

Not the time.

With a flick of her wrist she twisted her hair up and clamped the cap atop the blond mass.

"They're coming," J.T. muttered as he gazed at some point beyond her.

"Yeah, I know." She planted her palms against the wall on either side of him and leaned in. "Keep your eyes open. Let me know when they're inside."

Then she planted her lips on his.

* * * * *

Will J.T. and Eve be caught in the moment?
Or will Eve get the chance to reveal
all of her secrets?
Find out in
THE BRIDE'S SECRETS
by Debra Webb
Available August 2009
from Harlequin Intrigue®

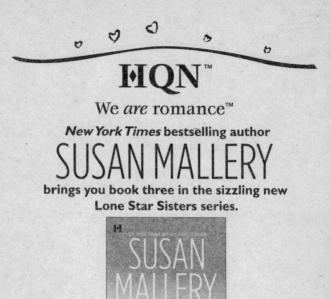